LEAVING MERIDIANA

UNCHARTED SERIES
BOOK 1

J A MORTIMORE

Sperrystone
Press

Ebook ISBN: 978-1-7393500-0-0

Paperback ISBN: 978-1-7393500-1-7

Cover design by 100 Covers

Edited by Vicky Brewster

This book is a work of fiction. Names, characters, places and incidents are either a product of the author's imagination or are used fictitiously. Any resemblance to actual people living or dead, events or locales is entirely coincidental.

Please note: I write using British English.

❀ Created with Vellum

CHAPTER ONE

Above Meridiana, as the last of the hastily converted fuel carriers joined the string of its fellows headed out towards the twin substream gateways, Flight Commander Zaran Atria flipped his firebird to look back at the planet. "Alpha patrol, that's the last of them," he commed. "Form up on the *Brightwing* as rear guard."

One by one his patrol confirmed status, the last, Sergeant Grus, adding mournfully, "I'd like to know who thought *Brightwing* was a good name for a fuel scow!"

Zaran smiled to himself, checking the holographic read-outs on his cockpit canopy as his patrol spread out to form the fuel carrier's escort. Once he was satisfied they were in position, he focussed his attention on the vista before him. From orbit, the planet looked unchanged; it was impossible to see the devastation, the fires and wreckage, that was all that was left of the spaceport, the twin mining towns of Prospect and Quarry, or the resort town of Devereau. Existing as it did at the rim of the substream network, the furthest node out from Sol, despite having been colonised for hundreds of years the planet had never attracted many settlers. It was – had been – a company planet, owned and operated by Galactic Fuel Incorporated, only viable because it was one of the known sources of seronium, the element that powered the current generation of pluslight and substream engines used throughout the Interstellar Union of Planets.

For all its emptiness – or perhaps because of it – Meridiana had been a beautiful planet. As a student, Zaran had visited the resort on vacation and remembered how much he had enjoyed the warm nights seated out under the sweep of stars drinking imported wine and arguing flight mechanics with his fellow cadets. He heaved a sigh; it seemed such a long time ago.

The decision to evacuate Meridiana had been made before the star cruiser *Atria* and her sister ship *Gemin* had arrived in the system. They had been sent to establish any truth behind the garbled stories the first evacuees had given on arrival at Bendos Wheel, the next station on the substream network – tales of amorphous aliens which had seemingly come out of nowhere and literally dissolved everything they touched.

Zaran's mother, Admiral Nashira, had been at the Academy at Bendos to give a speech and had pulled rank, ordering the *Atria* and *Gemin* to investigate. Two star cruisers, she had opined, should be enough to deal with what was probably just some natural phenomenon. Nobody, including Zaran, had been especially surprised when the flamboyant admiral had boarded the *Atria*, the ship she had once captained, to take a look at the Meridiana situation first hand. The current captain, Asterion, had even managed to keep his expression neutral. He was a quiet man, and Zaran couldn't claim to know him well, but he was sure the captain must have been put out by the admiral's presumption.

Nashira had been forced to eat her words when the *Atria*

and *Gemin* had emerged from the substream to be greeted by an automated message from the Meridiana Wheel which controlled the twin substream gateways stating that due to an emergency, the planetary system was closed, and all ships should take the upstream back to Bendos without delay. This was followed almost immediately by a holo from Wheel Commander Neno Rockspire, gushingly grateful to have two star cruisers come to assist with what he had confidently described as a planned evacuation.

As flight commander, Zaran had been briefed on the holo conference between the admiral, the two star cruiser captains, the Wheel commander, and Artur Greybridge, the planetary director. The latter had been quite clear that nobody had any idea where the aliens – if that's what they were – had come from; they had just started to appear. Initially, they were concentrated around the seronium refinery and the spaceport, but in a remarkably short space of time, they had spread out to attack the two mining towns. At first it seemed like the resort town might be spared, but eventually even that location had been threatened. The creatures seemed to multiply at a phenomenal rate, and they continued to spread until they were threatening infrastructure across the colonised areas of the planet.

The GFI directors had tried everything to stop the creatures, but nothing seemed to work. They did retreat from fire and various explosives but seemed to take no permanent harm from anything. Walls didn't stop them – they ate through them – and even dropping rocks on them had allowed only a temporary respite. Both laser streams and the various types of explosives available to the GFI had failed to make any noticeable impact on the creatures, and as more and more refugees streamed into the holding areas the company had managed to set up, it became obvious the situation was unsustainable.

In the end, unable to protect either his workers or his vats of refined seronium – Zaran wasn't entirely clear which of these Greybridge had been most concerned about – the man had made the difficult decision to try to get everyone off the planet. All available shuttles, whether commercial or private, had been co-opted to ferry refugees to the wheel, from where the docked merchant ships were persuaded to take as many people as they could and head for Bendos. The Wheel commander had started turning away new arrivals, whilst on the ground the company's manufacturing arm had worked frantically to refit the pods normally used to carry fuel into people carriers, and prefects had been sent out to try to round up those hardy souls living off-grid. If nowhere on the planet was safe, then they would just have to evacuate as many people as they could until a solution to the infestation could be found.

As for the resort town, the resort director had been surprisingly unwilling at first to evacuate, stating that attractions had to be preserved so that when the emergency was over customers would again be able to enjoy the planet's ambiance. Zaran believed the 'ambiance', which currently consisted of smoke and debris, would only attract those with an unhealthy desire to experience ongoing catastrophe. When pressed by Admiral Nashira, the stubborn director had finally conceded the need to vacate but as the resort's supply ship was in orbit they would use that and didn't need the IUP's help, thank you very much.

Zaran appreciated that evacuation had to be better than being under constant siege, but he suspected the passengers on board the converted fuel carriers were in for a particularly miserable ten weeks' transit through to Bendos. The vessels were typical cargo ships – a long spine onto which pods were docked. There was little privacy in the converted pods, with shared freshers and cooking facilities and racks of bunk beds.

Each of the twelve-pod carriers had ten pods containing people and two pods of seronium, sufficient to fuel the ship as far as Bendos with enough left over to pay the salary of the company employees forced to evacuate. Zaran shook his head; it would undoubtedly be a claustrophobic and uncomfortable journey.

With one last, lingering look at Meridiana, he banked his firebird and accelerated up behind the departing *Brightwing*. He was aware there were still people on the planet: the director had called for volunteers to rescue as much of the store of seronium as possible, as well as some of the more portable assets. Additionally, a skeleton crew was manning the remains of the port in the hope that the last few stragglers who had left the towns to live off-grid would get the evacuation message and make their way to a pick-up point. The last evacuees would be taken to the wheel until either the emergency was over or they could be put onto transport that would carry them upstream.

The two star cruisers were holding orbit, looking to protect and escort the last to leave. At the same time, their science teams were endeavouring to find out exactly what the destructive invaders were. In the latter respect, Zaran mused, they weren't having much success. To date, nobody had managed to devise a method of collecting a sample of something that ate through every substance they had tried to use to contain it. As a result, they still had no idea whether the blobs, as they were calling them, were a genuine life form or some recently manifested chemical reaction, an accident of fate.

The *Gemin* and the *Atria* dwarfed the fuel carriers. Like most of the ships that plied the substreams, they were long, comparatively slender vessels, but there the resemblance ended. Designed to be always on the move, the star cruisers were towns in their own right, carrying a large number of people as well as the firebird flights. They were the leviathans of space, larger by far than any other vessel. From their rounded noses to the blocky pluslight engines at their tail, star cruisers were vast cylinders pocked with bays, manoeuvring jets and, at their centre, the ring of thrusters that enabled them to pass through the substreams. Nobody would ever call them beautiful, but they were undeniably impressive.

The fuel carriers – seven in total – might be ungainly by comparison, but they were accelerating nicely towards the twin substream gateways, which at present were little more than an occlusion of the stars, a darkness beyond the brilliance of the Meridiana Wheel. The wheels which controlled the substream gateways had been constructed when the network was first developed, and were all of similar design: an outer rim to handle the docking, unloading and refuelling of ships – either those that weren't going as far as the planet, or those from the planet which weren't headed through the substream gateways - and six stubby arms that reached inward from the outer rim to the inner hub of the station, from which the gateways were controlled. Zaran had passed through the Meridiana Wheel on his vacation all those years ago, but as a visitor, he had only had access to a quadrant of the outer wheel and hadn't been there long enough to do any serious exploration. His impression had been that it resembled all the others he'd visited: utilitarian, stark and determinedly practical.

"Alpha Patrol Two to Alpha Leader."

Zaran smiled a crooked smile as his wingman's holo popped up in the lower left of his cockpit canopy. "Receiving, Alpha Patrol Two," he returned, the special mic in the collar of his safesuit already open. "What's your status?"

"I'm all zippy here," returned Lieutenant Raffi Forrester cheerfully. "Alpha Patrol is holding formation on *Brightwing*. It's nice to be off the *Atria* for a change!"

"We all love to fly—" Zaran began, but his comm was overridden, an unfamiliar face popping up alongside Raffi's holo.

"*Atria* Patrol, this is *Gemin*. We can't explain how, but … we think you've got blobs on your tail."

"Alpha Leader receiving, *Gemin*," he returned, frowning. "Can you clarify your message, please?"

"Alpha Leader." The flight commander didn't need to even glance at the new holo alongside Raffi's to know the *Gemin*'s captain had taken over the comms. He had heard his father's voice too often to mistake it. "We were monitoring the lake of blobs at what used to be Quarry," Captain Decrus said, "and some of the things just streamed straight up into, and beyond, orbit."

"In what?" Zaran asked blankly.

"In nothing; in themselves," Captain Decrus returned, sounding impatient. "They're headed straight towards the evacuation convoy!"

"Received, *Gemin*." Zaran shook his head slightly as he tried to comprehend what was happening. He opened comms to his entire patrol, their faces forming a block in the bottom left of his screen. "Patrol, this is not a joke. Look out for blobs incoming. Advise when sighted."

"Blobs in space?" Raffi sounded as incredulous as Zaran felt. "Flight, how in the seven hells are we supposed to spot unlit blobs against a black background?"

"Star occlusion?" suggested Allenda, the patrol's other lieutenant.

"I don't think they absorb energy," put in Sergeant Navi Redwind. "They should reflect light."

"Go to battle stations," Zaran said crisply. "*Gemin*, do the blobs show up on radar?"

"Yes, Flight, they do," Decrus informed him.

The patrol's firebirds spread out, circling the *Brightwing*.

"I think I've got something," Lieutenant Allenda reported. "Coming straight up from the planet's surface ... how in the seven hells are they tracking us?" His half-sister, Zaran thought, was picking up bad language from his wingman.

"Tracking implies agency," Zaran noted, peeling off towards Allenda's position. "Alpha Patrol, keep scanning. *Gemin*, has anyone advised the *Brightwing*?"

"Negative, Alpha Leader," Captain Decrus returned. "No need to panic her captain."

Because the sight of his escort suddenly zipping all over space wasn't going to alert the ship's captain, Zaran thought. He was still trying to comprehend how a simple escort role had become so much more urgent. "Acknowledged."

"Alpha Leader, they're spreading out," Allenda reported. "They're closing fast. Orders?"

"Once they get close enough, hit them with lasers," he said. "By all reports, that won't kill them, but it might deflect them. I am authorising laser initiation." He hoped his voice sounded steady; he couldn't help but remember that the last time he'd given that order, many of his pilots hadn't survived the ensuing firefight.

"Firing now, Alpha Leader," Allenda reported.

As soon as his lieutenant opened fire, faces popped up all along the bottom of Zaran's canopy – his patrol were all still there, now joined by Admiral Nashira, as well as the captain of the *Brightwing*, and a young woman he didn't recognise. The latter appeared puzzled.

"Patrol from the *Atria*," she said crisply, "are you firing on something?"

Zaran tapped her holo. "Welcome to the party, whoever you are," he said. He was peripherally aware that *Gemin* control was telling the *Brightwing* captain to maintain course for the substream gateway.

"Oh, this is Meridiana Wheel Traffic Control," the girl

replied, as if that should have been obvious. "Monitoring the evacuation arks. I repeat, are you firing on something?"

"Blobs," Zaran replied flatly.

"Wouldn't you need to be in close orbit to do that?"

"They're not on the planet," Zaran returned. "Don't ask how, but they're right up here with us. Meridiana Wheel, if you have nothing useful to add, we're a little busy right now."

"*Atria* Patrol, the first four arks have entered the substream," the girl advised. "Can you hold the – whatever they are – off for half an hour? That should give the others time to drop into the 'stream."

Zaran brought his firebird alongside Allenda's, and the amorphous shape on his battle screen was suddenly visible – a pulsating shape – yes, blob really was the best description – a thing whose method of propulsion was beyond his under-standing, as was how it could operate in the vacuum of space. He joined his laser fire to Allenda's, but all that happened when their twin beams struck was that their target split into two equally pulsating blobs which altered trajectory towards their two attackers.

"Uh-oh," he heard Allenda murmur, although he suspected she would deny it later. "Alpha Leader, suggest you back off and let me handle this."

Zaran frowned, irritated by her tone. He knew his half-sister had expected to be promoted to flight commander and was nursing a grievance because he'd scored higher at inter-view, but this was hardly the time for sibling rivalry.

Before he could come up with a non-confrontational reply, Captain Decrus's image pulsed. "Alpha Leader from *Gemin*, we're seeing more and more of the things leaving the planet. The *Atria* reports the same. We're targeting them with torpedoes to try and keep them on the ground. I've ordered our flight commander to launch a full detachment –

designation *Gemin* Patrol. They will swing in behind you and assist with the escort. Protect the *Brightwing*!"

"Acknowledged, *Gemin*." Zaran tapped communication holos. "Alpha Patrol, Grus and Kaitos, stay with the *Brightwing*. Adden and Navi, trailblaze, please. Allenda, Raffi, lay down a fire pattern across the path of the blobs; let's see if we can deflect them. *Brightwing,* this is Flight Commander Zaran. Hold course for the substream gateway."

Trusting his commands would be obeyed, the flight commander throttled back to put some distance between himself and his patrol. What became almost immediately apparent when he could see the bigger picture was that, despite both star cruisers now having firebird patrols actively opposing the blobs, the evacuation convoy and its escorts were becoming increasingly outnumbered. Confused reports from other ships implied that the blobs were no longer coming just from the planet but from every direction, homing in on the hapless *Brightwing*. To make matters worse, the evacuation ark's captain seemed to be panicking; instead of putting on speed towards the substream gateway, his vessel was making frequent course changes which only served to slow it down. His holo had disappeared from Zaran's screen, and his efforts to raise the man met with no response. There was a suspicious silence also from the *Gemin* and the *Atria*, which led the flight commander to suspect that the two captains (not to mention the admiral) were bickering about who had seniority.

"*Atria* Patrol, Meridiana traffic update: all the arks are safely through into the substream except the *Brightwing*," reported the young woman from the Wheel control room. "One incoming vessel has been diverted. Please advise whether you wish our defensive patrol to launch."

"Thanks, Traffic, but I don't think that will help." Zaran was feeling increasingly helpless and frustrated. The

Brightwing was closing on the upstream gateway, its course wobbling and erratic. Alpha Patrol swooped around it like a flock of gulls around a ship at sea, but despite their best efforts one of the blobs finally penetrated their field of fire and splashed onto the side of the carrier. In the blink of an eye, several more followed, and then they seemed to be coming from everywhere. "*Brightwing* is now taking damage."

"Flight, I've also acquired an unwanted passenger," Sergeant Grus reported. "My ship's haemorrhaging seronium. Best I can suggest is slamming my firebird into an asteroid. I'll switch on my emergency signal when I evacuate and await pick-up."

"Understood, Sergeant," Zaran responded. "May order prevail."

"Alpha leader." The woman in the Wheel control room was starting to sound a little shrill. "Under the circumstances, I am trying to advise *Brightwing* to divert away from the substream, but I think her comms array is out. Can you head her off?"

"We can try," Zaran said. "Alpha Patrol, converge on my signal. Let's form up ahead of the *Brightwing* and try to get her to turn."

"Alpha Three and I won't get there in time, Alpha Leader," responded Allenda. The slight flickering of her holo indicated she was nearly out of range. "We're several minutes away."

"Join us when you can, Lieutenant," Zaran said flatly, gliding his firebird into formation with the rest of the patrol. The *Brightwing* was, he realised, getting dangerously close to the point of no return, the substream gateway a flare of light against the darkness of space. Raffi brought her ship alongside his, with Kaitos and Navi close behind. The four firebirds swooped in front of the *Brightwing*, trying to force the captain to change course, but instead the fuel barge seemed suddenly to open out like a flower. It took Zaran a moment to realise that the captain had ejected all the ship's pods.

"Hell's blazing pits!" Raffi swore, banking hard to avoid colliding with one of the pods, the surface of which was almost entirely covered by pulsating alien matter which swirled and eddied, making the shape difficult to focus on.

"Oh, no," Zaran breathed, watching helplessly as the pod split open, spilling its contents into space – and into the swarming black blobs, where it was rapidly, but not rapidly enough, dissolved away.

"I think I'm going to be sick," Raffi said.

"You're cleaning it up if you are," Zaran shot back, pulling himself together. He could grieve later. The lumbering remains of the *Brightwing* were still falling towards the substream gate, faster now as if the captain thought he could somehow escape the fate that had befallen the pod. But his ship was swarming with the aliens, and Zaran suddenly realised there was only one action that could be taken to prevent this catastrophe from threatening all the worlds linked by the substream. "Meridiana Wheel Traffic," he said. "Are you in a position to initiate emergency shut down of the outbound substream?"

"What?" the girl said, her image blinking at him. She wore her hair very short, its ends spiking out from her head, framing a face that was striking rather than beautiful. "Flight Commander, do you realise the implications …?"

"Of course I do," he snapped. "Can you do it?"

"Not without the appropriate orders," she stuttered.

"But are you able to do it? How long would it take?" he pressed.

"Emergency shutdown takes five minutes." The girl looked away from the holo pick-up, obviously operating controls. "I can do it, but is there really no other choice?"

"No." Zaran steeled himself. "There isn't time to argue

about it. In less than ten minutes, the aliens will be into the substream. Close it down. I will take full responsibility."

She stared him in the eye for a long moment, but then he saw her shoulders slump. "On it, Flight Commander," she said, "but you'd better get over here and explain it to Commander Rockspire."

"Give me clearance to dock at the hub," he instructed her briskly.

"Clearance granted."

Zaran checked out his tactical display. "Raffi, keep track of the loose pods. Meridiana Traffic, do you have a rescue barge? If so, it needs to get out here and get to work picking up any pods that aren't … destroyed. Grus, I thought you were abandoning ship; my panel says you're still on board. Report!"

"I … don't understand," the sergeant replied. "My fuel finished flushing so I have no manoeuvring ability, but the aliens seem to have lost interest. I guess something more edible came along."

"Confirmed. Stay put unless the situation changes," Zaran ordered. "Gemin Patrol, be aware of a dead firebird in Gamma Sector."

His gaze was caught as the great, glowing ring that held open the outbound substream gateway flickered and then spun inward, irising smaller until with a final burst of light it vanished, leaving the inbound gateway suddenly, starkly alone.

"By … all … the … gods," breathed Allenda. "Zaran, what have you done?"

"My order, my responsibility," the flight commander growled. "Track the pods, Lieutenant. I'm headed down to the Wheel to face the music."

CHAPTER TWO

"… And then the drink server said …"

Cristal Feltspar closed her eyes wearily and braced for trouble. She'd been trying to contact one or other of the senior officers remaining on the Wheel ever since it had become clear that the evacuation wasn't going to plan, but nobody had responded to her increasingly desperate attempts to call them. The Wheel commander was about to discover just how seriously wrong things had gone, and she wasn't looking forward to the fallout from her actions. She opened her eyes reluctantly and focussed on the holo suspended above the main control podium, on which the scale of the tragedy that had occurred was quite clear. Just doing her job, she told herself, making sure that nothing *else* was going wrong.

"Controller Feltspar." There was a disbelieving note in the Wheel commander's voice as he gazed at the holo that was the central focus of the Wheel's hub. "The substream gate … what happened? Did it become dislodged?"

"I initiated shutdown of the outbound substream." Cristal

forwarded several incoming calls – undoubtedly from ships docked at the Wheel wanting to know what was going on – to the shipping office and tapped in a quick update so that the duty officer could make a decision as to what to tell them. She resolutely ignored the disbelieving query that elicited.

"You ... what?" Commander Rockspire literally staggered. "Do you have any idea what you've done?"

"The evacuation barges!" Artur Greybridge, the short, stocky planetary director, was close behind the Wheel commander. "Did they make it through safely, Controller?"

"All but one. That ... oh." She indicated a flickering light on the central holo. "I think it just broke up completely," she said hollowly. "I have search and rescue out trying to pick up the pods ..."

"You idiot!" Rockspire exploded. "You've stranded us all! What were you thinking? I'll have you up on charges!"

"Hold." Cristal swallowed in relief as the flight commander from the *Atria* strode into the control hub. He had evidently wasted no time docking, for which she was grateful. He was shorter than she'd expected and somewhat more muscular than his holo had indicated. The maroon of his uniform safesuit was a sharp contrast to the grey of the tunic and safesuit the Wheel commander was wearing. The flight commander's hair was clipped very short, and Cristal's eyes were drawn to the zigzag blaze of the scar that bisected the left side of his face from his hairline down his cheek and over the line of his jaw. She looked away quickly, hoping he hadn't seen her stare.

"Who are you?" Greybridge faced off to the new arrival whilst Rockspire reached out a shaking hand for a chair and sat down, staring fixedly at the holo, all the colour gone from his face.

"Flight Commander Zaran Atria." The man came to

parade rest. Cristal felt a vague shiver of unease; the fact that he used his ship's name as his surname made it clear he was one of the Elite, who had a reputation for regarding Wheelers and planet dwellers as beneath them. "I gave the order for the substream gate to be closed," he said. "The Traffic Controller, er ..." He glanced towards Cristal, as if suddenly realising he had no idea of her name.

"Followed that order, Commander Rockspire," she said, her attention firmly on her displays. It wouldn't do to have something *else* go wrong during her watch.

"Where are the rest of the duty team?" The flight commander looked around the room in obvious puzzlement. "Surely one traffic controller isn't sufficient to deal with this evacuation!"

"Rostering on the Wheel is my concern, not yours, Flight Commander," Rockspire growled. "As it happens, as a precautionary measure I took the decision to temporarily evacuate all but the most essential Wheel personnel to Bendos. And just as well I did, since you've managed to bring the entire system to a complete halt. You realise the substream can't be reopened from this end, don't you? They'll have to send us a new link, and that will take weeks ..."

"We can't reopen the gateway." Zaran's tone was bland, but he straightened noticeably and Cristal got the impression he wasn't used to having his actions challenged by someone not in his chain of command. "My flight reports that the aliens are all over the gate infrastructure. Since the admiral left instructions that no more ships were to be sent through until she reported back, there should be no new arrivals..." He broke off, frowning, and turned to Cristal. "I seem to recall you said there was a ship arrived during the battle, Traffic," he said. "What lunatic disobeyed Admiral Nashira's direct order?"

Cristal looked up from her duties. "It was an Elite ship, Flight Commander," she said. "I directed it into an escape trajectory. They'll be out of contact for a few days until they circle back toward us."

"Good thinking." Zaran nodded approval. Cristal frowned, suspecting he was patronising her, as had happened when she'd come into contact with Elite ship crew before, but she opted not to comment.

"You had no right to order the gateway closed," Greybridge blustered. "No right at all! Company assets are at stake here, and our constitution clearly states ..."

"I believe IUP regulations override company rules," the flight commander said. "Where were you when the decision had to be made?"

"I should have been consulted!" Greybridge insisted.

"Commander, I tried to contact someone when things started to go wrong," Cristal said, "but I couldn't raise anybody."

"You can't have tried very hard!"

"Gentlemen." Zaran made an obvious attempt to cool down the rapidly escalating situation. "I believe the controller is still on duty. I suggest we refrain from recriminations and deal with the situation as it stands."

"Oh." Greybridge deflated visibly. "Of course, I ... what is the current situation, Traffic?"

"The aliens – blobs ..." Cristal wished someone would decide what the things *were* so that she could refer to them in a sensible fashion. "Most of them are now either on the substream gateway infrastructure or congregated around the remains of the *Brightwing*. Our S&R patrol have managed to recover one of the pods and are heading towards the outer ring to dock and unload the passengers. The *Atria* pilot who was stranded ..."

"Sergeant Grus," the flight commander supplied, nodding approvingly.

"... is being picked up by one of the cargo pilots who offered to help with the recovery," Cristal continued, grateful for Zaran's support, although she was still suspicious of his motivations. "There are three more pods being escorted by firebirds, and two more that were ... sadly destroyed."

The three men all looked at her, their expressions clearly showing their horrified reaction to realising that any passengers aboard those pods had been lost.

"*Atria* is breaking orbit," she finished, turning her head slightly to take in the wide area holo occupying the part of the control room wall she always thought of as the front of the room, although in fact it was completely spherical.

"Captain Asterion to Meridiana Wheel." *Atria's* captain, whose holo popped up beside the wide area holo, both looked and sounded surprisingly calm. "The exodus of those things from the planet's surface seems to have come to a halt. Under the circumstances, the *Gemin* will be remaining in orbit to oversee the evacuation of the remaining inhabitants ..."

"Evacuation, sir?" Cristal dared to interrupt. "Captain Asterion, are you aware that the substream gateway is closed?" The captain's expression didn't change, but one of his eyebrows rose slightly and she blushed. "I mean, of course you're aware."

He nodded gravely. "I believe you have my flight commander on board?" he said.

"Here, sir," Zaran said, moving into line with the holo pick-up.

"I shall look forward to your full report," Asterion said. "Do you also have Commander Rockspire with you?"

"Yes, sir," Zaran said.

"Well, we can't leave anybody on the planet." The captain shrugged. "Nearly all the available food was sent with the evacuees, and the situation on the surface is critical. Many of the displaced persons will have to be housed on the Wheel temporarily until a decision is made as to what further action will be taken."

"Captain ... uh, Asterion." Commander Rockspire seemed to have found his voice. "The Wheel will, of course, be only too happy to take a few of the dirt-hugger refugees ..."

"Employees," Greybridge growled, glowering at the Wheel commander. "I'll thank you to remember we're not talking about any old planet dwellers, Neno. These are primarily GFI employees, and regulations state that the company will take good care of them."

"I guess we do have some temporarily empty quarters," Rockspire murmured, half to himself.

The control room door swished open, and Jedda Granit, Cristal's relief, wandered in. The tow-haired young man was gazing at his chrono thoughtfully, and was several steps into the room before he realised there were people other than Cristal present. He came to a halt, looked around curiously, and then took in what the holos were telling him. His mouth dropped open. "Um, has anyone noticed the substream gateway has gone weird?"

Cristal found herself hiding a smile as Rockspire, Greybridge and even the flight commander shook their heads – a smile which didn't last. This had been the worst thirty minutes of her life to date, and she rather thought the fallout was going to be just as awful. When word got around the Wheel as to what had happened and who was responsible, she suspected her life wasn't going to be worth living. As Rockspire and the *Atria's* captain continued to discuss their next actions, she stepped back from her duty post and waved Granit into her place.

"Handing over," she murmured formally, tapping her ear. "Check the log for an update on the situation," she added.

"Hand-over acknowledged," Granit said, mimicking her gesture and, like her, keeping his voice down.

"Enjoy your duty period," she said, and added, somewhat unnecessarily, "It's all gone horribly wrong."

"So I see," he returned as he initiated the log playback and watched the record roll past. "And I was hoping to get off early for gravityball practice." He frowned. "Even if we have only got a scratch team right now. I guess that league scout we were expecting won't be coming any time soon, will he?"

"Since nobody can get here, no. One ship did arrive during the exodus," she said. "Designation Gold One, an Elite cruiser. I sent them on a wide swing trajectory to avoid the fight. I'm not sure how long it will take to get back in range."

"Understood." The other traffic controller gave her an unusually cold stare – one she was, she suspected, going to be seeing a lot in the near future. "It would appear it was you who ..."

"Under orders," she murmured.

"Commander Rockspire ...?"

"*Him.*" Cristal nodded towards the flight commander, who was discussing the availability of shuttles.

"Flight Commander Zaran." A new holo popped up on the display, and Zaran straightened noticeably.

"Sir?"

"I shall await an explanation of your extraordinary order in the fullness of time," the man said. Unable to make her escape due to Director Greybridge blocking the doorway, Cristal stepped quietly back to allow Granit full access to the controls. The new speaker was, she saw, the captain of the *Gemin*.

"I'm sure Captain Asterion – or Admiral Nashira – will be happy to furnish you with a copy of my report," the flight lieutenant said.

"Perhaps if you hadn't let the aliens get that close to the *Brightwing*..."

"Captain Decrus, with respect, nothing seemed to stop them. Just as you were unable to stop them leaving the planet, nothing we tried stopped them attacking the *Brightwing*. Under the circumstances, I had no choice but to give the order I did. I couldn't let the aliens, or whatever those things are, get into the substream. We've yet to find anything that inhibits their attacks; everything we've tried just seems to make matters worse. Until we have an answer, I wasn't about to subject the entire IUP to an infestation."

"I'm sure Admiral Nashira will have her own opinion," Decrus said.

Zaran paled visibly, making the red slash of his scar even more obvious. He noticed Cristal looking at him, and turned his head, as if embarrassed by the flaw. He was correct about the danger – she'd realised that even before he gave her the order, which was one reason she'd obeyed him without argument, despite knowing her action would cut them off from the rest of civilisation. She was only relieved that her father and sister and most of her closest friends had already left, their duties not considered essential to the work of the Wheel, unlike her own. Of course, she was going to miss them, but at least they were safe. She hoped she hadn't unconsciously allowed her family's status to influence her decision.

"Captain, I took the only sensible action open to me," Zaran said.

"The admiral has called a meeting for tomorrow." Decrus was frowning, apparently unsatisfied with the flight lieutenant's answers. "We'll discuss then whether you would have made better choices from the control room of the *Atria*."

Zaran saluted the holo as it vanished, and then pulled a face. Cristal looked away, hoping he hadn't noticed her listening so overtly. Rockspire and Greybridge seemed to have calmed down and were now discussing where in the Wheel they could house the evacuees, including those being brought in from the *Brightwing's* pods.

"Of course, quarters are only *temporarily* empty," Rockspire was saying. "Once the emergency is over, people will expect to be able to come back to their homes. Let's discuss it further over a glass of something cool," he suggested, gesturing toward the door, and the two went out with barely a backward glance.

"I guess I'm in charge, then," Granit said.

"I guess you are, Jedda," Cristal replied. "You lucky boy."

"Controller ..." the flight commander said, and then hesitated visibly.

"Flight?"

"Uh ... I apologize." He inclined his head to her. "May I know your name?"

"It's Cristal. Cristal Feltspar."

"I take full responsibility for the order I gave, Controller Feltspar," he said, for some reason she didn't understand touching his fingers to his shoulder in the IUP salute. "I realise there will be people who ... won't be happy that, despite not being in my chain of command, you chose to follow it. I just wanted you to know that if you find yourself getting into difficulties, you should direct people to me and I'll put them straight. I believe we did the right thing, and I hope you can come to believe that, too."

"I ... yes, um, thank you," she said, a little flustered. The flight commander's gaze was very direct, and she noticed that his eyes were an unusually warm shade of brown. He really was a very attractive man, she thought. The scar gave him a rakish air, making him seem more approachable than the usual, perfect Elite. But he *was* Elite, she reminded herself, her smile fading a little. And she'd always been told the Elite couldn't be trusted.

Her back straightened. "Thank you, Flight Commander," she said. "I appreciate your concern. Now, if you'll excuse me, I'm off duty, and there's a cup of coffee with my name on it. Good evening to you." She saluted crisply and made her escape.

CHAPTER THREE

Zaran relinquished control of his firebird to the docking arm on the side of the *Atria* and unfastened his safety harness whilst his vessel was recovered into the interior of its gigantic mothership. As it was drawn into its docking pod and the *Atria's* skin irised closed, he blinked several times to adjust to the increased light levels inside the larger vessel. His craft clunked into place, and his cockpit array informed him that the chamber outside was cycling. Once the readouts told him the pressure was fully equalised, he cracked open the canopy and swung himself out onto the ladder along one strut of his ship's cradle. Descending slowly, he took a moment to check out his ship's skin for signs of damage. The pluslight envelope tended to repel most space debris, but it was better to be safe than sorry. Once he reached the bay's floor, he walked across to check the other side before operating the airlock door that led out into the pilots' ready lounge.

He had grown up on the *Atria* but had been away from her since he was old enough to enter the Academy, serving on several other vessels before finally applying for his current post, which had become vacant when the *Atria's* previous flight commander had retired. He was conscious that everything seemed ever so slightly smaller than he remembered, and nothing was in quite the same place as it had been on his previous postings.

The lounge was empty save for his wingman, Raffi, who had been his best friend since Academy days and had transferred to the *Atria* once his application had been approved. She was lounging in one of the bucket chairs, her maroon safesuit unfastened at the neck. The pose drew attention to her non-regulation boots, the thick soles of which made her feel, she claimed, less like a dwarf amongst the Elite. Zaran would have censured her for the discipline breach, but she'd pointed out that she'd had them made so that they sealed to her safesuit just like regulation boots would, and he'd had to agree that they weren't a safety issue.

The curly-haired pilot had a glass of something orange in her hand and toasted him with it. "Welcome back, Zar. Got to warn you, you're not the most popular person on the ship right now. Lots of people are a touch vexed that you've cut them off from hearth and home."

"At least their hearths and homes aren't being devoured by … whatever those things are," he told her ruefully.

Raffi shook her head. "They function in *space*, Zar - how's that even possible?"

"If I ever figure that out, you'll be the first to know." He shrugged. "Not that I'm expecting to. Figure it out, that is … I'm babbling; I'm tired. How's Grus?"

"The Wheel's recovery team got to him before his safesuit's emergency air supply ran out," Raffi advised. "He seemed pretty calm about the whole experience, but I sent him to debrief with psych to be on the safe side."

"Good thinking." Zaran flopped into the chair across the table from Raffi and contemplated closing his eyes and going to sleep right there.

"I wouldn't get too comfortable," she told him. "Your mother wanted to be informed when you docked."

Zaran pulled a face. "I thought I'd escaped her when I took this posting," he said. "I should've remembered that the universe has a sense of humour." He heaved a sigh. "Anybody else asking for me?"

"Justice Rydon came by. He didn't say what he wanted, but I think we can both guess. And your Uncle Ashwood came by, as well."

"Ashwood?" Zaran was genuinely startled. "I didn't think he ever left his office these days."

"... especially with your mother on board?" Raffi laughed. "Did I say you weren't the most popular person around? The number of people looking for you suggests otherwise!"

Zaran managed a faint laugh, tiredness sweeping through him. The adrenalin he'd generated during the firefight was all but used up now, and he wanted nothing more than to find his bunk and fall onto it. "I'd better go and see Ashwood," he decided. "It might be important, and he may be the only person who doesn't want to lecture me." He levered himself out of the chair, resolutely ignoring the knowledge that what he should really be doing was writing his report. "You should hit your bunk, Lieutenant," he told her. "I can't guarantee we won't have to fly again tomorrow. In fact, I'd lay odds we'll be spending a lot of time in our firebirds in the near future."

"Good point." She peered into her nearly empty glass. "Do the same yourself, Flight, and we'll see what tomorrow brings."

The pilots' ready room was towards the rear of the ship. Zaran walked up to the central thoroughfare of the *Atria*, a vast cylindrical space which ran from the prow of the ship to its stern. This was the heart of the ship, navigated either by moving walkway or, for those in a hurry, via the magrav pods that sped overhead. At ground level, coffee shops, bars and restaurants jockeyed for space with outlets from which all kinds of commodities could be purchased. The less expensive shops sold goods created in the ship's replicators, whilst others offered pricier items produced on planets or manufacturing stations. Trees and art installations broke up the space, and higher up neat lines of office windows offered snapshots of activity. Like the core of all the star cruisers, it was brightly lit during the day watch, whilst the lights were dimmed during the ship's 'night' period.

Deciding that he was too tired to hurry, although his destination lay toward the front of the vessel Zaran hopped onto one of the moving walkways rather than taking the steps up to the magrav pod boarding point. It was towards the end of the ship's day, but there were still plenty of people around. Although he recognised some faces, he was aware that many of his mother's contemporaries had transferred off the ship when she left it; she had rewarded her team well. Some of them he'd thought of as friends, and he missed their familiar faces. He found himself wondering whether, cut off as they were, he'd ever see any of them again, and shook his head. Of course he would; things couldn't possibly be *that* dire. He refused to contemplate the fact that if they were, it might just be his own fault. He let the belts carry him towards the front of the vessel and Ashwood Atria's lair.

Because his mother had been captain of the ship and therefore too busy to spend much time with him, the young Zaran had, along with his half-sister Allenda, run a little wild; but, where Allenda had always aimed to be underfoot in the pilots' ready lounge, Zaran had preferred the company of his small, eccentric uncle, whose office was filled with all kinds of wondrous things. Most Elite, living as they did in ships and space stations, kept few belongings; Ashwood, however, was something of a hoarder. Books, paraphernalia, mysterious objects and intriguing diagrams filled every surface in his clut-

tered space. Zaran had lost count of how many happy hours
he'd spent exploring the fascinating room. That was probably,
he thought, why everyone had expected him to follow in his
uncle's footsteps and become some kind of scientist. They
underestimated just how much he'd fallen in love with flying,
once he'd been given the opportunity to try it.

When he reached Ashwood's office, he found the door
open and his uncle behind his desk, squinting thoughtfully at
a holo of the day's battle. Zaran hesitated, seeing his own firebird roll across behind one of the alien blobs, his lasers laying
down a pattern of fire.

"Come in, dear boy." His uncle waved a hand to pause the
recording. "Fascinating creatures, aren't they?"

"I'm not sure I'd call them fascinating," Zaran admitted,
taking the chair his uncle indicated. "Horrifying, perhaps.
Infuriating. Devastating. And very, very trying."

Ashwood steepled his fingers and rested his chin on them.
"No doubt, Zaran," he said, "but did you figure out what
makes them move?"

"Was I supposed to?" Zaran asked. "There was nothing
visible. No exhaust pipe, no engine flare, no manoeuvring jets.
Just blobs, being ... blobby. I do wish somebody would come
up with a sensible thing to call them. Are they sentient creatures, or are they operating on some sub-intelligent, instinc-
tive level?"

"Possibly tardigrades," Ashwood mused. "Almost definitely a form of extremophile. I'm not an astrobiologist, and I
don't think we have one on board these days, but I do know a
little about panspermia ..."

"That sounds uncomfortably reproductive," Zaran
commented wryly.

"It's a theory concerning the transmission of life in the
universe through space," Ashwood told him, smiling a little.
"So I suppose it is, if you take it literally!"

"Sorry, Uncle Ash," Zaran laughed, "but I sincerely hope they're not alien sperm!" He sobered. "Frankly, I don't think I can tell you anything about the blobs you can't see for yourself. They arrived, they pretty much ignored our attempts to deflect them, and they dissolved things."

"*All* things?"

"There really wasn't time to check, but it certainly looked like it."

"Your mother and the captain wouldn't let me go down to the surface and examine them myself," Ashwood sighed. "They said I was too valuable ... which is all very flattering but doesn't help me identify what they are."

"We need to find a way to deal with them, whatever they are," Zaran said, resisting the temptation to be drawn into a conversation about his mother.

"Well, obviously, dear boy. Finding out what they are is one step of that." Ashwood shook his head. "We just don't have the knowledge in our databases any more," he said, half to himself, and then looked up. "Were you aware, Zaran, that we no longer carry any research papers?"

Zaran frowned. "We don't? That seems strange. Have they just been filed somewhere else? Sorry, obviously you will have checked."

"Star cruisers were once the fount of all knowledge," Ashwood mused, "collating and comparing research from all over the system. But somewhere along the way, somebody took the decision that only proven facts should be shared, and our library dwindled accordingly. Our Academies were discouraged from innovation ... and, you know, not just our database was slimmed down. Once, a ship like this would've had a whole team of scientists working on developing new things. Nowadays, my department is seriously undermanned, and the title 'head scientist' is a bit of a joke, just as we have a thirty-year-old entitled 'Surgeon General' just because he's the most senior doctor on board, and ..." He broke off. "I'm sorry, I suspect the last thing you need is to listen to me complaining. I'm feeling a little old today."

"You're not old," Zaran said, quite correctly as, at sixty, his uncle was less than halfway through his projected lifespan.

"I'm just disappointed that you don't have more information for me," Ashwood admitted. "But I suppose I shouldn't be surprised – no mystery is solved quickly."

"I was a little preoccupied with trying to save the *Brightwing,*" Zaran pointed out, and yawned wearily.

Ashwood frowned at him. "You're exhausted, boy," he diagnosed. "Go and get some sleep."

Without further comment, the small man turned his attention back to the holo, unfreezing it, and Zaran left him there, fingers steepled, dark eyes brooding as tiny firebirds zipped through the space in front of him, and the *Brightwing* endlessly repeated her final voyage.

Zaran made his way to his quarters and was not especially surprised when, turning the final corner into the passageway that housed the senior officers' quarters, he found himself confronted by his mother. She would, of course, have been checking on his whereabouts via his locator chip, and he'd had a suspicion she would want to speak to him privately before he had a chance to file his report.

Admiral Nashira was annoyingly tall, so that he had to look up at her. Her hair was in a tight bun, making her look older than her years, and the robe she wore over her safesuit was one of her most official, with the ribbons of her awards pinned to the left shoulder.

"Zaran," she said. "I expected you to report to me earlier."

Zaran bit off the retort that he worked for Captain Asterion, not her, and came to attention instead. "I beg your pardon, Admiral," he said. "I was not aware that you required me to report directly to you."

"Perhaps if you had we wouldn't be in this situation," she said tartly. "Really, Zaran - ordering the substream closed down without checking with anybody first? What in the seven hells were you thinking? I've got Captain Asterion and your father demanding to know what kind of a son I raised. Director Greybridge has threatened to make a formal complaint, and Justice Rydon is considering whether to have you arrested. Why, by all that's good, didn't you ask before you took such a calamitous action? It's going to take a great deal of time and effort to sort it out. I hope you enjoy your deserved notoriety."

She strode off without giving him the opportunity to respond, leaving him with his mouth half-open. He closed it and shook his head, turning to key his personal code into the pad adjacent to the door of his quarters. His mother was upset, he told himself, because she'd made the decision to accompany the *Atria* rather than remaining safely at Bendos. She'd been there to oversee the annual graduation ceremony, after which he understood she would have returned to Sol Academy. There was a vacancy on the Board of Trustees, and strong rumours that she would only have to turn up to be appointed, the youngest trustee in the history of the IUP. Instead, now it was quite likely she had no better idea than he did how long it would take to get back to IUP space, and the decision to go to Meridiana might have destroyed her career.

That didn't excuse her attitude toward him, he thought, but then they'd never really got along, and she'd been horrified when she'd discovered he'd been appointed to the vacancy on the *Atria*.

He entered his quarters and ordered the door closed behind him. He unsealed and kicked off his boots, then stripped off his safesuit and hung it carefully in the locker, where it would be refreshed. Frowning, he headed for the fresher. He always found that standing under the jets of water helped him think, and Ashwood's words had worried him.

Star cruisers had always been multi-taskers: they were cities in permanent flight, patrolling the substream and servicing the various settlements at the nodes. They carried correspondence, news and entertainment materials, no way of sending communications by any faster method having been found to date; they spread the word about new discoveries in the sciences and medicine, and dealt with outbreaks of disease; they updated planetary databases on new laws, and the Justice team undertook investigations and trials of matters considered too high profile or difficult for planets to manage themselves; and very, very occasionally they acted as police, shutting down pirates and those who would cheat traders, ensuring no planet developed the desire or the wherewithal to attack another.

If the knowledge they were sharing was no longer innovative, what did that say about the IUP?

They had bigger things to worry about right now, he thought. In all the years since the substream had been developed and the star cruisers had begun their endless voyages, no lifeform bigger than a microbe had been discovered. Planets were seeded and colonised entirely by the IUP. This – if these were true aliens – he believed to be a first, and Zaran sincerely hoped if this was typical of the other life forms in the universe it would be the last.

He turned up the pressure and braced himself as the streams of recycled water massaged his aching body. He couldn't remember the last time he'd spent so long in his firebird, and however much he loved flying, the cockpit didn't allow for much in the way of exercise. He'd been beginning to experience cramps before he finally docked at the Wheel.

Thinking of the Wheel reminded him of the wide-eyed traffic controller who had had the misfortune of being on duty when he'd given the order to shut down the substream. Cristal Feltspar, by her name, wasn't from the Elite class, and indeed she didn't look much like an Elite woman. They tended to be tall, polished and graceful. She was pale and slender, and the spiky hair he'd noted on her holo had turned out, in real life, to be streaked with rainbow iridescence. When he'd been standing close to her, he'd noticed a light perfume that reminded him of summer days at the Academy, although he wasn't entirely sure why. It was likely she was Wheeler born, although he supposed it was possible she might have been born on a planet and moved to the Wheel later in life.

He realised he felt a strong sense of guilt where Cristal Feltspar was concerned. She was going to get just as much disrespect from people as he was for shutting down the substream and trapping them all here with the rampaging ... things. He should try and make it up to her, he thought. It would be a kind gesture.

But first he'd better write up his report.

CHAPTER FOUR

Normally, Cristal managed two full circuits of the outer wheel before breakfast. Today the running track was milling with confused-looking strangers, presumably evacuees, and she opted to slow to a stop at the end of her first circuit. She made sure to do her full bends and stretches before jogging the rest of the way to the hatch that marked the end of her morning run. She tapped in the entry code and stood back as the heavy door opened with a hiss. She smiled as the strong aroma of vegetation washed over her.

One entire arm of the Wheel was given over to hydroponics, a warm, green jungle of fruit and vegetables along with some purely ornamental foliage grown for aesthetic purposes. After ensuring the hatch was fully closed, Cristal touched her wristcom to open her throat mic. "Thom? Where are you?"

Her friend's holo popped up above her wristcom. "Breakfast is being served at Station Six".

"I'll be right with you." Cristal jogged gently down the aisles between the tanks with their burgeoning greenery, emerging eventually into a small area under a spreading tree where a table was laid for two.

"Coffee?" The hydroponics chief, already seated at one of the places, held up the carafe.

Cristal grinned. "Have I ever said no?"

"There might be a first time."

"It won't be today!"

As her friend poured, Cristal sank into the chair opposite him with a contented sigh. She loved this space, in some respects the lungs of the Wheel, which supplied its oxygen, helped to cleanse its air, and offered a peaceful haven away from the more crowded thoroughfares.

Thom Redwood was a tall man, well built, with a mass of curling dark hair and an utterly unfashionable moustache and beard. He had the kind of looks that had the singles on the Wheel sighing after him, but to the best of Cristal's knowledge, he had never shown any interest in any of them, of either gender. Her own friendship with him had resulted from him taking pity on the sad-eyed child he found wandering in his arboretum. She had adopted him as a kind of big brother, someone she could talk to when Ruby was being problematic, or her father was being particularly difficult, or she had argued with her friends.

With the coffee came a plate of mixed fruit, freshly picked; but today Cristal found herself pushing it around the plate, not especially hungry.

"Don't waste it," he said. "I hear you had a tough duty yesterday."

"Word travels fast." She sighed, pushing her hands into her hair in a gesture of frustration. "I had no choice, Thom. If those things had got into the substream, it could've been the end of our civilisation. Nothing seems to touch them. They swarm in space as if vacuum and lack of gravity mean nothing to them. Nobody even seems to know how they propel themselves. It was terrifying," she admitted. "It just felt like we were utterly defenceless. They cracked open one of the pods from the *Brightwing,* and all the people on board died ... I may have nightmares about that for the rest of my life. What if they get onto the Wheel?"

"I'm sure the IUP admiral will have a plan," Thom said ironically.

"Have you ever met her?" Cristal wondered.

"No. But I know of her. Admiral Nashira used to be captain of the *Atria*, and I've talked to crew from the other star cruisers that have docked here. She's a formidable woman, by all accounts, destined to be a Trustee."

"Oh, fabulous," Cristal sighed. "And I'm willing to bet she won't like the fact Zaran and I just stranded her here and left her with a bunch of Wheelers, planet dwellers and aliens to juggle!"

"Ah, yes, Flight Commander Zaran." Thom grinned, as if she'd said something funny, although she couldn't think what it might have been. "He's her son, you know."

"He is?" Cristal was surprised. "It never occurred to me ... of course, it's easy to forget these Elite are so inbred. Their entire society is built on nepotism."

"More like pragmatism," Thom said. "They are the ones who chose to live in space, either at their orbital headquarters at Sol or one of the Academies, or on board the star cruisers. It's not a closed society as such, but they tend to prefer to match with someone who understands their way of life. I know your father wasn't keen on them, but I've found some of them to be quite reasonable."

Cristal shook her head, unwilling to enter into an argument. "I don't think I want to think about Elite, or aliens, or anything else much this morning. Distract me – how are the plants? Anything new to report?"

"Well, the irises are coming into flower." Thom loved plants, and as soon as he started to talk about them his whole demeanour changed. "You should go by them and take a look," he said. "They're over in bed twenty. And the maize is just about ready to harvest. Oh, and the runner beans have picked up since I changed their carbon filters. I've been told I need to increase the potato production, since although half our own population has been evacuated, we're taking on a lot of evacuees whilst the crisis plays out." Off her look, he shrugged. "Cristal, we can hardly pretend it's not happening. When I heard what was going down yesterday, I went up to the observation deck and watched the fighting. I think I was the least surprised person there when the substream gateway closed down. Last time I checked, the blobs were doing a great job of demolishing the infrastructure. I have to tell you, I don't think that gate's going to be reopened any time soon, even if Bendos Wheel attempts to send a new link through."

"So what's going to happen to us?" Cristal wondered.

Thom shrugged again. "I do plants, not prophecies. On the positive side, we have not one but two whole star cruisers here to help us."

"Didn't you get offered a job on one once?" Cristal queried. "I seem to remember you telling me that happened before you came to the Wheel. Do you regret not taking the post?"

"I ... would have liked to see more of the network," Thom admitted. "But I was born on a planet, and after managing an entire farm I wasn't prepared to take the menial job I was offered on a star cruiser. This ..." He indicated the space they were in. "This is a challenge I enjoy, and I'm my own boss."

And that was the problem with the nepotism inherent in the Elite system, Cristal thought as she made her way out of the hatch at the hub end of the hydroponics arm. Assuming that all else was equal, she would still be expected to turn up for duty in the control room. It wasn't always the case that the best person got the job - it was the best-connected person. Her father had told her that an Elite would always take precedence for star cruiser appointments over anybody else, no matter how clever they were. Take Flight Commander Zaran - Thom said he was the admiral's son, and she guessed that meant he'd risen through the ranks easily.

She frowned. On the other hand, the man she'd met in the control room hadn't seemed snobbish, and what she'd seen of his flying appeared to her eyes more than effective – even inspired. She couldn't think of any way he could have used his patrol to better effect against the impossible creatures they were fighting. No weapon seemed to work against them, and once they'd started flying around in space a disastrous outcome had seemed inevitable. She remembered the way the flight commander had looked at her when he'd told her he would take the flak. He'd really meant it, she was sure. Maybe she should rethink her preconceptions about the Elite, or at least give this one the benefit of the doubt until she found out otherwise.

The inner hub was busy, and Cristal encountered a number of other Wheel employees, all of whom she knew at least casually. Some nodded politely, whilst others glowered at her in obvious annoyance. Word of who was responsible for initiating the gateway shutdown seemed to be spreading; she guessed it had been too much to hope that her name would be kept out of it. She wished fewer of her friends had been evacuated. Apart from Thom, there wasn't really anybody left she thought would take her part.

As she made her way around the passageway that surrounded the hub of the Wheel, she encountered a group of five young men standing around a girl who was gesticulating enthusiastically.

"... I'm telling you they have a really *good* team on the *Gemin*, and I'm sure the *Atria* has one, and ..." The girl's voice tailed off as she spotted Cristal. "Oh, good morning, Cristal," she said, sounding less enthusiastic. "We're trying to set up a tournament with an Elite gravity ball team. Will you be available to play?"

Cristal wondered why the cargo handler thought she might not be. "I guess so, Meran," she said. "Have you asked the star cruiser teams?"

"No, but I'm sure one or the other will be happy to give us a game," Meran enthused. "I can't imagine either star cruiser doesn't have a team. You talked to the duty comms officers last night, didn't you, Jedda?"

Jedda Granit, the man who had relieved Cristal in the control room the previous evening, yawned widely. "We talked a lot about gravity ball," he said. "They didn't seem to know we had a really, really good team here, even with half our players evacuated. We've still got our best player: me!"

The others groaned, and there was some good-natured jostling. Normally Cristal would have joined in the banter, but this morning she felt as if there was a barrier between her and her fellow gravity ball players, most of whom were younger than her twenty-five years.

"We need to beat them," Jedda continued, "so that when the new substream is open and the league scout gets here, they can tell him to tip us for the league."

It was, Cristal was aware, Jedda's sole ambition to get into the league and appear in all the gravity ball championships they saw on holo, often months after the matches had been played.

"Did they say there would be a new substream set up?" she heard herself ask, and hunched her shoulders a little defensively as a couple of the players frowned at her.

"Not in as many words," Jedda said. "But it stands to reason, doesn't it? What else can they do? The star cruisers will get rid of the aliens, and everything will go back to normal."

Cristal wished she could believe his optimism had any

basis in reality, but after seeing the blobs dissolve the *Brightwing* she didn't hold out a great deal of hope. "Are we going to practice at the usual ..."

She broke off as her wristcom chimed. "Controller Feltspar, please attend Commander Rockspire's office immediately."

"I have to go," she told her fellow players. "Um, I'll talk to you later." She hurried past them, a leaden feeling in her gut.

Rockspire's office was on the outer edge of the inner hub, some distance from the control centre. Cristal called up the duty traffic controller. "Henny, I'm going to be late," she said. "Do you mind holding the fort?"

"I guess I don't have much choice," the controller she was due to replace responded. "What's the delay?"

"I've been called to speak to the commander."

"Oh." Henny hesitated. "Uh ... good luck, I think."

"Thanks," Cristal said. "I need it!"

When she reached his office, Rockspire called her straight in but didn't offer her a seat. She stood at parade rest in front of his desk, her hands behind her back and her fingers crossed where he couldn't see them. "Reporting as ordered, Commander," she said crisply.

"Controller Feltspar." Rockspire put down the stylus he had been fiddling with when she came in and straightened in his chair. He looked her up and down, his brow creasing as he frowned. "You've caused us all a great deal of trouble, Controller." He shook his head. "When the evacuation started to go wrong, you should have made more effort to contact me. As it is, you rashly took it upon yourself to use a set of instructions that were intended for the direst of emergencies. Whether or not the circumstances were as calamitous as Flight Commander Zaran seemed to think is up for discussion. There's a distinct possibility he overstepped his mission remit and will be brought up on charges. It's even possible that the justices on the *Atria* and the *Gemin* might see their way to bring charges against the Wheel."

"Charges?" Cristal said faintly. It hadn't even occurred to her that the legal arm of the IUP might have an interest in what had happened.

"Wilful destruction of IUP property; stranding persons of the IUP and the GFI for an indeterminate period; failure to follow procedures ... I'm sure the joint justices will have plenty to say," Rockspire said grimly. "You can rest assured, Controller Feltspar, that those charges will be directed at you, not me. I don't intend to take the fall for your dereliction of due process. Do you understand me?"

"Yes, sir." Cristal stared straight over his head, too terrified to meet his eyes. Her heart was thundering in her chest as she wondered what the penalty might be for the kind of charges Rockspire was suggesting. She wanted to laugh a little hysterically – half a cycle earlier, her major concern had been whether she'd still be alive by the end of the day. Now, as well as that, she was under threat of being blamed for the results of the order she'd been given. She found herself feeling hugely relieved that her father had already been evacuated and wouldn't witness her disgrace, and at the same time angry that the commander didn't seem more shocked by the loss of life. "Flight Commander Zaran ..." she began, her voice shaking slightly.

"Isn't part of your chain of command, Controller." Rockspire glanced at his wristcom and rose to his feet, tugging down the robe he wore over his safesuit. "I would love to spend more time telling you just what I think of you," he said, "but Admiral Nashira has called a meeting to discuss our situation. I've offered her our Star Chamber as a suitable venue, and the meeting is due to start."

"Yes, sir," Cristal said again, expecting him to dismiss her.

"Your presence is required at the meeting, Controller. I

suggest you make your way to the Star Chamber immediately." He looked her up and down and shook his head slightly as if her uniform safesuit wasn't quite the attire he would have expected her to be wearing. If she'd had some warning, she thought crossly, she would've put on her dress robes.

"But I'm supposed to be on duty," she said, a little stupidly.

"Oh, for ..." He looked ceilingward. "Must I do everything? Call your line manager and advise them to reschedule your duty. Dismissed, Controller."

Chastened, aware that her face was flushed, Cristal turned and left his office.

CHAPTER FIVE

Zaran docked the shuttle from the *Atria* on the outer rim of the Meridiana Wheel. Admiral Nashira disembarked first along with her aide, Colonel Kovis, with Captain Asterion of the *Atria* close behind them. The *Gemin* and the *Atria* were supervising the evacuation of the remaining people from the planet to the Wheel. When Zaran followed the others through the hatch into the dock circuit, he found it crowded with people meandering apparently aimlessly in one direction or another. They looked dirty, dishevelled and in some cases had obvious injuries. The GFI uniform didn't include a safe-suit as standard, Zaran realised, and he hoped someone had thought to increase the production of clothing suitable for off-planet life. The evacuees were both male and female, but he saw no children. Of course, he realised, the children had been sent off first in the pods. He thought about the ill-fated *Brightwing* and swallowed the lump that rose in his throat, hoping there had been no children on board that doomed vessel.

Their deputation was met by a Wheel engineer, who chivvied them somewhat apologetically towards a small transit cart. The vehicle had seen better days, its cream canopy fraying and its fabric seats stained. Zaran found himself crammed on the back seat between the more muscular Asterion and Kovis. All of them were wearing their dress robes, which didn't help matters. His mother, similarly clad, sat more comfortably beside the engineer as he drove them through the throng. Their journey took longer than it might have since they had to keep stopping to persuade groups of confused and distraught evacuees to make way for them, and Zaran wondered how many bruises he was going to have as a result of being jostled between the two bigger men.

"This isn't going to be easily resolved," the colonel murmured, gesturing to the milling throng.

The captain shook his head. "You're right there."

The two men seemed very comfortable with each other, Zaran thought. He didn't think they'd served together in the past and was a little surprised that they gave every appearance of being good friends. He wondered whether the admiral's aide, who had served with her for as long as he could remember, was acting as a buffer between his occasionally antagonist mother and the captain of her old ship.

Their vehicle turned in-Wheel through a security door and entered an area which seemed sparsely populated after the outer ring. The cart sped up as they passed along a corridor that was as utilitarian as the outer area, though the grey metal had at least been broken up by holos of the space outside and the occasional clump of ferns and tropical trees. Zaran noticed the area was warmer than the dock circuit had been.

The engineer brought their conveyance to a final halt outside an open door. "The Star Chamber, Admiral."

"Thank you." Nashira descended regally, took a moment to tidy her robe and the ribbons of her rank, and then swept through the doorway, the other men scrambling a little to keep up with her. Zaran caught Colonel Kovis's eye and the older man dropped him a wink. The flight commander found himself feeling a little better about things. It appeared not everybody thought he was a walking disaster area.

The Star Chamber was a large lecture theatre with a stage against one wall and tiered seating around the other three. When the invitation to the meeting had been issued, Zaran had been surprised that the Wheel had an appropriately large gathering place, but he'd established that it was apparently used for training lectures and holos as well as festivities. The room was already packed with people and very noisy – everyone there seemed to be talking at once. There was an undercurrent of alarm, apprehension and despondency in the exchanges Zaran overheard as he hesitated at the top of the steps. His eyes were caught by the holo at the rear of the stage showing a view of the system which included the substream gateway apparatus. With only one gateway open, it looked unbalanced, as if the gigantic structure was, like Kovis had, winking at him.

Admiral Nashira started to descend the steps, and Zaran followed behind her aide and the *Atria's* captain. At the foot, a prefect waved the admiral and her aide towards the stage, whilst he and the captain were directed to a pair of vacant seats in the front row. Zaran found he had been allocated the seat next to Traffic Controller Feltspar. As he sat down, adjusting his robe self-consciously, he noticed she was wearing the same perfume as the night before, which he still couldn't identify. "Good morning," he greeted her.

"I don't think it's good," she said. "Sir." This last was added bleakly and, he thought, perhaps a little uncomfortably.

"I will take full responsibility, Controller Feltspar," he assured her. "I said I would, and I meant it. Please don't be afraid."

"Afraid?" she countered, bristling visibly. "Frankly, Flight Commander, I can't decide which of the various things that went wrong yesterday terrifies me the most, although aliens eating everything in their path might *just* overshadow fear of public censure."

Zaran smiled wryly, accepting that he'd just been put firmly in his place. He realised Feltspar didn't like him very much – possibly because he was Elite and she wasn't – and decided against attempting to reply. The order bell rang, the groups of people who had been chattering in the aisles of the room were chivvied by a number of prefects to find seats, and the hubbub slowly quieted. Zaran spotted his uncle Ashwood seated nearby with a small contingent of scientists from the *Atria*, and behind him the imposing figure of Lord Chief Justice Rydon. He wasn't surprised to find most of the audience to be strangers to him; there had to be representatives from both the planet and the Wheel here. Everyone had a stake in how they dealt with the situation they found themselves in. He noticed his father, Decrus Gemin, further along the front row, and managed to avoid making eye contact.

Admiral Nashira and her aide walked onto the stage and the room finally fell silent. His mother was in her element here, the focus of every eye; even Kovis, whose exceptional good looks usually drew attention, was eclipsed by her presence. Whilst the admiral stood at centre stage, the colonel situated himself to one side, his dark eyes scanning the seating, alert for any trouble.

"Is everybody here?" Nashira smiled. "Good morning to you all. I'm Admiral Nashira from the IUP, currently using the *Atria* as my flagship. As the ranking officer of the IUP, Director Greybridge and Commander Rockspire have ceded the chair of today's meeting to me." She looked around at the gathering, which was now almost unnaturally silent.

"Gentlefolk," she said, "I must open by offering condolences to all here who have lost friends or family in the evacuation of Meridiana." She bowed her head for a moment in respect and then straightened. "What has happened in this star system is unprecedented," she said. "For the first time ever, we have encountered something which gives every indication of being an alien lifeform. I am therefore going to call it such, although it is still possible that we may discover it to be simply some hitherto unknown element reacting to our presence. Whatever those things are, whatever they want, we are in some ways privileged to witness these events, however calamitous. Director Greybridge, can I ask you please to open with a recap on the arrival of the ..." She gestured a little helplessly. "Aliens."

The GFI director rose to his feet and made his way up to the platform. The short, stocky man didn't have anything like Nashira's charisma, Zaran thought. Kovis brought a chair for the admiral, and she sat down, folding her hands on her lap. Zaran noted that she was wearing her full honours, even some she didn't normally bother with, her ribbons a splash of colour against the dark maroon of her robe. Her grey hair was, as always, swept back into a bun.

Rockspire described again how the aliens had appeared, apparently from nowhere, and how they had slowly but inexorably encroached on the planet's infrastructure. Nothing the inhabitants of Meridiana had done had slowed the things, nor done any apparent damage. "This is predominantly a mining planet," he finished. "We don't have biologists. We don't know anything about aliens – who does? As far as we know, nobody has ever met one before – and if they did, they've kept very quiet about it!"

"So you learned nothing about them before you decided to evacuate the planet?" Nashira queried.

"Only that they don't want to communicate with us. All they want to do is destroy." Rockspire shrugged. "Like I said, nothing we could do seemed to stop them – and frankly, Admiral, nothing the IUP have done to date appears to have stopped them, either. If anything, you've made matters worse!"

Zaran winced; he had a point. Until the star cruisers had arrived, the things had confined their activities to the planet's surface. Of course, their leap into space coincided with the departure of the majority of the residents, which could also have been what gave them their impetus.

The room quieted as Ashwood Atria wandered onto the stage, almost as if he hadn't noticed where he was, but Zaran realised that his uncle's apparent absent-mindedness had served to deflate the tension created by Rockspire's accusatory words. Rockspire gave him a puzzled look and then retreated to stand by Nashira's chair, effectively ceding the floor to the chief scientist.

"For those of you who don't know me," Ashwood opened, "my name is Ashwood, and for my sins I'm chief scientist aboard the *Atria*. I've got some things to say and a suggestion to make, but I'm going to start by talking about the past." He tapped one finger against his mouth for a moment as if thinking, before he continued. "When our ancestors first set up the substream network, they created a system that allowed them to access sufficient resources to give their – our – civilisation everything it needed to prosper. There came a point when there was no longer any profit in expanding further. Establishing the co-ordinates, the nexus, for each substream pair took time and effort. As you all know, in all the time the network was being constructed, no-one ever found identifiable life on another planet. We spread our crops and our livestock where they would thrive and created a bubble of similarity." He paused, considering his audience thoughtfully. "Have we now, for the first time, encountered another life form, one that has no ties to our mother planet? To be honest, I don't think we can answer that question yet. The blobs – to give the things their colloquial nomenclature – have performed in a way that leads us to conjecture that they have self-agency - but their behaviour could still be accounted for by a chemical reaction or by some other unknown stimulus. Their recent behaviour would suggest that they came to Meridiana from somewhere else; but that may not be the case, despite their now proven ability to maintain structure and perform actions in the vacuum of space."

Ashwood paused, his expression pensive. "The point I'm trying to make is that we need far more information than we currently have in order to establish what is causing them to behave as they are. In the meantime, until we are able to learn more than we currently know, we don't have – and I don't think we *can* have – a good defence against them." He looked thoughtfully across at his sister, and then inclined his head to her. "I'm going to save my suggestion for later, Admiral, if you don't mind."

"Thank you, Chief Scientist." Nashira frowned slightly as her brother wandered off the stage with the same air of absent-mindedness with which he'd arrived.

"Interesting," Zaran heard Cristal say, and turned, assuming she was addressing him, only to find that she was speaking to a dark-haired man he didn't recognise who was seated on the other side of her. "Do you rate him?"

"He may not look it, but he's a genius," the man murmured in reply. "I've watched all his vids. He's an inspiration."

Zaran raised an eyebrow. It sounded like his uncle had an admirer.

Nashira summoned Captain Decrus to the stage. Zaran sank down in his chair, having a strong feeling things were about to get very uncomfortable for him. His father, a tall man whose mop of hair was now almost completely white, described the evacuation as seen from his vantage point on the *Gemin*, including the fate of the *Brightwing*. "I confess to a feeling of incredulity when the blobs launched themselves into space without taking any apparent harm." He shook his head. "Both the *Gemin* and the *Atria* focussed lasers on them, but we were unable to alter, or even slow, their trajectory."

"Thank you, Captain." Nashira's gaze sought out Zaran, and he braced himself. "Flight Commander Zaran, if you would join us, please?"

Zaran stood up, straightening his robe self-consciously. He made his way to the ramp at the side of the stage, and as he strode up it he found himself looking over at the still seated Cristal. He offered her a wry – and he hoped reassuring – smile, but if she noticed, she showed no sign. He swallowed and adopted his best professionally neutral expression as he stood to attention to one side of the stage.

"Please take up the story, Flight Commander." His mother's tone was very sweet, which he knew indicated she wasn't at all happy with him.

Zaran described the aerial fight, his interactions with the star cruisers, the Wheel, and the evacuation vessels. His parade voice carried, and as he described the moment when the blobs struck the *Brightwing*, he saw people as far as the back row of the auditorium wincing in sympathy. He explained the way the alien matter seemed to spread out across the surface. "Exactly," he said, "the way oil spreads out if you throw a glob of it at a flat surface." He saw Ashwood, back in his seat, nodding thoughtfully.

"The worst of it was there seemed to be nothing we could do," he went on. "Our laser fire deflected the things only temporarily and seemed to do no damage to them. The *Brightwing* captain wasn't answering our hails – we assumed his communications array was offline – and he took it upon himself to eject his pods." Zaran swallowed. "His action saved

... some of them, at least. The pod that was destroyed ..." He closed his eyes for a moment. "That moment will haunt me for the rest of my life."

"And then," Admiral Nashira said, "you ordered the Wheel traffic controller to close down the substream gateway."

"We were unable to deflect the *Brightwing*," Zaran replied flatly. "The only other choice would have been to fire on her directly, and the crew were still on board. With the gateway closed, there was a chance the *Brightwing* crew might be rescued, but if the vessel entered the substream the blobs would be on their way to Bendos and might have gone on to infect the entire substream network."

"So," Nashira said, "let's get the facts straight, Flight Commander. You took a decision, without referring the matter to your superiors, to have the substream gateway closed. Is that correct?"

"Yes, ma'am."

"Why did you not refer the matter to a higher authority?"

"There wasn't time to have a debate about it," he said flatly. "We had a matter of minutes, and the Wheel traffic controller told me it would take that long to initiate the shut-down."

"That would be Controller Feltspar?"

"That is correct, yes," he said. "As senior officer in the field, I gave her a direct order to close the gateway. The responsibility is entirely mine."

"Is it?" The tone of Nashira's voice indicated her displeasure. "Justice Rydon, do you have any comment to make at this time?"

The tall, hook-nosed justice rose to his feet and turned to address the audience. "This is an unprecedented case." Rydon's tone, usually laced with sarcastic undertones, was at its most bland and officious. "Substream gateways have been closed in the past, but only when a planet was deemed to have become too dangerous to be connected to the substream network. I think it can be argued that this is an analogous case; the threat to the IUP was self-evident. However, I will have to undertake more research on legal precedents to establish whether the flight commander was correct to take that decision without first referring it to a senior officer."

Zaran blinked, surprised. He would have thought Rydon had had plenty of time to reach a decision, and wondered why he was straddling the fence.

"And was the Wheel traffic controller correct in accepting the order given?" Nashira pursued.

"Again," the justice said, "I would need to spend more time examining the rules and regulations that apply on a Wheel. I would have liked to consult with a member of the Wheel judicial department, but I am informed that they have already been evacuated." He sat down.

"I see." Admiral Nashira glared at the justice. That was interesting, Zaran thought; Rydon had been on the *Atria* when his mother had been captain, and he wasn't aware of any disagreements, but there seemed to be a tension between them now. He frowned, trying to remember whether the lord chief justice had risen to his present position before or after his mother was promoted off the ship.

Commander Rockspire was summoned and bustled onto the stage. "How can I help, Admiral?" he asked.

"I understand, Commander, that your traffic controller was alone in the control room at the time of the evacuation and subsequent incident. Is it normal for there to be a single person on duty in the Meridiana Wheel traffic control?"

The commander nodded several times rapidly. "It is," he said. "Out here on the rim, we don't see the kind of traffic you get nearer the centre and it's not so important to keep a large staff on duty, particularly when traffic has been further reduced by the embargo on new arrivals placed by your good self. There are procedures in place to alert someone if any emergency should arise ..."

"What procedures are those?" Nashira interrupted him, her tone sweet. She didn't like the man, Zaran thought, and wondered whether everybody found his mother's temperament as easy to read as he did. Not yet dismissed, he stood to attention and tried not to make eye contact with anyone.

"Well, the controller should contact his or her superior officer," Rockspire blustered. "Or myself, of course. Controller Feltspar failed to do so ..."

An involuntary glance at the audience told Zaran that Cristal Feltspar was furious. They were discussing her and her actions without any recourse to her, which he felt to be entirely wrong. "Controller Feltspar attempted to contact you," he interjected. "I saw her do so. She couldn't get a reply."

"Perhaps you can tell us where you were at this time, Commander?" Admiral Nashira said, with a sweetness that Zaran knew concealed irritation.

"Director Greybridge and I were discussing how to proceed once the majority of the personnel on the planet had been evacuated," Rockspire said, drawing himself up. "It was very important to establish how Galactic Fuel's assets would be preserved, and in particular how the remaining refined seronium was to be stored pending the situation stabilising."

"In other words, you were discussing tactics," the admiral said. "Was it necessary to be out of the control room whilst you did this? Particularly bearing in mind that the evacuation was taking place at that time."

"I didn't expect there to be any problems," Rockspire blustered. "If there were, I expected the controller to make every effort to contact me. I certainly didn't expect her to ...

to follow orders from someone outside of the Wheel. Or to take such a decisive action without referring it to me."

"I see." Admiral Nashira nodded and then turned to her son. "Flight Commander, consider this a reprieve. However, the possibility of penalties for you as a result of your action still exists. Commander Rockspire, I leave it up to you whether you wish to suspend your traffic controller pending further investigation. Now," she continued, dismissing both Zaran and Rockspire with an impatient wave, "we need to talk about how we should proceed."

Zaran made a hasty exit from the stage, headed for his seat, but came to a halt when someone in the audience called out, "Admiral, I protest! I want action taken against your flight commander."

"And you are ...?" the admiral asked, as everyone else reacted with surprise.

The red-faced woman who rose to her feet was unfamiliar to Zaran, but he noticed Cristal wince slightly. "I'm Dolor Stile, Director Greybridge's aide, and I can't begin to tell you how furious I am. We have been stranded – stranded! – here, because of the actions of your flight commander. You've got nothing to lose – your family's right here with you! But some of us have families – families and friends – on the vessels that have already left. Families we might never see again, thanks to you!"

"I understand your frustration," Admiral Nashira said, although Zaran wasn't entirely sure that she did. He reached his seat beside Cristal and sat down, meeting her gaze with a rueful expression. He wanted to tell her that he had done his best to defend her and would continue to do so, but rather got the impression she was still angry that she hadn't been called to answer for her own actions.

"I'm not sure you do," Greybridge's aide complained.

"Regardless," Admiral Nashira said, "as I said, we have to

decide how to proceed. Fortunately, a large percentage of the population was evacuated before the situation ... escalated. Those remaining on the planet have now mostly been repatriated to the Wheel. I'm sure the IUP will be considering ways to re-establish the upstream from Bendos, so what we need to decide is how to accommodate one another until such time as that happens."

"But what if the aliens go on attacking?" somebody else in the audience wanted to know. Indignant conversation broke out throughout the chamber, and Zaran winced.

"That's the only plan she has?" Cristal said, not to Zaran but to the man on her right. He hushed her, and she sat back, folding her arms with an angry exhalation.

Ashwood wandered back onto the stage, and even Admiral Nashira gazed at him in surprise. "You have something to add, Chief Scientist?" she said.

The audience quieted as the small man cleared his throat. "As I mentioned earlier," he said, "I would like to propose another possibility."

"Oh?" Zaran got the impression his mother was unimpressed that she hadn't been warned about this in advance. Ashwood and Nashira were chalk and cheese, he thought – the one self-deprecating and cheerfully eccentric, the other self-aggrandising and severe.

"Yes." Ashwood looked around a little vaguely at the audience and then smiled his most charming smile. "Friends," he said, "has it occurred to any of you that we might travel to rejoin our civilisation the *long* way around?"

"The long way around?" Admiral Nashira repeated blankly.

"Yes," Ashwood said. "It would take a few years, of course, but it's perfectly possible to get to Bendos without using the substream."

"Even using pluslight it would take at least ten years,"

Nashira reminded him. "Nobody travels that kind of distance by pluslight. I'm not even sure it's possible. And not all the ships here are pluslight enabled."

"Well yes, it might take that long," Ashwood agreed. "But only if we don't devise a methodology to enhance our movement capability. All the vessels will have to travel together in overlapping pluslight envelopes, of course. Our propulsion systems and scanners have remained unchanged for generations." He paused, and then grinned. "I'm sure if we put our minds to it we can find ways to shorten our journey."

"By all the stars," Zaran heard himself say.

Conversation had broken out again, and this time it took Admiral Nashira longer to call the meeting to order. "I think the possibility suggested by the chief scientist is … interesting," she said, "but our situation is not yet so serious that we should take such an irregular step. I suggest we take a break at this point for refreshments and reconvene in an hour. Gentlefolk, thank you."

"Um … Controller Feltspar?" Zaran said quickly, before the girl could rise to her feet.

"Yes, Flight Commander?" she said, a little coldly.

"I … wondered if I might buy you lunch," he said. "If you would like to join me, that is," he added, and winced, suspecting he sounded ridiculous. From the way she was looking at him, he was fairly sure she was going to refuse, and he took a step backward, casting around a little desperately for a polite response.

CHAPTER SIX

Cristal had intended to have lunch with Thom, but as she was about to speak to him, the chief scientist approached him. "Am I correct that you are Thom Redwood, the Wheel's hydroponics expert?" he asked.

"I am," Thom replied warily. "Can I help you?"

"Oh, I certainly hope so." The chief scientist smiled up at the taller man. "I think we are about to have something of a food shortage, and I wondered how we might help each other to cater for the evacuees as well as our usual clientele. I hear you've achieved increased production by utilising some interesting variations on filters and nutrients, and I wanted to ask you some questions, if I might?"

"I ... guess I'd be happy to talk to you, Chief Scientist," Thom said, sounding flustered. Cristal wondered whether that was because he was surprised the *Atria's* chief scientist had heard anything about him at all.

"Over lunch?"

"Oh." Thom gave Cristal an apologetic look. "Yes, I'd ... like that."

Cristal blinked, noticing a slight blush on her friend's face, and then turned to Zaran. "You wanted to buy me lunch?" she said. "Did you have somewhere in mind?"

He smiled. She thought he was surprised that she'd accepted, and felt a little guilty that she had in fact been about to refuse. "I'm not altogether familiar with this part of the Wheel," he said, his tone apologetic. "I've only ever eaten in the visitor area, and that was some years ago. Do you have a suggestion?"

"There's a bistro a short walk from here," Cristal replied, after a moment's hesitation. She was conscious that, unlike most of the other people around them, she wasn't wearing formal robes, only her well-worn safesuit. "The food's basic," she went on, "but I think most of the people here will eat at the restaurant next door, so hopefully we'll get served quickly."

"Good idea," Zaran said. "Lead on." She led him through the throng, managing to avoid the senior officers, none of whom she had any great desire to speak to. As she had expected, most of the people from the meeting were headed into the adjacent restaurant; she turned in the opposite direction.

As Cristal had hoped, the small bistro near the hub was not overly busy, although several acquaintances gave her odd looks when she came in with the flight commander. She led him to a small table adjacent to a large potted palm, one of Thom's carefully nurtured trees which was growing in a large tub surrounded by ferns. She wasn't quite sure why Zaran had offered to buy her lunch and wondered whether he was just being polite. She ordered a salad, and he followed her lead, commenting only on the wide variety on offer.

Cristal considered her companion thoughtfully, trying not to stare at the scar on his face, which she would have expected Elite medics to have removed. "So," she ventured, "why did you want to have lunch with me?"

He laid down his fork and focused his attention on her. "I wanted to apologise," he said. "Admiral Nashira should have asked you to speak for yourself in the meeting. I have no idea why she didn't do so." He shook his head, looking flustered and rather younger than she'd first thought him. "I didn't know what she was going to say," he continued. "She can be a little intimidating."

"Isn't she ... I heard you were related," Cristal ventured. Behind him, she noticed Thom and Ashwood seating themselves at a corner table. They appeared to be getting along rather well. Ashwood was talking rapidly and gesticulating widely; Thom was nodding and smiling, interjecting the occasional comment.

"Nashira's my mother," Zaran said, and she gave him her full attention. "And if you don't already know, I should warn you that Captain Decrus of the *Gemin* is my father."

"Oh," she said, realising he was embarrassed. "That must be ... interesting."

"You could say that. But never mind me." He gave her a small smile. "Do you have family? I mean, on the Wheel, or are they already ...?"

"My family — my father and my younger sister — left on a merchant carrier a few days ago," she told him. "I'm kind of glad, because they're on their way to safety, but I'm also worried about how they'll manage without me. Oh," she finished, shrugging. "That sounds dreadful. My father tends to be very focussed on his work, and I'm usually the one who deals with Ruby's needs."

"I hope they won't be worried about you."

"I think they will be," she sighed. "But I'm glad they were evacuated. The commander ordered all non-essential personnel to leave. Perhaps he had a premonition that things were going to go wrong. More wrong," she noted scrupulously. "Obviously, what was happening on Meridiana was terrible."

Their meal arrived, and Cristal took refuge in sampling it. The conversation felt awkward, as if what they were talking about wasn't the real subject at all, although she couldn't imagine what else they would have to say to each other. Star cruisers had been calling at the Wheel all her life, though she couldn't recall the *Atria* being one of them, but the Elite she'd encountered had pretty much acted as if she was beneath their consideration. She had no idea why this partic-ular Elite was behaving differently and seemed to want to talk to her.

The bistro wasn't one of the best on the Wheel but was convenient – although, seeing the limp lettuce and badly sliced tomatoes on both their plates, she rather wished she'd suggested somewhere a little more upmarket. Zaran made no comment about the food, however, and ate with apparent enjoyment, so she decided against commenting.

"That was an interesting suggestion, that we go the long way around," she said finally, to break the strained silence. "Nobody does it, of course, because it takes so long to get anywhere, but I've always wondered what's out there. I mean, the substream is quick, but there could be all kinds of inter-esting systems and planets between here and Bendos that nobody's seen since the original probe passed in search of resources."

"I was surprised when Ashwood suggested it, but when you stop and think, it's not as crazy as it sounds," he replied. "It would hopefully get us all away from the things – the blobs, aliens, whatever they are – and it might be better than sitting here waiting for something we can't guarantee will happen. I'm not sure we'll find anything that interesting, to be honest. None of the planets we've discovered up until now have had any life larger than a microbe. But I prefer to be

doing *something* rather than sitting around waiting for somebody else to act."

"Me too," Cristal agreed. "But if we stay, we might find
out what the things are, or what they want."

"I'm not sure they want anything more than to destroy
everything in their path," Zaran said ruefully. "And we don't
know why they do that. We don't know whether it gives them
pleasure, or energy, or anything else. Their behaviour seems
to be little more than instinct." He gestured helplessly.
"Maybe our arrival triggered all of this – the increase in their
attacks, their explosion into space. Are we cause or coinci-
dence? I don't know."

Cristal was surprised that he seemed so impassioned
about the situation. She realised she was finding him increasingly attractive and reminded herself firmly of a friend who'd
been foolish enough to believe the fairy tales of romance
whispered in her ear by an Elite sergeant who'd been just
passing through – and who had left on schedule, leaving her
friend heartbroken. At the time, her father had commented
that he wasn't surprised; the Elite didn't have a reputation for
treating Wheelers or planet dwellers well. She thought she'd
do well to remember that, no matter how rakish Zaran's scar
might be or how appealing his smile.

"Cristal?"

And who, she thought, closing her eyes wearily, had
decided that Cargo Handler Penn was essential to the operation of the Wheel? She'd grown up with the man and had
never liked him much, but had once made the mistake of
letting him bully her into going to a dance with him in the
mistaken assumption that if she caved in, he'd stop pestering
her. She'd been regretting it ever since. The big man had
turned out not to have grown out of the bad temper he'd
often displayed as a child, and although she'd told him she
wasn't interested, he'd acted insanely jealous of anybody she

looked at twice — not that there had been anyone who'd caught her eye in recent years. She'd been much too busy studying or looking after her sister.

"What are you doing with this ... person?" Penn wanted to know. He glowered at Zaran. He had two of his friends with him, Cristal noticed, which was probably what gave him the courage to be so rude.

"This is Flight Commander Zaran of the *Atria*," she said, deciding her best bet was to pretend she hadn't noticed his attitude. "Zaran, this is ..."

"Oh," Penn interrupted, "so *this* is the Elite halfwit who gave you an illegal order and left us all stranded. Is he bothering you, Cristal? Just say the word and we'll teach him a lesson he'll never forget."

"You tell him, Penn," one of the other men said, grinning in obvious anticipation of a brawl.

"May I ask who you are?" Zaran said. Cristal winced, hoping the flight commander wouldn't respond to Penn's obvious attempt to pick a fight. She risked meeting the flight commander's eyes, and was relieved to see that his features were schooled to impassiveness.

"I'm a friend of Cristal's," Penn half-snarled, turning on Zaran. "You leave our women alone, spacer. They're too good for the likes of you."

"I think you should leave us," Cristal said stiffly, rising to her feet. She was irrationally annoyed about their attitude, despite the fact she'd been thinking negative thoughts herself about members of the Elite only moments earlier. "We're just having a quiet lunch, and who I have lunch with is none of your concern."

"But Cristal ..." Penn said, managing to sound both domineering and ingratiating at the same time.

"Enough, Penn," she said flatly. "Go away. I don't want to have to tell you twice."

The cargo handler hesitated, but as Zaran showed no sign of allowing himself to be drawn into a brawl, he and his friends walked off, still loudly voicing their opinion of Elite halfwits.

Zaran sighed and put his fork down on his empty plate. "I'm really sorry," he said. "I didn't realise offering to buy you lunch would put you in such an embarrassing position. I should have thought about it more. I just wanted to ... I mean, I got you into this and ..."

"No, you didn't," Cristal sighed, sitting down again. "I'm a big girl, Flight Commander. I knew what you were asking me to do, I understood why, and I did my job – nothing more and nothing less."

"It shouldn't have been up to you."

Despite herself, Cristal felt her heart give a little flutter as their eyes met. His gaze was mesmeric. "Probably not, no," she agreed, "but it was, and that's over and done. And Penn's just annoying. Can we talk about something else?"

"What would you like to ...?" Zaran broke off, apparently startled, as alarm klaxons began to howl. A holo bloomed from the emergency apparatus.

"Attention all Wheel residents. Emergency breach in corridor 22C. The corridor will be sealed. All personnel in the area unable to get clear in time must activate safesuit protocol one. Attention all Wheel residents. Additional breach in arm 9. All personnel in the area ..."

"Is that us?" Zaran asked, looking around worriedly for signage.

"Other side." Cristal suppressed a shiver of fright and queried her wristcom for further information. She frowned, looking up. "But they've just closed the bulkhead between us and the Star Chamber for safety. You're cut off from your friends, Flight Commander."

Zaran nodded and tapped his own wristcom. "Flight to

Colonel Kovis, I am cut off from your location." He glanced across the room. "Ashwood's with me." He beckoned to his uncle to join them.

"Understood, Flight," a rich, deep voice replied. Cristal hadn't heard the handsome aide speak before, but thought the voice fitted him. "The creatures just hit the outer ring of the Wheel, completely swamping a merchant ship. I'm headed to the shuttle with the admiral and the captain. Are you able to return to the *Atria?*"

"I'll find an escape pod."

"Make sure you bring Ashwood along – we can't afford to lose him. Or you."

Zaran raised an eyebrow. "Understood."

Ashwood and Thom came over, the former fumbling with his safesuit gloves whilst Thom was already half-wearing his hood. Both of them had shed their robes, and Zaran did the same, automatically checking his boot seals. The emergency holo was still reporting bulkhead closures and breaches. It was apparent the creatures were swarming the Wheel.

Cristal reached up to release the hood of her safesuit from its concealment in her collar and checked her own seals. If the creatures had got onto the Wheel, they were all in serious jeopardy. The bistro was emptying, the few diners hurrying out, their expressions varying from anxious to terror.

"I have to save my seed stocks if I can," Thom said. "We can't afford to lose the varieties, or the livestock genomes. We can still get to the hydroponics unit at the moment – will you help me rescue at least some?"

"Can't we rescue it all?" Ashwood asked, blinking.

"I don't know about you," Thom said, "but I can't carry more than one tree!"

"But the hydroponics unit should detach from the wheel." Ashwood grinned, his expression mischievous. "I recall reading that they were designed that way, in the event of an emergency. I'm sure we could initiate the release protocols."

"Even if we could detach it," Thom said, "and I don't know how we'd do that, we don't have anyone who can fly it."

"I can fly it." Zaran folded his arms, and looked up as the alarm holo abruptly cut off. "And right now I don't think we have any time to argue." Cristal looked at him in astonishment, as did Thom, but the chief scientist was smiling.

"Shouldn't you be, um, out there defending us?" Thom asked.

Zaran shook his head. "I'm not irreplaceable. The flight lieutenant from the *Gemin* can organise the firebirds." He smiled a little grimly. "And flying a hydroponics unit? It'll be a worthwhile challenge. Let's do it."

Cristal shook her head, convinced what they were suggesting was improbable, if not completely impossible. Thom caught her arm and she gave him a rueful smile, allowing him to draw her in the wake of the other two men.

CHAPTER SEVEN

The corridors of the hub seemed strangely empty as Thom led the way at a run back to the inner ringway. He, Ashwood and Zaran had abandoned their robes in the cafe, standard practice in an emergency. Zaran assumed most people would be headed to the outer ring where the ships were docked, trying to get off the Wheel if it was badly threatened. His wristcom had finally latched on to the Wheel's emergency broadcast, but all he was getting were garbled messages – there were lots of aliens; there were just a few aliens and only a few ships affected; half the available ships couldn't leave; people were going to be left behind; nobody would be left behind. The flight commander from the *Gemin* was launching and requesting the B Flight from the *Atria* form up with his people. Zaran reported his situation, but didn't get more than a brief acknowledgement in response – he understood that the *Atria*'s control was stretched to the limit.

As they ran, the klaxons still roaring out their warning, he noticed Thom speaking to a group of flickering holos above his wristcom, presumably members of his hydroponics crew, since he was requesting they meet him at hydroponics.

"I've never seen any flight controls in the hydroponics area," Cristal said. She was very obviously keeping her speed down to accommodate Ashwood, the oldest member of the group, and didn't seem even slightly short of breath.

"You spend a lot of time there?" Zaran asked her.

"I pretty much grew up there," she replied shortly.

They skidded to a halt outside the bulkhead door that led to the hydroponics arm of the Wheel. Thom keyed in the pass code and the door slid open. "Will the controls be at this end or the other?" Zaran asked his uncle.

"I have no idea, dear boy," Ashwood said. "We'd better look for them, hadn't we? Thom, may I suggest you would be best occupied tying down anything that might take damage from manoeuvring?"

"We'll do what we can." Thom turned as two men ran up to him. "Gos, Graf - thank you for responding. We need to tie down as many of the bigger plants as we can."

"We aren't taking them to a shuttle?" one of the men asked, scratching his head.

"Apparently the hydroponics unit can separate from the Wheel," Thom said, exchanging a look with Ashwood.

The older of the two men shook his head. "Who knew? I'll take the starboard beds."

"Thank you. Graf, come with me – we'll deal with the peas and beans." Thom and the younger man strode away purposefully.

Ashwood and Zaran examined the bulkhead door, and the scientist pointed out the thickness of the entryway. "I suspect there are bolts holding it in place in the Wheel. If we can find the controls, there will be a way to release them."

"I kind of thought you knew where they are." Zaran tried not to sound accusatory. "Or would at least have some idea!"

His uncle gave him a thoughtful look. "I'm not infallible, dear boy," he said. "It's some years since I encountered the note about this functionality. I suggest we start looking for them."

"Should we check whether there's anybody else to evacuate?" Cristal asked.

"At the moment, we're not even sure we can evacuate ourselves," Zaran pointed out. There was nobody in sight in the corridor outside, and he closed the door and spun the lock.

"What can I do?" Cristal asked. "What exactly are we looking for? If you can explain it to me, I can at least tell you where you *won't* find it. I know this area like the back of my hand."

"Holo projectors, a helm ... or something a helm might be contained in," Ashwood told her. "Are there any places where you think there might be a hidden room, or a wall panel that hasn't been opened in years?"

"No, I ..." Cristal paused, something apparently occurring to her. "It doesn't have to be at either end of the arm, does it? Ship controls can be anywhere in the vessel, can't they?"

"It's quite likely with something like this unit, which was only intended to be flown for short distances in an emergency, that the controls would simply be tucked away somewhere."

"I think I know where we're going, then," Cristal said. "Follow me!"

She led them down past the iris bed and the burgeoning runner beans, then stepped up onto the edge of a bed of tomatoes. In the bed's centre was a luxuriantly fruiting grapevine that clung to netting, covering a pillar wider than Zaran's arms could stretch. It reached from beneath the growth medium up to the roof. "The pillar," she said. "It's an anomaly, right in the middle of a bed. There's nowhere else in the unit like this, and it doesn't make sense for it to be structural."

"Don't worry about the carbon filter," Ashwood said to Zaran as he started to clamber up after Cristal. "I'm sure Thom has spares."

Zaran squelched across the bed, attempting to avoid the dangling crop of tomatoes, and when he reached the pillar he pushed the grape foliage out of the way anxiously. At first, he couldn't find anything and thought Cristal might be wrong, but then his questing hands found a small indentation behind a vigorous grape stem. He wriggled his hand in through the netting and found a small, inset handle.

"I've got something," he said, "but this vine is really in the way."

"I think finding out if it's what we're looking for is more important than a few grapes," Cristal observed, taking hold of the vine and tugging at it, attempting to lift it far enough away from the pillar for him to move the handle. Zaran noticed she had removed the gloves of her safesuit and followed her example before starting to tear off leaves and stems. Their efforts were rewarded when he saw that the handle was now clear enough to turn. His wristcom caught on a protruding branch and switched to the *Atria's* wavelength. Ziff, the communications chief, was apparently struggling to direct the ships full of evacuees whilst pilots attempted to deflect the blobs away from the Wheel, or any ships they got too close to. So far, none of them had collided, but from the increasingly shrill note in Ziff's voice, it might only be a matter of time before they started seriously endangering each other.

Reaching for the handle a second time, his eyes met Cristal's. He noticed that her irises were a translucent shade of turquoise green, but his attention was mostly caught by how calm she seemed.

"Attention!" the emergency holo cut in again, making them all jump. "Access to gates 14 to 18 is suspended. All evacuating personnel please go to the nearest emergency docking point as indicated by the flashing lights."

"It sounds like the blobs are widening their attack," Cristal said flatly as he strained to turn the handle.

"I know, I'm trying ... ah!" The handle finally gave, and with a grinding sound the entire outer casing of the pillar started to try to glide upward. Zaran and Cristal found themselves desperately trying to fend off the vine as the netting slid down and grapes fell in festoons around them.

"Ah, good." Ashwood peered across the bed toward the podium exposed by the lifting pillar. "The controls. Are they usable, Zaran?"

The flight commander unwound himself from a cocoon of vine leaves and passed a bunch of grapes that had ended up on his head to Cristal, pretending not to notice her amusement. He did a slow walk around the podium. "Hm." He ran a hand over the deck and nodded as buttons lit up. "A little old fashioned, but ... ah!" A holo popped up over the centre of the podium, showing the hub of the Wheel. With some manipulation, he turned the view outward and they could all see the confusion of ships cluttering the local space, firebirds zooming in and out like sheepdogs with a particularly disobedient flock. They could also see the spreading splash of prismatic colour on the exterior of the Wheel which was the blob incursion.

"They're close, but we have a little time," Ashwood said reassuringly. "Can you see the release for the bolts holding this spoke of the Wheel in place?"

"I think ... yes, it's labelled. I'll disengage and hold us in place for the moment." He put one hand firmly on the raised hemisphere that constituted the helm and initiated the release sequence for the bolts. They had to be massive, he thought, to be holding the entire spoke in place. Whilst trying to keep track of the general situation, he watched the indicator lights for the bolts flash from red through orange and to green – except one of the four stuck at orange. He blinked, and looked at it, tapped it, and muttered a quiet imprecation. "Ashwood," he said. "You used to fly shuttles – can you handle this helm?"

"I haven't entirely forgotten everything I once knew," his uncle said cheerfully. "Why?"

"Because I need to check why the fourth bolt hasn't released. If you could hold us in position ...?"

"Of course, dear boy." Ashwood picked his way fastidiously through the tomatoes and the wreckage of the grapes to take over his nephew's position, one hand on the helm.

Zaran opened his link to the *Atria* control room. "*Atria*, this is Flight Lieutenant Zaran. An additional vessel may shortly be joining the fleet."

"What ship?" Ziff returned, sounding exceedingly harassed.

"We're going to try to fly the Wheel's hydroponics arm out to meet the *Atria*," Zaran said. "We can't afford to lose the food supply. Flight crew is Ashwood Atria, myself and Controller Cristal Feltspar. Call sign, uh ..." He thought of the plants they'd passed on the way in. "*Iris*." He turned to Cristal. "I may need your help," he said.

"Aye, sir," she said, a brief grin lightening her words.

He thought about it for a moment, checking on the still determinedly orange light one last time. "Take me to the outer rim, right-hand corner."

Her grin widened. "This way, Flight Lieutenant." She set off at a run and he tucked in behind her, admiring the ease with which she swerved in and out of the verdant greenery. He was less agile, and was conscious of knocking several fruits from trees as he dashed past. They passed one of

Thom's hydroponicists, who was battening down a potted tree. He frowned at them as they raced past, but Zaran decided against trying to explain their mission.

The right-hand corner, when they reached it, had several bolted inspection hatches. The spanner to unfasten the bolts sat in a glass case on the wall. Cristal gave the glass a sharp rap with her elbow. It shattered, and she reached carefully through the remaining shards to take out the spanner. "Which one?" she asked, raising her voice to be heard over the blare of the klaxon, which was directly above them.

Zaran shook his head. "I'm guessing," he shouted back. "Let's start with the largest?"

It turned out to be a good guess. Once the panel was removed, what was revealed was a long, narrow, horizontal crawl space with a series of handholds along one side and a set of manual controls just visible at the far end. Zaran knelt down and looked into it, comparing the width of his shoulders with the available space. "Was this ship built by children?" he wondered. "I might *just* fit in this ..."

"Just as well I'm skinny, then, isn't it?" Cristal said, handing him the spanner and pulling on her safesuit gloves. She tugged up her hood, which had fallen down when they were running, and closed it over her mouth so that she was breathing from its built-in air supply. He moved out of her way and watched as she pulled herself into the tube, completely disappearing into it. She still seemed calm, although like Zaran she had to be aware that time was passing and the blobs were undoubtedly expanding their toehold on the Wheel.

She was quite a girl, he thought: independent, capable, brave, and pretty in a way no Elite woman ever would be. She was, somehow, more real, more vital, than the women amongst his peers. Her build was athletic rather than effete, and her iridescent, spiked hair gave her an urchin quality which he realised he found very appealing. He reminded himself that he was promised elsewhere, but it was a long time since he'd found a woman attractive and he couldn't help thinking about how nice it would be to run his fingers through Cristal's pale, straight locks. He gave himself a stern lecture about inappropriate distractions, although he couldn't resist trying to imagine the look on his mother's face if he were to hook up with a Wheeler girl.

"The control's stuck," came Cristal's voice, echoing back along the tube, slightly distorted by her safesuit's voice relay. "Can you pass me that spanner? I'm going to try giving it a thwack."

He knelt and peered into the tube. She was edging back down, one hand stretched back toward him, and by cramming his shoulders into the narrow space he was able to reach the spanner up to her. "Sorry, I'm blocking all the light," he said, and a moment later her safesuit lights came on and he shook his head. "Sorry," he said again, his voice echoing oddly in the confined space. "I seldom have to engage my safesuit."

"Star cruisers must be nice, safe places compared to Meridiana Wheel," she said. "I'm going to seal my hood before I hit this thing. If it releases without the hatch closing, I could get dragged out into space. I suggest you do the same, in the event the seals fail."

Zaran tugged his safesuit hood into place, then hunched himself down a bit and by hunching his shoulders managed to squeeze a little further into the tube. "I'm going to take hold of your foot," he warned her. "Just in case."

"Thanks."

There was a clang that echoed in the confined, metal-lined space loudly enough to hurt Zaran's ears, and then another. The third blow must have done the trick, as the alarm klaxon fell silent, presumably separated from the Wheel's feed. Zaran felt the vessel lurch and tightened his hold on Cristal's foot. "Clear?" he called, very aware that he couldn't hear the hiss of escaping air.

"Clear!" she confirmed.

He edged back out of the tube and, as the ship lurched, fell backward onto the floor. She emerged in rather better order behind him, tugging off her hood as they both got to their feet. "The outer hatch sealed when the bolt released," she reported, pushing a stray lock of hair back from her face.

"Zaran to Ashwood," he commed. "Hold her steady if you can. We're on our way."

The two of them headed back toward the control column. Thom appeared from between two beds. "The klaxons shut off," he said. "Does that mean we've separated from the Wheel? We're really flying?"

"It seems we really are," Zaran said.

"Outstanding!" Thom fell in beside them. "We really couldn't afford to lose all our seed stocks."

Back at the controls, the three of them found Ashwood standing absolutely still, both hands on the helm. "We're holding steady," he reported. "Please take over, dear boy. I think I'm getting cramp in my shoulders."

"Of course." Zaran trudged through the increasingly wrecked tomatoes and the absolute ruin of the grapes, and slid his hands across the helm to replace Ashwood's. The scientist moved back to stand beside Thom.

"Sorry about the grapes," Cristal said.

"Least of our worries, I believe," Thom replied. "We can always grow more. I wondered what that column was for."

"Didn't you try the handle?" she asked.

"There was a handle?"

Zaran found himself smiling at the banter. "I suggest you

all find something to hold onto," he said. "This could get ... interesting." He took a moment to get the feel for the ungainly craft – now the good ship *Iris* – before dropping it down away from the plane of the Wheel. Once he was sure they were clear, he switched on the manoeuvring jets and began to move towards the *Atria*.

Captain Asterion's holo popped up to one side of the field of flight, and Zaran reached out to tap it. "Sir?"

"Thank you for joining us, Flight Lieutenant. We have a cargo ship, the *Bellevue*, alongside us with a docking slot reserved for you." Zaran shook his head slightly. The *Atria*'s captain didn't seem in the slightest bit surprised or inconvenienced by the impending flight of the *Iris*.

"Thank you." At least he had somewhere definite to fly his current command to, but there were still far too many ships in a relatively small area of space, and the erratic paths they were weaving made it difficult to hold to a straight course.

"Flight." Raffi's voice. "I've got Grus and Kaitos escorting you. Hold steady, and don't worry about the aliens."

Zaran realised he hadn't been, and hoped Cristal, who had joined him at the control pillar and taken hold of one of the anchor loops, hadn't noticed. Most of the ships on the side of the Wheel where the blobs were impacting had now lifted clear, although some, with increasing levels of panic, were reporting unwanted passengers. Zaran shook his head, edging his ungainly vessel clear of the Wheel. "The direct course will take us altogether too close to the sun," he murmured.

"Of course!" Ashwood exclaimed from behind him. "I'm an idiot! Zaran, tell control to order the infected ships to fly as close as they can to Meridian 264."

"To ..." Zaran said blankly.

"The local sun!" Ashwood said impatiently.

"Will that kill the aliens?" Thom asked.

"I can't answer that, but it ought to inconvenience them. We can decontaminate anyone who gets too large a dose of radiation." Ashwood sounded surprisingly cheerful under the circumstances, but then, Zaran thought, his uncle had always been a law unto himself.

Zaran passed the message on to the *Atria*, and almost immediately several of the ships that had reported problems veered hard over toward the star, which had the added bonus of clearing him a corridor towards the *Atria*. As two members of his patrol took up positions alongside the *Iris*, he flew the hydroponics unit in a cautious, but somewhat wobbly, curve, aware that it had far less manoeuvrability than just about anything he'd ever flown before.

The next few minutes were nail-biting, with a melange of cargo and passenger vessels zagging about the sky, whilst fire-birds lay down barrages to try to drive the blobs away. One vessel, which Zaran identified as a seronium carrier, split apart and was almost immediately swamped by the blobs. This allowed more of the vessels to get clear, the *Iris* amongst them.

One swerving cargo vessel caused Zaran to take evasive action, and Ashwood exclaimed sharply as he skidded side-ways. Thom, who had taken a firm hold of the construct around which the tomato plants were anchored, fielded the smaller man with one hand. "Hold on to this," he advised.

"Thanks," Ashwood said. "You keep an exquisite garden, sir," he went on, as though utterly unconcerned. "I wonder if I can persuade you to take up a temporary position on the *Atria*?"

"I prefer to work for myself," Thom replied, his tone guarded.

"I meant as chief of hydroponics," Ashwood returned. "We don't have one right now, and I think you could teach our people a thing or two about yield – and not just yield, but also growing things for their own sake."

Zaran shook his head; trust his uncle to take the opportunity to try to enhance his department!

"We will have to think about how we expand hydroponics to feed the additional evacuees," Thom noted thoughtfully.

"Indeed. Perhaps you would like to move to the *Atria*?"

"I don't know …"

The disintegrating seronium carrier seemed to be holding the blobs' attention, and Zaran was able to bring the lumbering *Iris* alongside the *Bellevue*. It took some careful manoeuvring, but eventually the hydroponics unit was safely docked and he was able to step away from the controls. Ashwood, he saw, was shaking hands with Thom, a pleased smile on his face, and he guessed that meant the hydroponics chief had eventually accepted his job offer.

Zaran glanced at Cristal and she grinned at him. "Nice flying."

"I … thank you," he said. "It's my job, after all. Although the *Iris* isn't quite as zippy as my firebird!"

"I guess not."

She was standing quite close, looking up at him, and he noticed the scent she always wore, finally identifying the aroma as vanilla. Her gaze was direct and slightly challenging, and he realised he'd rather like to kiss her, and that she didn't seem entirely adverse. He found himself starting to lean forward …

"Zaran, I need you to report to me immediately. A shuttle is on its way to the *Bellevue* to pick up you and Ashwood."

He jerked back, startled. "Admiral?" he said, then shook his head, tapping his wristcom and repeating the query.

"At once, Zaran," his mother said. "The medical ship *Gold One* is inbound from an entirely inappropriate slingshot trajectory directed by that young controller on the Meridiana Wheel."

"Medical ship?" he said, a little stupidly, and then realised what the admiral was telling him. He swallowed and stepped back, realising how close he'd come to something that would have been decidedly embarrassing. "We're on our way."

CHAPTER EIGHT

Cristal felt numb. The Wheel was completely lost. Engulfed by aliens, visible holes were beginning to appear in its superstructure, and entire sections were breaking away and drifting. She watched the destruction on the hydroponics unit's control holo, distantly aware of Thom and the two assistants who'd joined them on their unlikely escape from the alien attack moving around in the background. A number of the more delicate plants had taken damage during the unit's short flight, and she knew Thom would be salvaging what he could and replanting what he couldn't. She knew she should probably offer to help, but still she stood amidst the ruined grapes and tomatoes, watching the only home she'd ever known ... dying.

"Cristal." Thom put his hands on her shoulders, turning her around to face him. "There's nothing you can do. Nothing you could have done."

"Henny's dead," she said, her voice sounding odd to her own ears. "She stayed in the control centre directing traffic and ... and my friend Jus, and Benni from the gravityball team, and Lowis ..."

"I know you're grieving," Thom said. "I do understand that. But you need to sit down, or even lie down, and get some rest. There's nothing you can do right now."

Cristal leant against her friend's shoulder, closing her eyes and wondering why she wasn't crying. It wasn't just the people she knew who'd lost their lives. The Wheel had been full of evacuees from the planet, many of whom hadn't had safesuits and had presumably perished when the Wheel's superstructure was penetrated. There simply hadn't been enough time or ships to evacuate everybody. For some, their last minutes must have been awful, knowing they were going to die and there was nothing they could do about it. She wondered how many had died simply because the people around them had panicked.

"I've made you up a pallet in my office," Thom said, keeping her firmly turned away from the holo. "I want you to rest for a few hours. Can you do that for me?"

"What about you?" she asked.

He smiled. "Ashwood is nagging me to do the same." He tapped his wrist to indicate the chief scientist had been comming him.

"You like him," Cristal said slowly.

"I knew he was brilliant," Thom replied. "I didn't realise he'd be quite so ... charismatic. Eccentric." He snorted. "And crazy. I can't believe I let him talk us into rescuing the hydroponics arm. If we hadn't been able to find the controls, we would all have died! Besides," he added, with a grin, "he's out of my class. Now go and lie down, and I don't want to see you on your feet until much later."

Cristal hadn't thought she'd be able to sleep, but she did, and awoke to find Thom shaking her shoulder gently. "Sorry to wake you," he said, "but our transport's here. Take a minute to freshen up – we're going to the *Atria*. I'm leaving Gos Hawthorn in charge."

"Oh." Cristal blinked sleep from her eyes and got to her feet, scrubbing a hand through her hair and wishing she had a comb. Except she didn't, she realised hollowly. Or anything else, either. She went into the tiny washroom to one side of the office and blinked at her appearance in the mirror. She looked ... tired, she thought, despite the sleep she'd had. Tired and sad and still quite numb.

Thom had a comb, and she wielded it to good advantage, taming the wire tangle her hair had become. Her ablutions completed, she found herself reluctant to leave the small room, to face what she suspected – if the aliens continued their attacks – to be a very bleak and possibly short future.

Thom was waiting for her when she finally emerged, a small holdall in his hand. "You're taking the job the chief scientist offered you?" she guessed.

"We're going to need all the food we can get," Thom said. "So, yes, I am. Also ... well, never mind that for now. This way, the shuttle's waiting."

"But why am I coming with you?" she queried, reluctant to leave the familiar surroundings.

"I think the *Atria's* captain might have a job for you," he told her.

"Me?" She blinked at him blankly. "Why would he have a job for me?"

Thom shrugged. "Perhaps because they don't have any decent traffic controllers of their own?" he suggested. "Let's go and find out, shall we?"

The flight to the *Atria* was only a short one, and before she knew it she was clambering out of the shuttle and on out of its docking pod into what appeared to be a lounge area.

Cristal wasn't sure what she'd expected the interior of a star cruiser to look like, but if asked she probably wouldn't have described wide corridors apparently boarded with pale wood, so that it felt more like she imagined being on board an old-fashioned sailing ship would have been. She found herself gawking around herself as Ashwood Atria, who had met the shuttle when it docked, ushered them through the massive space cruiser.

"This is one of the higher levels of the ship," Ashwood explained. "Residential quarters are lower down, although they're a bit crowded right now due to the people we took on board when the Wheel was evacuated ..." He broke off, frowning to himself. "I'm sorry," he said, reaching out a hand and touching Thom's elbow. "I don't know if you're aware, but I'm afraid the Wheel is ... completely lost. We evacuated as many as we could, but ... there were casualties."

"We were aware of that," Thom said, meeting the smaller man's eyes. "Your flight commander left the helm of the hydroponics unit live when he left."

"The second substream gateway has been infected, too," Ashwood murmured. He seemed to realise he still had his hand on Thom's elbow and stepped back.

"What are we going to do?" Cristal asked. It was difficult to take in that the place she had been born and grown up, the place she knew literally inside and out, was lost to them, along with all her belongings. Like most Wheelers, she kept her possessions to a minimum, but as things were all she had was the safesuit she stood up in. "I ... have nothing," she heard herself say. "No job, no way of earning a living, no possessions ... nothing."

"I appreciate that you've lost a very great deal," Ashwood said, turning to look at her, "but please don't despair." He smiled ruefully, and she found herself thinking that he was more sensitive than she'd expected an Elite scientist to be. "I do have an offer to make you," he continued, "and I promise I'll explain everything shortly - but let's get somewhere we can sit down first."

"I'm sorry," Cristal said. "I just ... it's a lot to take in."

"I do appreciate that."

As they continued along the passageway, Cristal looked around herself. After a moment, she realised she was looking for Zaran, which was ridiculous on a ship the size of the *Atria*. She wasn't sure why, but he'd seemed suddenly cold just before he left the *Iris*. One minute she had thought he might actually be thinking about kissing her, and the next, he just walked away. She shook her head, telling herself she was being ridiculous. She had much worse things to worry about – and suspected she was focussing on the flight commander to avoid thinking about them.

She assumed that the ship must be full of evacuees, but there was little sign of them as they proceeded. They passed some people, many of whom nodded to Ashwood as if they knew him, all of whom wore safesuits in a variety of colours that she knew indicated what section of the ship they worked in.

Ashwood was talking to Thom. "I appreciate that your own hydroponics unit is what you regard as home," he said, "and I won't mind if you feel more comfortable living there rather than moving to the *Atria*, but I want you to see what we've got here, so that we can discuss how to improve things." He glanced down at the bag Thom was carrying. "Do you have a sleeping place in your unit?"

"Once or twice I fell asleep at my desk," Thom confessed, "but I didn't go as far as putting in a bed, although I kept a few personal items there." He hefted the holdall thoughtfully. "I had a rather plain cabin on the Wheel." He looked around. "This seems very pleasant. The Wheel decor was mostly hard surfaces. Are the quarters equally congenial?"

Ashwood laughed. "For some, undoubtedly ... but for everyone?" He shook his head. "I know you probably think we Elite are soft and self-aggrandizing, but actually we have to earn our rank just like you do. I'm not going to say we don't have advantages ... but we live our lives as travellers, our home a ship rather than a planet, with all the hardships that type of living involves. With rank comes greater responsibility – but also nicer quarters." He shrugged. "I think that's the same the universe over."

He led them on through what seemed like a maze of passageways until eventually he gestured to an open door. "We can talk here."

'Here' turned out to be a small lounge area with tables and chairs, currently unoccupied. The walls were lined with the same pale wood as the corridors, and one of the walls was enhanced with two large paintings of planetary scenes. "Now," Ashwood said, sitting down. "Refreshments?"

"I can't remember the last time I had a hot drink," Thom admitted, dropping gratefully into one of the chairs. Ashwood tapped on the table's edge and a column rose from its centre with the same kind of water heater they had on the Wheel. There were mugs to one side and a choice of drinks. Thom chose a strong herbal tea, gaining a nod of approval from Ashwood, whilst Cristal was pleased to find that chocolate was one of the options. She was feeling a little less numb, she realised. The rest had obviously helped, as well as the fact they were doing something, even if she wasn't entirely sure yet what that was. She had no idea why the ship's chief scientist was spending so much time on them, although seeing the way he was looking at Thom she wasn't sure his assistance was entirely altruistic.

"Now, Cristal," Ashwood said, clasping his hands together on the edge of the table. "About that job. I've been talking to Captain Asterion, and he believes that you and the other traffic controllers from the Wheel have skills the ship needs. Star cruisers don't usually have a whole fleet of other ships around them, so traffic control has never been a priority before – but it certainly is now. I'm told there have already been a couple of collisions and more near-misses. We'd like you to join the alpha watch, and to be honest if you could start straight away that would be wonderful."

"Oh! But I'm not an IUP employee," Cristal said blankly. "I mean, I work for the Wheel ..."

"Old roles and allegiances are pretty much suspended for the duration of the emergency," Ashwood said.

"I don't know what to say," Cristal admitted. She really didn't have much choice, she realised. Currently she had no job and no home; she was being offered both. "I'm willing to help however I can," she decided.

"Is that a yes?" Ashwood asked.

"I ... guess it is."

The door swished open and a woman came into the room, the ribbons on her maroon safesuit indicating that she was a lieutenant. She was tall, with long dark hair worn in a plait, and had a pleasant but unremarkable face. "Ah, Charra," Ashwood greeted her. "Excellent timing. Thom, Cristal, this is Charra Atria. Charra is the chief helmsman."

"Hello," Charra said.

"Cristal has agreed to help us," Ashwood said. "Cristal, Charra has offered to share her quarters with you."

"It will be nice to share with someone with so many different experiences." Charra's smile revealed dimples and Cristal found herself smiling tentatively back. She was used to the small suite she'd shared with her father and sister, but knew she would never see that again, nor probably have the same level of privacy. "I've only seen ship life," the lieutenant confided, "and the Academy, of course, but I'm sure being on a Wheel must be very interesting."

"Thank you," Cristal said. Charra seemed pleasant enough, and if they didn't get along she had a suspicion Ashwood would help her find another bunk.

"We all need each other to get through this," Charra said.

"Ashwood, are you aware they're taking your daft suggestion seriously now?"

"Going the long way home?" Ashwood grinned. "I'm not surprised. Until we can find a way to deal with the aliens ..."

"Oh, that reminds me, Ashwood," Charra said. "The captain was impressed – your solution to the infected ships worked. Not all of them made it, but some did, and the crew weren't so irradiated we can't save them – especially now the specialist medical ship has joined us." She turned to Cristal. "We work long shifts," she said. "And unless you're too tired, I can take you to the bridge now and show you the ropes. You'll be on the Alpha Watch with me, at least initially. I'll explain more as we go. Are you ready?"

"Oh ... yes, that's good." Cristal rose to her feet, leaving her half-drunk cup of chocolate on the table. She still felt numb, and had the decided impression that somehow the situation had got away from her. Thom gave her a smile and then turned his attention back to Ashwood; the two were already exchanging ideas about growth mediums as the door closed behind her, and she thought they were intellectually well-matched.

Cristal had expected to feel very alone in her new surroundings, but the first face she saw in the corridor was, to her surprise, Jedda Granit, her fellow controller.

"Oh, they got you, too," he greeted her, frowning. "You got the Alpha crew, and I got the Beta. Hope by the time I get up there, you'll have sorted out all the idiots flying around like there's nobody else in the dome." He hurried past, leaving Cristal somewhat lost for words.

"He's right about the chaos," Charra admitted. "It doesn't help that the ships are all overcrowded and full of panicking people, many of whom haven't got a thing to their name and aren't even sure where their next meal is coming from."

"I don't either," Cristal said. "Know where my next meal is coming from, I mean."

Charra laughed. "Don't worry, we have a ready room off the bridge, and I've arranged for us to take our breaks together in the short term. Captain Asterion ... well, you'll see. He's an excellent captain, but at present we think he's feeling a bit put out because of the admiral being on board. People keep taking things to her instead of bringing them to him. He may be a bit short-tempered at the moment, although he's very good at not showing it, so I recommend keeping your head down!"

Oh great, Cristal thought. *First day in a new job and the boss is in a temper!*

And then they emerged from the passage into the central core of the ship, and Cristal's mouth fell open. Looking in both directions, she realised she couldn't see the end of the vast open area − and that, if nothing else, brought home to her just how big the star cruiser was. Everywhere there was noise, and people, and lights, and windows, and doorways, and shop fronts, and market stalls, and foliage, and the moving walkways, and the pods zipping past overhead ...

Charra grinned at her expression but tactfully said nothing and led her onto the moving walkway that went towards the prow of the ship.

The bridge, when they reached it, was circular, with the usual 3-D holo of surrounding space at the centre, the *Atria* shown as a blocky red rectangle. Immediately Cristal could see the problem: between the *Atria* and her sister ship, the *Gemin*, was a confused jumble of ships, from gigantic company tugs carrying fuel and other company assets down to tiny, privately owned yachts. In between were the Wheel's own evacuation shuttles with clusters of recovered escape pods clinging to them, one white rectangle she guessed must be the medical ship Charra had mentioned, a number of merchant vessels, and some she didn't recognise at all. At a quick guess, there were half a hundred ships milling around. She tried not to look at the ruins of the substream gateways, or the oddly misshapen Wheel. "By all the gods," she said, blinking. "This has got to be sorted out!"

Charra pulled out a seat alongside the holo and gestured to the blank desk area. "Swipe to pull up coms. Can you operate this?"

Cristal sat down, bringing up the communication channels with one hand whilst her gaze was focussed entirely on several impending disasters outside. "What's my call sign?" she asked.

"*Atria* Traffic Control."

Cristal tapped icons impatiently, reading off the identity numbers of a couple of ships on a very definite collision course. "G1524, this is Atria Traffic," she said firmly. "Please alter your course to Azimuth 624; you are currently on a collision course." On the holo, one ship swerved, and she winced. "G1524, please avoid accelerating unnecessarily."

The next several hours went by in a whirl, as Cristal argued with a series of captains who thought they knew better than she did, but eventually she had the tangle of shipping sorted into some kind of order. It was a bit like herding escaped chickens, she thought, sitting back with a sigh. Someone applauded, and she looked up in surprise and blushed. She had no idea who any of the people on the bridge were, but they all seemed impressed by her achievements. "No, really," she heard herself say, "I'm just doing my job!"

"Thank you, Controller Feltspar." Cristal blinked at the tall man in the immaculate maroon safesuit who was smiling at her. She'd seen him in the star chamber, and didn't need to read off his rank ribbons to identify that he was the captain. The captain whose fleet she had just been ordering around without having even been introduced, she realised, and blushed.

"I'm sorry," she said tremulously. "I didn't think …"

"I'll overlook the insubordination on this occasion," Captain Asterion said. He had dark hair with sideburns, and his maroon safesuit was immaculate, the ribbons of his rank aligned with precision. "I think you've single-handedly averted several nasty accidents. Well done. And welcome to Alpha Watch. I think you'll fit in very nicely."

Cristal stuttered some kind of thank you, and was grateful when one of the other crew members, a tow-haired man, came over and offered to relieve her. "It's more than time you had a break," he said. "And Charra's been holding off on taking hers until you were ready. I'm sure I can keep this zoo in order long enough for you to get something to eat!"

"Thank you." She rose to her feet and stretched.

Charra led the way into an adjacent room, separated from the bridge by a clear bulkhead. The door swished closed after them, and the noise of the bridge was immediately muted.

"I can't believe you got all those ships sorted out!" Charra said. "That's a really impressive talent you have there."

"Some days are really quiet, but on others you get a lot of ships through the substream at once," Cristal said. "It's kind of like playing gravityball - you have to know where everybody else is in the dome and how fast they're travelling. Have people been told yet that the fleet is moving out? Do you know when that's likely to be?"

"The admiral is making a statement later today," Charra replied, gesturing to a series of covered hotplates at the side of the room. "That's today's choices," she said. "Help yourself to whatever you fancy, and I'll tell you a bit more about how our duty rosters work."

CHAPTER NINE

"Oh, so *this* is where you're hiding!"

Zaran pulled himself out from under his firebird, spanner in hand, and scowled at Raffi. "What do you mean, hiding?" he said. "The ships took a beating in that last battle. I'm just giving the ground crew a hand."

"Yeah, right." Raffi crossed her arms and grinned at him annoyingly. "So you're not hiding from your mother and her new best friend, then?"

Zaran groaned, sitting up and rubbing a slightly greasy hand across his face. "Did you want something, Raffi?" he asked. "Only I am quite busy here …"

"Doing someone else's job." She reached out a hand to tug him to his feet. "Come on, Zar, we've known each other a long time – don't you like Doctor Medwen?"

"She seems very nice," he said cautiously.

"Well, I like her." Raffi folded her arms and frowned at him. "But then, I've actually bothered to spend some time with her."

Zaran winced. The arrival of the medical ship with his match on board had not been happenstance; his mother had been expecting the ship to arrive at Bendos when she decided to accompany the *Gemin* and *Atria* to Meridiana, and had left orders that, if the captain thought it appropriate, he should follow them. The *Gold* had been the only ship with permission to enter the substream after them, and it had done so, the captain presumably disbelieving the stories of omnivorous aliens as much as the admiral had.

Zaran's first meeting with the woman to whom he had been matched was under the eagle eye of his mother, who had taken obvious delight in introducing them. Zaran thought Medwen was ... well, a typical Elite: tall, beautiful, elegant and accomplished. At his mother's direction they had exchanged a chaste kiss, and there had been nothing there – no spark, no feeling of desire, nothing. Zaran knew it didn't matter to the Elite whether he actually liked the woman – there were too few Elite for genetics not to play a major role in their procreation. He just didn't feel comfortable making up to a woman for whom he didn't actually hunger.

"Did you come here to nag me?" he asked.

"No." Raffi grinned. "I came to tell you your father's on his way here to talk to you. In fact ..." She cocked her head, listening, and they could both hear approaching footsteps. "... I think that's him now," she finished brightly.

Decrus Gemin was, as always, immaculately presented, and Zaran was very conscious that his safesuit was dirty and creased and he probably had grease on his face and in his hair. Although facially he resembled his father, he was much shorter, and his black hair was in sharp contrast to his father's pure white locks.

"Ah, there you are, boy," Decrus greeted him, and nodded politely to Raffi, who took the hint and beat a retreat. He frowned at Zaran. "Don't you have ground crew to deal with that sort of thing?"

"Our firebirds came under considerable stress in the

attempt to keep the blobs at bay," Zaran said bluntly. "Personally, I want to be sure my ship's in good condition before I take her out again."

Decrus nodded, dismissing the explanation. "I ... wanted to talk to you," he said. He hesitated noticeably, moving to parade rest, his hands clasped behind his back, before continuing. "I don't know if you're aware, but it's been decided that the *Gemin* should remain here at Meridiana whilst the rest of the fleet moves out. The ..." He sighed. "I'm going to call them 'aliens' because whatever they are, they're alien to our understanding. They have eaten huge holes in the outbound substream gateway, but the inbound is astonishingly still functional. I would have expected the authorities at Bendos to have closed it by now, but presumably they're still refusing to believe what's happened here."

"You think there might still be ships in the substream?" Zaran queried. He was uncomfortable in his father's presence, only just barely resisting the urge to stand to attention. Like most Elite children whose parents were from different vessels, he had had little contact with his father as a child. Occasionally the *Atria* and his father's ship had met up, but his father had always seemed a distant stranger. Decrus had been a trainer at Bendos Academy when Zaran had gone there, and he'd found him terse and judgemental, presumably careful not to show his son any favouritism. He had never approved of Zaran's love of flying, insisting that he would do better to learn to orchestrate a fire fight from the overview of a star cruiser's control room. Today, the older man's speech seemed forced, and Zaran really had no idea where the conversation was going.

"We can't sidestep the possibility," Decrus responded. "There might be a rescue team inbound – not that a rescue would work, but someone has to stay here in case. Additionally, there may still be civilians on the planet in need of rescue. It's unclear whether the settlers who'd moved away from the mining centres have all got to pick-up points, and some of Meridiana's prefects are still out searching. And obviously it's important to try to keep the things from pursuing the fleet." He hesitated visibly and then went on, "Son, I know I've been tough on you. I just don't want us to part on bad terms. I'm sure the *Gemin* will re-join civilisation in due course, but just in case ... you understand."

"Sir," Zaran started, and then shook his head. "Father. I appreciate we disagree on the best way to manage a flight, but I hope I haven't disappointed you in other respects."

Decrus sighed. "I would have liked to see my grandchildren," he said. "But I think you and I are more alike in that respect than your mother appreciates. I thought you should know ... your mother and I were never matched."

"You weren't?" Zaran said blankly.

Decrus shook his head. "I was matched to a girl I never met," he said. "Before I could, I met your mother, and ... things happened." He shrugged. "We were sufficiently far apart on the genetic charts for your birth to be acceptable to the Board, but after you were born, your mother felt we should ... stay away from each other. She went on to meet her correct match, and your half-sister was the result of that." He paused, obviously as uncomfortable with the revelations as Zaran. "I think perhaps you understand," he said. "I ... decided to focus on my career, rather than take what, for me, felt like second best. I believe my match was rematched and is perfectly content about the situation. As for you ..." He sighed. "Zaran, Doctor Medwen seems like a very nice girl. I hope you'll give her a chance. But if you find she isn't the one for you ... I would understand that, even if your mother is less forgiving. I wanted you to know that before we parted. I am, and always have been, proud of you."

"You're a difficult act to follow, sir," Zaran said, a little ruefully. "I can only do what I think is right. And I'm sure we'll see each other again."

"I certainly hope so." Decrus nodded. "Good luck, Zaran."

"And to you, father."

Zaran swallowed as his father walked away. It was difficult to imagine a world without Decrus in it, and equally difficult to imagine a world where his mother did something as unexpected as mating outside of her match. He'd always assumed that, for some reason, her match with Decrus had been annulled and she'd rematched later. They'd never been close enough for him to ask her about it, and he'd thought it inappropriate to ask Ashwood. He wondered ruefully if his father would have been as proud of him if he'd admitted that, at this moment in time, the girl he couldn't get out of his mind was a Wheeler.

It wasn't unheard of, of course, for a matched Elite couple to do their duty and have children together whilst carrying on affairs on the side, but Zaran realised he was uncomfortable with the idea of having children with a woman he didn't care about.

One of the ground crew came in and Zaran shrugged off his discomfort. He updated the woman on the state of his firebird, then headed back to his quarters to change out of his oily clothing. His progress was interrupted several times by people wanting to ask him about the proposed exodus, and on several other occasions he noticed people giving him cold glares, obviously aware that he was the reason they had to take this action. It was a relief to get out of the public eye.

He leant against the door of his quarters and looked around thoughtfully. Bachelor quarters suited him – he liked his compact room with bed and desk conveniently close to each other, with the communications array that allowed him to speak to his team should an emergency arise whilst he was there. He liked the warm, sand-coloured paint on the walls and the only picture, a painting of a sunrise. He'd bought it on the spur of the moment in a market at Bendos, and it had graced the wall of his quarters on several different ships. Accepting his match would mean a move to larger quarters; it would mean someone else sharing the space with him, and he acknowledged with a sinking feeling that the woman he wanted to see smiling back at him when he came in from a hard day's work was not the Elite woman to whom he was matched, but rather the elfin traffic controller.

His mother, he thought irritably, had got away with *her* indiscretion – the one that had resulted in *him* – because she had erred with another Elite. Had she got herself pregnant by a non-Elite, her chances of one day becoming a Trustee would probably have been severely diminished.

It wouldn't do, he told himself. He would be letting down decades of careful matching, the best efforts of his people to avoid inbreeding — and he would be letting down his mother, who wanted grandchildren about whom she could boast, not ones she would be embarrassed to claim.

Zaran had had no reason to see Cristal since she had come aboard the *Atria*, but had heard she'd impressed Captain Asterion with her ability to convince the captains of the many small ships that formed the fleet to stick to a desig-nated flight path. The incidences of collision had dwindled to nothing, much to everyone's relief, and the focus had switched to identifying which ships had too many people aboard, which had space for more, and how they could grow enough food to feed them all. He was aware that the captain had caused some friction within the fleet by insisting that the personnel retained on the *Atria* were security cleared and used to being in space, on the grounds that the star cruiser's job was to protect the fleet, and it couldn't do that if half the personnel on board had no idea how to conduct themselves in an emergency. It had been largely, but not entirely, Wheelers who had benefitted from this dictum. The ship's shuttles had subsequently been busy transferring people. Those rescued from the Wheel had largely been returned to their own ships, whilst planet evacuees had been spread across what little space could be found for them on other ships.

Zaran had a feeling this redistribution of personnel would be going on for some time. Already, Lord Chief Justice Rydon was calling for volunteers with prefect experience or who were interested in training as prefects, and he wouldn't be the only one whose department would be stretched by their current situation. Most of his pilots had been asked to share quarters, at least in the short term, and he was keeping a weathered eye on them in an attempt to deal with any friction before it got out of hand.

Ashwood and Thom had been working together to identify locations where hydroponics units could be located and issuing instructions on how the existing units could improve their output. This was, of course, vital, since food was the one thing replicators couldn't reproduce. Zaran rather thought the two men were growing closer than just a common interest would indicate, and thought it would be nice if his rather solitary uncle had someone in his life.

The aliens – Zaran decided to follow his father's lead and call them that rather than the descriptive 'blobs' – had remained focussed on the Wheel and the substream gateway, as well as still being active on the planet's surface. Admiral Nashira had opted not to send down teams to investigate what was happening on the planet's surface in case that stirred them into further activity.

Having freshened up and changed into a clean tunic, Zaran decided to head over to the bar favoured by his crew rather than go to the officers' lounge where he might encounter Medwen. He knew he was treating her badly, but felt unable to pay court to her when his mind was occupied with thoughts of another. He tried to convince himself that if he just put a little space between himself and Cristal, his attraction to her would fade.

He was about to step onto the walkway when someone ran past him and he felt a distinct push that carried him across the outer walkway onto the faster central belt. He staggered sideways and fell badly against the handrail. He lay for a moment, as much startled as hurt, and then another passer-by stopped to help him up. Zaran thought he recognised the man as the proprietor of one of the replicator clothing outlets.

"Had one too many, Flight Lieutenant?" his rescuer asked coldly.

"I ... think someone pushed me," Zaran said, trying to decide whether that had really happened or it had just been someone careless, in a hurry, not looking where they were going.

"Not surprised," his rescuer grunted. "I doubt he or she will be the last. After all, you're the loon who got us all into this mess."

A fact I can't deny, Zaran thought as he limped on his way, favouring his left leg, which he suspected was going to have some magnificent bruises. However much he thought closing the substream had been the right choice to make, there would always be those who believed otherwise.

CHAPTER TEN

The control room of the *Atria* was very quiet, almost as if everyone was holding their breath, as Astel, the chief navigator of Alpha Watch, keyed in the flight co-ordinates and Charra placed her hands on the helm. At a nod from Captain Asterion, the helmsman tracked the helm to the new course and reported, "Helm engaged." Around the star cruiser, the fleet of smaller vessels moved out along with her. At the traffic control station, Cristal murmured instructions to the vessels which threatened to drop out of the pattern. With some juggling, each of the larger vessels was now accompanied by smaller vessels with some laser functionality to deal with any space debris large enough to get through the plus-light field. The population had been evened up as much as possible, taking into account the passenger space available on each vessel. They were still overcrowded, and both food and other supplies were dangerously low, but there was work underway to ensure that the replicators were producing the most urgent needs first, stores were properly catalogued, and hydroponics units across the fleet were co-ordinating production.

The secondary reason for the layout of the fleet became apparent when Captain Asterion gave the order to go to pluslight. Not all the vessels were pluslight-enabled, but so long as they remained within the pluslight envelope of the larger vessels, they were carried along with them. It had taken Ashwood's team some considerable time to calculate the precise layout to ensure the pluslight envelopes would work safely together and not negate the *Atria's* scanners.

Directly behind the *Atria* sat the *Gold One*, the small medical response vessel that had arrived in the midst of the evacuation and which, Cristal had been told, carried the woman to whom Zaran Atria was matched. Cristal wasn't at all sure how she felt about that. She had known that all Elite were subject to matching, but because the flight commander had seemed unencumbered, she had somehow thought he would always be that way. Obviously, she'd been wrong, and any attraction she might have thought she could feel between the two of them must have been her imagination, or something that could never be. Zaran had been conspicuous by his absence in the few days she'd been aboard the *Atria*, although she wasn't sure whether he was actively avoiding her, was spending all his time with his match, or was just staying out of the way of his mother, who came by the bridge several times a day.

A part of her felt an anticipatory glee as the star cruiser swung away from Meridiana at the beginning of her long voyage back to Bendos. They were going to traverse tracts of space which no ship had visited since the substream gate was established centuries earlier. She rather hoped they might see wonders along the way, things no living human had ever seen. Or, she reminded herself, it could all be just emptiness and incredibly boring. She wasn't entirely sure which she would prefer. After all, she'd already had far more excitement in her life than she would have chosen.

She was still surprised by how welcoming the rest of her bridge watch had been. Captain Asterion had set the tone, visibly impressed by her management of the confusion of small ships that surrounded his star cruiser. Charra had proved to be good company; she had a wicked sense of humour and loved to gossip, which meant Cristal had learned far more than she'd expected about the *Atria*'s crew in a remarkably short space of time. Ziff, the communications chief, was a tall man whose conversation revolved around his wife and three children, whilst Melas, the bridge technician, seldom spoke.

Charra and Cristal often took their break with Astel, the petite navigator, who seemed very popular with the unmatched Elite men on board. "She likes to tease," Charra had confided in Cristal when the other girl wasn't around, "but nobody takes her too seriously. They all know they'll meet their match in the fullness of time."

Because the Elite had adopted the 'match' terminology, planet dwellers and Wheelers also talked about getting matched, but they were free to choose their partners.

Admiral Nashira, Cristal was told, had run a tight ship when she'd been captain of the *Atria*, and had spent little time with her two children. Cristal had been surprised to learn that one of Zaran's co-pilots was his half-sister, and learned from Charra that the younger sibling was jealous of her older brother's rank. When the admiral visited the bridge, Cristal tried to keep out of her line of sight, as she suspected that the woman didn't rate her very highly, although she had no basis for that belief beyond a nagging feeling that somehow obeying Zaran's orders had made her, more than him, responsible for the situation in which they found themselves.

She was still finding the *Atria* a strange place. There was very little about the star cruiser that reminded her of the

Wheel, which had been a workmanlike structure with not much in the way of luxury about it. The *Atria* used soft wood to disguise metal, and the corridors were dotted with alcoves containing artwork and sculpture. The central core, with its bustle of adults and children moving in and out of its shops and food outlets, never ceased to both astonish and charm her. The air smelled fresher, and the people seemed less concerned about their safety – she even saw the occasional person not wearing a safesuit.

"They're clerks, shopkeepers, restaurateurs and the like," Charra explained when Cristal asked. "There's no need for them to go outside the ship or put themselves into dangerous situations, so some of them opt never to wear a safesuit."

"But they're hygienic," Cristal said, a little shocked. "They collect skin cells that would otherwise form a layer of dust ..."

"Not all skin cells," Charra said cheerfully, "and not all the time. I don't sleep in mine - do you?"

"Always," Cristal said blankly. "What if there was an emergency ...?"

"I guess star cruisers are safer than Wheels," Charra sighed. "Don't you think feeling the need for a safesuit all the time is a bit ... paranoid?"

"Not really," Cristal said. "My mother died in an accident when I was quite young. Her safesuit didn't save her, so I grew up very aware of the worst that could happen and I'm used to being careful. I don't feel very comfortable outside of my safesuit."

"Must make dalliances difficult," Astel teased, joining the conversation.

"You can still have fun." Cristal gave what she hoped was a sufficiently secretive smile to hide her lack of recent experience in that direction.

The quarters Cristal shared with Charra had obviously previously allowed the helmsman an office separate from her sleeping space; now her room combined the two, and Cristal had the other room to herself, with a bed and desk.

"I really don't mind sharing," Charra insisted when Cristal observed she felt a bit bad about it. "We're actually way better off than some of the other folk in the fleet, and I quite like not having to go far in the night if I have an idea I want to check out, or I can't sleep and want to watch a holo."

The room Cristal had inherited had pale mauve walls and a soft carpet on the floor. The only carpets she'd encountered on the Wheel had been of the tough, hard-wearing variety, and she still wasn't sure whether she approved of this level of luxury. The fresher was pretty much identical to the one she'd shared with her family on the Wheel, though, and the credit award she'd received in return for accepting the traffic control posting had enabled her to pick up soap and shampoo, a hair-brush, and some of the iridescent gel she used. The only clothes she owned were her old grey Wheeler safesuit and the three brand new maroon star cruiser command crew safesuits issued to her by stores.

"I don't know why you do that," Charra said, the first time Cristal spiked her hair.

"I think it's neat," Astel said. The navigator had long, dark hair which she tended to wear in a variety of plaited styles. "Do you think it would suit me?"

"Everything suits you," Charra sighed.

The helmsman was, it transpired, an avid reader. Cristal, who of all her belongings most missed her data pod library, was pleased to find that Charra had recordings of some of her favourites and was happy to share them. She had some re-enactment comics as well. "But if you're really into those," she confided, "the person to talk to is our surgeon general, Nazif. He's got the entire run of *Shell Maiden.*"

Cristal found herself thinking that she'd been very lucky with the roommate she'd ended up with and wondered whether Ashwood, who had apparently arranged it, had known they would get along so well, or whether it had just been good luck.

On the Wheel, Cristal had done her shopping in the malls in the public areas. There, merchandise en route to and from the planet had been readily available to purchase. On the *Atria*, goods fell into two categories: those which could be replicated, which were less expensive, and those which had come from a planet, which were more expensive and likely to become even more so. The chief storekeeper, a tight-lipped older woman Cristal had seen on the bridge but had never spoken to, had to have her work cut out for her keeping track of what was available across the fleet, identifying potential shortages and ensuring that the right things were being produced.

Thom and Ashwood were busy planning improvements to the fleet's hydroponics and livestock production. On one occasion when Cristal had joined the two men for a meal in the chief scientist's quarters, she'd found them so preoccupied with their task that it was all they seemed to be able to talk about, until in the end Ashwood laughed and apologised to her for monopolising the conversation.

Meals on the star cruiser were also different than Cristal was used to. On the Wheel, animal products had been relatively easy to get hold of, since Meridiana had supported cows and sheep which had unfortunately had to be abandoned to the blobs. On the *Atria*, fish and meat were luxuries reserved for special occasions, but eggs were available from the ship's flock of chickens, which occupied a large, open area in the bowels of the ship. A wide variety of vegetables, nuts, roots, pulses and grains made up the rest of the normal diet.

Cristal had yet to find anywhere she felt comfortable running in the way she'd run on the Wheel, but there was a gravityball court, and she'd spent a cycle each day practising with a team made up of personnel from the Wheel. They had already challenged the star cruiser team to a game and were preparing, as Jedda insisted, to wipe the floor with them. The star cruiser's gravityball court was on one of the lower decks near the pilots' ready room, and Cristal always found herself looking out for Zaran, although whether that was because she wanted to see him, or because she wanted to be sure to avoid him, she wasn't entirely sure.

She still needed to use the star cruiser's location finder to get around. The walkways and tubes all looked the same, the only clue as to where she was often the colour of the security coding on them. Her role as traffic controller for Alpha Watch meant she had one of the highest security clearances, something that had initially surprised her, until Charra had explained that if the bridge was ever out of commission, they might be expected to fly the ship from any one of a number of other places.

Cristal learned later that normally the science areas of the vessel would have been outside her security clearance, but Ashwood had insisted that she should be able to visit her 'family' on the ship, Thom, whenever she wanted, and hence she had been given clearance for that area as well. In fact, the only areas of the ship she didn't have access to were engineering and the flight deck.

The evening of the third day out from Meridiana, she was en route to the practice area after her watch had been relieved. She had left Jedda frowning at the neat line of ships, and rather hoped he wouldn't make too much of a mess of it during his duty, as she was getting bored with ushering everybody back into place every time her duty followed his. She rather thought his heart wasn't in the job; he was much more focussed on the impending gravityball game. He really was obsessed with the sport, she thought, but then perhaps it was his way of taking his mind off what had happened to their home.

After adding elbow and knee pads to her safesuit, she pushed off from the gravity plate into the freefall bubble that formed the gravityball practice area. She limbered up with a few simple push-offs and landings and then, since at that time she had the bubble entirely to herself, went into a more complicated routine of rolls and tucks. The exercise was welcome after a day hunched over the traffic control desk, and she found herself relaxing in a way she hadn't since this whole sorry mess had started. Energised, she requested a ball, and the added calculations required to ensure she and the ball both ended up where she wanted exercised her brain. She remembered remarking earlier that the mental arithmetic she undertook in order to avoid her fellow players and score goals in gravityball was much the same as that which she used to keep track of the ships of the fleet.

A final back flip and roll enabled her to tuck the ball neatly into the goal, and she somersaulted back towards the gravity plate. It was only then that she saw that she had an audience. She had no idea how long the flight commander had been there, watching her, but as she saw him, he ducked his head and turned away. He hurried up the approach ramp and disappeared into the changing rooms beyond. She frowned, annoyed that he wasn't intending to acknowledge her, and dropped into her landing, putting one hand down to compensate as she crossed the plateline and was once again subject to normal gravity. She pushed herself upright and hesitated, deciding that if he really didn't want to speak to her, she would give him time to get clear rather than embarrass them both. But then the lights in the changing room unexpectedly went out and she heard someone shout, "Get him!"

Puzzled and alarmed, she jogged up the ramp, triggering

the lights on her safesuit. She just had time to glimpse Zaran, something over his head, struggling with three black-clad figures before, with a muffled curse, somebody grabbed her from behind. She twisted, attempting to either throw or kick her assailant, but before she could get sufficient traction, something struck her on the head, and the world went black.

CHAPTER ELEVEN

Zaran recovered consciousness slowly, utterly confused for a moment as to where he was and why he was in so much pain. His head, ribs and arms ached and he swallowed as nausea swept through him.

"Hold still and give your safesuit time to stabilise you," a soft voice said. The nausea slowly subsided, and he opened his eyes to find Cristal kneeling over him, her expression anxious.

"What happened?" He struggled to sit up, but she put a gentle hand on his chest to hold him in place.

"Give the anti-nausea medication time to take hold," she said. "We're in a bit of a mess, and frankly vomit would only make it worse."

"Vomit makes everything worse," he agreed, deciding to worry about the rest of her sentence when he could think more clearly. He waited patiently for the waves of sickness to settle down.

"How much do you remember?" she asked.

"I remember going to the gravityball changing room," he said. "I was supposed to be meeting Raffi and some of the other team members." He frowned, considering. "I got a message from her inviting me to join a practice game. When I got to the changing rooms, there didn't seem to be anybody there. I walked up the ramp ..." He broke off, remembering how amazing Cristal had looked in the weightless bubble. She had built up considerable speed, pushing off from the various hard surfaces, keeping a practice gravityball moving around the bubble. Watching her had stirred him in a way he hadn't felt in a long time, and he'd felt he could have stood there all day.

And then he'd thought, with a surge of guilt as he remembered that he was matched, maybe this was some kind of a trap. Maybe she had faked the message from Raffi to get him there, to talk to him. And then he'd felt doubly guilty, both for his misplaced desire, and for wanting it to not be his fault. She had done nothing to make him suspicious of her, or indeed to indicate that she was even interested in him. He'd turned back toward the changing room, feeling conflicted and unhappy ...

"Somebody jumped me," he remembered, and then, "Where are we?" He put his hand to his wrist to check on his wristcom, and was startled to discover it was missing. "My wristcom ..."

"They took mine, too," she said sourly. "We're in an escape pod, and I think we're moving. I'm afraid I can't tell you much more. I didn't pass the aptitude test for learning to fly."

"Did you kidnap me?" he asked, completely bewildered.

She snorted. "Why would I do that, Flight Commander? We're both in this mess together, since my pathetic attempt to come to your rescue when you were attacked only resulted in me being knocked out and dumped in here with you. I came round first ... I don't think they hit me as hard as they hit you, or as often. You may have some impressive bruises. If ..."

Her voice broke off, and she shook her head. "Anyway," she went on, "here we are, wherever here is. The gravity plates are enabled, which is something, but I know they use a lot of seronium, so I guess if we can we'll have to disable them to conserve fuel."

With her assistance, he sat up and looked around. As she had said, they did indeed seem to be in a small escape pod, probably a ten-person one. It had a scruffy, run-down look about it, and he was sure it wasn't one of the *Atria*'s pods. He guessed it must have come from the Wheel or one of the other vessels.

"Have you contacted the *Atria*?" he asked, wondering whether she was right that they had been jettisoned or whether they were, in fact, still safely docked. He really didn't want to disbelieve her, but the whole thing seemed so absurd. He decided to at least go along with her until his head stopped swimming and he could check it for himself.

She was shaking her head. "I'm afraid somebody has ripped out the comms array," she said. "I pulled up the navigation holo, but ... frankly, I'm not a navigator. I have no idea where we are."

"There weren't any other ships in range?"

"Not a one," she said. "And the star configuration is ... well, we're not close to Meridiana, wherever we are. Which would make sense, because the fleet has been moving away from that star system at pluslight for some time and ..." She broke off again. "I can't think of anything else to try," she finished quietly. "I was rather hoping you'd have some ideas. Do you think you're well enough to get up now?"

"I think I'd better try," he said, and accepted her help to stand up, trying not to notice how pleasant her hand felt holding his. He managed to get his feet under him and put out a hand to steady himself against the nearest wall, closing his eyes and waiting for the room to stop spinning around him. He remembered being struck repeatedly during the struggle before he'd lost consciousness, and his right arm and ribs ached almost as much as his head. The readout patch on his safesuit indicated that he hadn't got any broken bones. He put a cautious hand to the back of his scalp, and winced when he felt stickiness and matted hair.

"I didn't want to touch that whilst you were unconscious," she said. "I don't think you lost much blood; head wounds always look much worse than they actually are."

She moved away from him to sit on one of the fold-down seats around the edge of the circular pod. He made his way cautiously across to the helm, wishing his head didn't hurt so much, and called up the navigation holo. As she had told him, there were no other ships in sight, no matter how far he pulled out, and no sign of Meridiana's system. It only took a touch to the helm for him to realise that she was telling the truth; they were really in flight, on autopilot, and what he could see on the holo was, presumably, also true. He swallowed hard and took a good, long look at the controls. It wasn't just the comms array that had been vandalised, he realised. Apart from the helm itself, without which the pod would have gone nowhere, very little was still operational.

"I doubted you," he said. "I'm sorry, that was very ill-mannered of me, but this all seems too … excessive. Crazy." He offered her a weak smile. "One piece of possible good news – this pod is pluslight enabled, and we're travelling at about the same speed as the rest of the fleet, so we shouldn't be left too far behind."

"Unless we're headed in completely the opposite direction?" Cristal suggested sourly. "Unless you've annoyed someone really badly over something else," she went on, "I'm guessing this is someone's warped idea of revenge. We stranded them all, and so ..."

"It could have just been me," he said. "If you'd kept out of it ..."

She shook her head. "They must have known I was in there, and I doubt they wanted to leave any witnesses. Did you ... did you get a chance to identify any of them?"

"In the dark?" He sighed. "They put something over my head, so there didn't seem to be any point in lighting up my safesuit. I was just trying to get them off me. How about you?"

"Three people, all wearing black," she said. "Medium height, medium build, and I never saw their faces. I'm sorry – as I said, my attempt at a rescue was sadly lacking. What do you think? Do you have any way of figuring out where we are, or any functionality in your safesuit that would enable you to contact the *Atria*?"

He shook his head, swallowing hard, and found he couldn't look at her. This was his fault. His action had brought this down on the two of them – on *Cristal*.

He couldn't explain his growing attraction to the Wheeler girl. She seemed so different to the Elite girls he'd grown up with, or even the girls at the Academy when he'd been a student. He was hardly an innocent, but the girls he'd dated had understood that because of the Elite matching rules, he wasn't in a position to get serious about them. He'd been fond of some of them, but he'd never felt more than a casual attachment. Since his graduation, he'd been focused on his career, knowing that in the fullness of time the council would arrange a match for him.

Now, however, realising the danger that he and Cristal were in, the desire to protect her welled up inside him until he felt he was choking on it. If he could physically throw himself between her and their fate, he realised, he would do so. The realisation both confused and distracted him; she was, he told himself, far too independent and strong to respond favourably to his instinct. "I think this is a one-way trip," he said hollowly.

The controller frowned at him. "Are you always this defeatist?" she asked. "However did you get to be a flight commander with an attitude like that?"

"I got to be a flight commander by being good at calculating the odds," he said, bristling slightly. "We appear to be on a trajectory to nowhere in a sky that might be full of aliens. We have no comms …"

"But somebody must have registered the ejection of this pod," she said. "Somebody must be wondering where we are – I'm certainly late for duty, and I would imagine your mother or your match or your team will be looking for you. I'm not a pilot, so I wasn't about to attempt it, but maybe if we flip the ship or something we can use the last of our fuel to head back in the direction we came from, and if we're lucky someone will pick up our suit signals. I've already switched my safe-suit's emergency beacon on, and you should probably do the same." She glowered at him. "We have air, and lighting, and at least for the moment we have gravity. The hull of this pod seems sound, and I don't hear any aliens hammering on the door to get in. The longer we leave things …"

"You're right," Zaran said, feeling his face flush with embarrassment. "I'm not thinking. Although it's not quite that simple." He reached for his wrist before he remembered that their attackers had stolen his wristcom. "Give me a moment," he said. "It's a while since I did this kind of math in my head. The pod must've been ejected at right angles – they're all set to do that – and assuming our speed is constant …" He went over the controls one more time, and discovered with some relief that the flight timer was operative, as was the fuel indicator, which registered a little under half full.

"Good," he said, refusing to think about the amount of fuel they had left. "Now I know how long we've been travelling, I can calculate where we are in relation to the fleet. It's fairly simple triangulation, although we have to work out where they're going to be in relation to ..."

He closed his eyes, again wishing his head didn't hurt quite so much, grateful he had spent his first few years in college memorising flight tables. He blanked out everything else and made the calculation. Eventually, he took a visual reading on the stars ahead of them, then reached out and disabled the autopilot, manually adjusting the pod's direction of travel. "I can't be positive this is the right course, because I don't have absolute confirmation that the pod fired at an exact right angle to the ship, but we should now be headed back towards the *Atria*," he said, locking in their course. "But outside bodies may have already affected our flight path." He checked the fuel level and winced. "We've got enough to keep going for a while," he said, "and I'll leave life support on for now. And I apologize – I panicked."

"I may be just a Wheeler," she said, "but I do know a few things."

"Just ...?" He stared at her for a long moment, trying to decide whether he had treated her any differently because of her origins. He didn't think he had. He'd been too busy being unexpectedly and inexplicably captivated by her. "Some of my best friends ..." he began.

She snorted. "You're Elite, Flight Commander. I know what you think. If you've got us back on course, why don't we search this vessel from top to bottom? You never know, we might find something useful."

Between them they searched every inch of the small ship – beneath and behind the seats, inside all the compartments, and even behind those panels they felt they could safely remove. The communications system had, as she had said, been thoroughly sabotaged, circuit boards, crystals and fuel cells smashed to smithereens. Zaran shook his head over the mess. "I don't think we can salvage anything here," he said.

"Mm, I was hoping there might be one or two intact crystals. We could have sequenced them into our safesuit signals to boost them," Cristal said, kneeling beside him. "But there's nothing usable."

There was little of use in the rest of the ship, either. There were no supplies, what water there was was stale and metallic tasting, and the lockers were completely bare. "It's weird," Cristal said. "This pod is pluslight enabled, which – correct me if I'm wrong – is actually quite unusual. Which ship has let a pluslight-enabled shuttle get into this state? It's not one of the ones from the Wheel – we were too paranoid about accidents to leave a pod semi-derelict."

"No star cruiser would have left a pod in this condition, either," Zaran assured her. She was kneeling quite close to him, and he was tempted to put an arm around her – except that she didn't seem to want comfort. She seemed remarkably calm about the situation, and he heard himself say, "I don't understand why you're not more … concerned."

"Oh, I'm concerned," she said flatly, "but I'm not going to panic. I spent my entire life being safety conscious, and everything I've learned tells me that there's always something you can do. You're the pilot, Flight Commander. Taking into consideration how much time passed between when this ship launched and when you turned her around, the normal fuel capacity of a pod and the amount we're using, are we going to get within shouting distance of the fleet?"

"The fleet is still moving, of course," he said, "and our course is the hypotenuse of the triangle, so … we may get close. But I don't know whether it will be close enough."

"But," she echoed, drumming her fingers on the arm of the chair in which she was seated. "I think we need to find a way to make this ship do something no natural object would do. I think that might make the *Atria* notice us, although it's going to use up some of our remaining fuel. If they're looking for us, which I'm sure they are, we need to draw their attention. How do you feel about a zigzag course?"

He nodded briskly. "It'll use more fuel, but ... I see what you're saying." He tried to imagine the scene back on the *Atria*: his mother would be white with anger, Captain Asterion would have patrols out in the direction the pod had left – assuming they had that recorded, but why wouldn't they? The fact a pod had left the fleet had to have been recorded on the log, even if nobody had noticed at the time it left - which, with the number of ships in the fleet, was possible. He couldn't believe Raffi wouldn't be doing *something* to find him. And Doctor Medwen ...

His thoughts broke up. He hadn't spent enough time with his match to have any idea how she would feel about the fact he was missing, and knew that was entirely his own fault. He sighed, uncomfortably conscious that he might be more like his father than he'd realised. At least, he thought, his father had had the sense to fall inappropriately for someone who wasn't *entirely* inappropriate.

"Strap yourself in," he said briskly. "I'm going to take the gravity offline; we're going to need all the fuel we can get. If it comes down to the line, we'll go on to the emergency air supply in our safesuits. Minutes could count."

"I hear you, and I'm good with weightlessness," she said. "Go ahead."

He pulled out the chair closest to the helm and strapped himself into it. As calmly as he could, he took the auto-trajectory offline and took over flying the ship. He felt the familiar serenity settle over him as he allowed their vessel to swoop from side to side, attempting to ensure that the behaviour of their pod was at odds with anything he'd ever seen in space.

Even the blobs tended to stick to a smooth trajectory. He jagged and dove and bounced their little pod. If somebody would just notice and come closer to investigate, they should pick up the emergency call from their suits. The minutes clicked past, one after another, and nothing familiar appeared on the navigation holo: no ship, no star system, no planet. He watched their fuel level drop. His comms link remained deathly silent.

"Should I carry on or give us more time with life support?" he heard himself say, with a sinking sense of dread.

He heard her sigh. "Go for it, Flight Commander," she said. "I'd rather have hope as long as possible."

Finally, he sagged back, admitting defeat. "That's as much as I can do," he said, a little raggedly. "I'm sorry; I don't think it was enough."

"We're not going to get out of this, are we?" she said softly from behind him. "I'm all out of ideas myself ... you?"

"I can't think of anything we haven't already tried," he said. "We've probably only got minutes of life support left before we have to switch to our safesuits."

"Then ..."

He froze for a moment, astonished, as she pulled herself onto his lap, her arms encircling him to lock her in place as she pressed her mouth to his ... and then felt himself relax, realising he could hardly object to something he'd been secretly dreaming about for what seemed like forever. Her mouth was as soft and supple as he had imagined it, and when he parted his lips she followed his lead and the kiss turned passionate.

Zaran knew this was wrong – she wasn't his match, she wasn't even Elite – and yet, it felt so right he couldn't deny her. He drew her closer, feeling his body respond to her proximity, guiltily aware that his attempts to deny this attraction had been cowardice. He had dreamed of running his fingers through her pale locks; now he did so, feeling the spikes collapse into silky softness at his touch. He touched the warm skin of her neck, his fingers tracking down to the collar of her safesuit. They were both breathing faster, and he realised they were using up their remaining air. They should be thinking about hooding up, using their emergency air, but it seemed pointless to do so when they could be together like this. He saw that her eyes were bright with tears and knew she felt as he did. He began to feel giddy, and not because of her – their air was running out rapidly. He saw her eyelids flutter, heard her begin to gasp for air, and somewhere in the distance he realised someone was calling his name.

With numb fingers and the last of his strength, he unfastened the hood of her safesuit, cursing his clumsiness as her eyes fluttered closed. He choked for air, knowing he wasn't going to get his own hood in place in time and not really caring.

It took him a long moment to realise the banging he could hear wasn't, after all, the pounding of his heart.

CHAPTER TWELVE

Cristal woke slowly, vaguely aware of a feeling of surprise. There was something on her face, and her questing fingers discovered a mask over her mouth and nose. With a sensation of shock, she came abruptly and fully awake, blinking blearily, tugging at the mask.

"It's fine. Everything's fine. You're safe on the *Atria*. Wait a moment and I'll get that for you." The voice was feminine and soft, and Cristal blinked again, bringing into focus the face of a complete stranger bent over her to unfasten the oxygen mask and remove it. The woman had dark hair caught back in a complex plait wound around her head, and had a serene beauty that caused Cristal to sigh a little in envy.

Then she remembered and jerked bolt upright, nearly smashing her head into the other woman's face. "Oh! Oh! I ..." The woman straightened, and Cristal felt her face heat with embarrassment. "I'm sorry," she managed, and then looked down and realised she was wearing a medical safesuit – standard sick bay issue, she realised. Apparently, the *Atria* got their medical provisions from the same supplier as the Wheel.

"It's fine. You were just on a little extra oxygen until your body recovered," the woman said. "I'm Doctor Medwen, and you're in the *Atria's* sick bay. Do you remember what happened to you?"

Cristal blinked, recalling asking that question of someone else very recently … and who that had been, and what had followed, and then winced. She hadn't expected to wake up ever again, and based on that belief, kissing Zaran Atria had seemed like a perfect ending to her life since she'd never get the chance again. It seemed they had been rescued after all. Or, at least …

"Is … is Zaran …?" Even as the words were leaving her mouth, she realised who this woman was and wondered whether whoever had rescued them had described what they'd found. "Is he alright?" she finished determinedly.

"Zaran is doing fine," Medwen said, still smiling softly. "He didn't get his safesuit up, so he was technically dead for a few minutes, but thankfully Lieutenant Raffi succeeded in reviving him before any permanent damage was done."

"My safesuit was up?" Cristal said, trying to conceal the surge of relief that had gone through her at the confirmation that Zaran was alive.

Medwen nodded, glancing up at the medical screens adjacent to the bed. "You would have regained consciousness sooner," she said, "but I decided to keep you under until your body had fully recovered. Zaran is still asleep, but I expect to release him from sickbay later today. How are you feeling now?"

Cristal considered. Relieved, embarrassed, cringing at the thought of facing the flight commander again. Perhaps she could pretend it had never happened? She swallowed, trying to pull herself together. Physically, she felt … absolutely fine. She said so, trying out a smile.

Medwen nodded. "That's good." She reached behind

Cristal to adjust the bed, encouraging her patient to lay back into the supportive surface. "Your indicators are all normal," she observed, "but I do have to repeat my question - do you remember what happened to bring you here?"

Cristal nodded. "Yes, I remember."

"Good. Deputy Chief Justice Hobart would like to ask you a few questions. Are you willing to talk to him?"

"Of course," Cristal said, her brow creasing into a frown. Why would anybody think she *wouldn't* want to talk to a Justice?

Medwen tapped her wristcom. "Hob, the patient is ready to see you now."

A moment later, the door swished open. The man who entered appeared middle-aged and wore a prefect's dark blue safesuit. "I won't keep you long, Traffic Controller." He smiled at Cristal. "I'd just like you to tell me in your own words what you remember, starting from before your abduction."

"I was practising for gravityball," she began, and proceeded to give her report concisely but comprehensively.

"Thank you," Hobart said when she concluded. "That corroborates what Captain Asterion pieced together from the logs. I expect we'll have a few more questions for you later, but that's all for now."

He departed, and Medwen came back over. "Lieutenant Charra has been waiting outside," she said. "I'll send her in with a replacement safesuit for you, and then you can go. Normally I'd recommend you take a day to recover before resuming duty, but the captain is insistent that you're needed on the bridge. I've told him to ensure you take things slowly, and if you feel you're not up to it, just say so."

"Thank you," Cristal said.

"Just one more thing before you go," Medwen continued. "I'm going to ask you to spend a few minutes with the ship's head counsellor to talk through what happened and how you feel about it. Are you all right about that?"

"I guess so," Cristal said. "Thank you," she repeated, a rush of guilt causing her face to heat up all over again. It had only been a kiss, she told herself. Surely Zaran would realise it was just the heat of the moment; it hadn't meant anything.

She suppressed ruthlessly the memory of how passionate his response had been, and how she had felt his body stir against hers.

Medwen went out, and Cristal sat up cautiously, swinging her legs over the edge of the bed. She really did feel fine, she thought, and looked around herself curiously. She was in a private diagnostic cubicle, just the one bed, and the desk on the opposite side, a door that probably led to a fresher, and a wall of closed cupboards. The walls were painted a pale green, and the floor was the colour of pine wood. There was a faint smell of pine in the air. It was quite different, she thought, to the cramped multi-bed wards of the Wheel's infirmary.

Charra was all smiles as she came in. "I'm so glad you're all right," she said, putting down the bundle of fabric she was carrying. "Here's a fresh safesuit for you. I got it from your closet. I hope that's okay. You have to tell me all about what happened - you're so lucky it was Zaran you got stranded with. I'm not sure who else would have got you safely back!"

Cristal unfastened the medical safesuit, and was vaguely surprised when Charra turned her back to give her privacy whilst she changed. Rather bemusedly, she realised that her friend was giving the flight lieutenant all the credit for the fact they were rescued, and she found that somewhat annoying. Once she was fully dressed, she asked how they had been found.

"I thought there was something odd when you didn't come back to our quarters that first night," Charra said. "But then, I thought ... you know, maybe you'd met up with someone. But then you didn't show up for work the next morning, and Jedda was furious because he was still on duty. Then Raffi reported Zaran missing, and mentioned that a lot of people were blaming the two of you for the substream closure – and Captain Asterion had the techs check for your safesuits, and we found out neither of you were on the ship.

"There had been lots of shuttles back and forth in the fleet since you'd last been seen, and it took time to check, but neither of you could be found on any of the other ships. Then Captain Asterion had Komin – I don't think you've met him, he's our chief data analyst – pull the navigation records, and we found an emergency pod originally from the *Canopus* had ejected from the *Atria*, and that it had left the fleet on a trajectory that took it away from anywhere we knew.

"Everyone was panicking, and then ..."

The door swished open and a tall, blond man entered. Cristal guessed that he was the promised counsellor. Charra broke off her account. "I'll tell you the rest later," she promised.

After Charra left the room, the man introduced himself as Jazen Atria. He engaged the room's privacy seal before speaking to her, and was calm and patient, seemingly uninterested in the detail of what had happened. He asked her a lot of questions about mortality and how she felt about her near-death experience, and left her feeling that she should be reacting more than she actually was. She had to admit to herself that the fact she'd nearly died didn't seem nearly as much of a problem as the fact she'd kissed the flight lieutenant – a fact she wasn't about to admit to the counsellor, even under a privacy seal, however much he probed. She got the distinct impression he knew there was something she wasn't telling him, but he didn't press the point.

"If you experience any problems sleeping, or any other changes in your normal thought pattern, come and see me," he said. "My door is always open. Otherwise, I think your friend is waiting to tell you the rest of her story. Take care now."

"I will," Cristal said. "Thank you."

Jazen escorted her out of the room into a circular atrium, where she found Charra waiting. The *Atria's* sick bay appeared quite extensive. There were a number of doors off the atrium, and several long corridors. The exit was prosaically labelled. As the two women left the sick bay, Cristal acknowledged to herself that she really wasn't feeling any after-effects from her traumatic experience; it was almost as if nothing had happened. She didn't even feel hungry, although she wasn't at all sure how long it had been since her last meal.

A moment later, she was swept off her feet by Thom, arriving at a run to hug her frantically. Ashwood wandered along in the bigger man's wake, a slightly bemused smile on his face.

"Ah," he said. "There you are. Thom has been worried about you."

"We've been waiting for Doctor Medwen to release you," Thom said. "Typical it happened whilst we'd just popped out to check on an experiment we're running. What happened, Cristal? How did you end up in an escape pod?"

She gave the two men the short version, and her old friend looked suitably horrified. "Who'd do a thing like that? You could both have been killed! Do you have any idea who was responsible?"

"I wish I could answer that," she sighed.

She thought about it all the way up to the bridge, Thom and Ashwood peeling off in the direction of hydroponics after extracting a promise from her to come and see them after she finished her tour of duty on the bridge. Thom seemed angry that Captain Asterion wanted her to work, but Cristal assured her old friend that she was fine about it, and that she was sure the justice department would be looking into the incident. After all, it was the *flight lieutenant* who had nearly died!

She wasn't so sure about working when she saw the traffic holo on the bridge. Many of the ships in the fleet were dangerously out of line, and Jedda, looking tired and harassed, was practically shouting at one of the captains. "No, no, I said *left* vector!"

"I'm here to relieve you," Cristal said politely.

"About time!" Jedda said angrily. "I've been stuck here for hours!"

She exchanged a look with Charra as the younger man stormed out, and then sat on the stool he'd vacated. To her relief, the other members of Alpha Watch seemed delighted to see her. Captain Asterion took the time to come over and tell her she'd been much missed.

It was almost as if nothing had happened. She cajoled the various captains to align their ships more neatly, the bridge crew worked on around her, and she was just beginning to think that maybe everything would return to her new normal when the officer on duty at the comms station exclaimed, "Captain! I'm receiving a message. It's faint and breaking up, but … I think it's the *Gemin,* and it sounds like they've got some kind of emergency!"

CHAPTER THIRTEEN

For a moment, when Zaran awoke, he thought he was still recovering from the battle at Pellan which had gained him his last promotion. They had been tasked with quelling an uprising resulting from a religious cult taking control of the planet's government and attempting to confiscate the cargo of any trader who had the misfortune to exit the substream at their Wheel. Zaran had lost four of his pilots in the battle and still had nightmares about their deaths. To that now was added a flash of memory of the *Brightwing's* pod breaking up, and of the number of deaths on the Wheel as a result of the alien attacks. With that, he recalled where he was and why – but not how he had got there.

"Lie quietly for a moment, Zaran," a soft voice murmured. "You're going to be fine, but at the moment there's still some neuron repair work ongoing."

Zaran opened his eyes, gazed up at Medwen Gold, and felt his face heat as a rush of guilt and embarrassment flooded through him. He realised that in his head and his heart he had betrayed his match, and he should tell her so. He couldn't go on pretending that he was free to court her when his principles told him otherwise. Whatever the outcome of his interactions with Cristal Feltspar, he had experienced a surge of attraction for her that he just didn't feel for his match. He opened his mouth, fully intending to explain, but what came out was, "What happened?"

"You were technically dead for a short period," Medwen told him. "Fortunately, Lieutenant Raffi reached the pod in time to revive you, and no permanent damage has been done. Most of the repair work was done whilst you were asleep, but I needed to wake you to check whether you have any phantom pain from the nerve damage. Do you feel any tingling anywhere in your body?"

"I ... don't think so," he said, experimentally moving his arms and legs fractionally. He was, he realised, wearing a medical safesuit, and felt his face heat to what had to be visible proportions. He wasn't self-conscious about his body, but acknowledged he didn't want the person looking at it to be his match.

If Medwen noticed his blush, she didn't react. She checked the monitors over the bed and then smiled at him. "Everything seems to be mending well. Do you have a headache? I've placed a temporary neuro-desensitiser, so you shouldn't, but please tell me if you do."

"I feel fine," he said. "I was dead?"

"Briefly," she said, and grinned. "Any memory of a long tunnel or a bright light?" she teased.

"None." He shook his head. "Raffi found me?" He was reacting slowly to what she had told him, he realised. "Is Cristal ... all right?"

"Her safesuit kept her balanced on the cusp until Lieutenant Raffi could recover her," Medwen said. "I believe she thought, since you were the one not wearing your safesuit hood, your rescue took priority." She lifted an eyebrow, and

Zaran decided he didn't want to pursue whatever she was thinking.

"I do feel a bit woolly," he admitted.

"You need to rest," she told him firmly. "But before you do, there's one person I can't keep out."

This person was, of course, his mother. Zaran swallowed, looking up at Admiral Nashira's anxious expression, which settled, upon seeing him, into its more normal, apparently serene indifference. "I'm pleased to see you recovered, Zaran," she said, and smiled thinly. "I was concerned by the condition in which you returned to us. I hope this wasn't an attempt to spend some quality time with your match."

Zaran opened his mouth, concluded there was nothing he could say that would salvage that misconception, and closed it again. "I wouldn't have endangered Controller Feltspar to do that," he said, a fraction before the silence became awkward.

"Didn't they teach you anything at the Academy?" Nashira went on. "I am astonished you failed to seal your safesuit. What were you thinking?"

Of someone other than myself, he thought, but just gave her his best polite smile. "I apologize for worrying you, Mother. I'll try not to do it again."

"Well, that's good," she said. "I received a preliminary report from the Lord Chief Justice, and I intend to speak further to the justice department about how they plan to progress the investigation into your abduction. Please do what Doctor Medwen says, and ..." She smiled again, in what he interpreted as a somewhat predatory manner. "Enjoy each other's company."

After she'd left the room, Medwen shook her head, but obviously felt disinclined to comment on what the admiral had inferred. "Actually, although you do need to rest, I think you should speak with Lieutenant Raffi first. She's been pacing back and forth outside the door for several hours, waiting for me to revive you. She seems like a very good friend."

As Medwen went out after his mother, Zaran realised his mouth was hanging open slightly. Did Medwen think he and *Raffi* ...?

The door slid open again and his lieutenant came in. She slapped a hand on the privacy seal button as the door closed again. "Well," she said. "You're an idiot, Flight Commander. Is there something you should be telling me?"

"I ... don't know what you mean," he said cautiously.

She gave him a look. "Zaran, the girl was in your lap and you didn't have your safesuit hood on. What were you thinking of?"

"I was thinking of putting *her* hood on before she asphyxiated," he said.

"She couldn't do that for herself? What's the first thing they teach us about safety? Put your *own* hood on first!"

Zaran wilted. "I'm sorry."

"So you should be." She pulled out a chair and sat down, looking at him. "So, you want to tell me what exactly is going on?"

"Someone tried to kill us."

"I got that bit."

"You rescued us."

"We did. You were zagging around all over the sky; we spotted you at once when we got close enough. It took a bit longer to get into communication range, and by the time we did, you weren't answering."

"I thought I heard voices," he said, remembering. He'd been a bit preoccupied at the time, he realised, and felt his face heat.

Raffi folded her arms. "I don't think I've ever seen you blush," she observed critically. "How long have we known each other? Since the Academy," she answered her own question, "when you were bright enough to realise I didn't have any right to be there. And I've never seen you do anything so stupid. Did you get knocked on the head and lose your mind?"

Zaran put a reflective hand to the back of his head. "Well, yes," he said. "But ... no, that wasn't when I ..."

"Oh, so something's been going on for a while, has it?" Raffi shook her head. "And you haven't told Medwen? I thought better of you, Zaran. If you're messing about behind her back, that's despicable."

"I'm not," Zaran protested. "I only ..." He broke off and shook his head. "Raffi, this isn't the time for this conversation. I need to think. I confess to being ... conflicted. It's nobody's fault but my own," he went on, realising that his lieutenant's loyalty to him might make her misjudge Cristal Feltspar. "Did anyone else see ...?"

"No, I was the only one who went into the pod."

"I owe you my life," he realised. He didn't ask if she'd told anybody else what she'd seen; he knew she wouldn't have.

"Several times over, probably." She sighed. "Look, like I said, I'm not happy. I've spent more time with Medwen than you have, and really, she's very nice – not at all stuck up like a lot of Elite."

Zaran gave her a quizzical look. Raffi had been born a dirt hugger, and had finessed an appointment to the Academy at Bendos by obtaining forged credentials that showed her to be a Wheeler by birth. The Academy took a small number of Wheelers to supplement the Elite, since birth rates weren't high enough otherwise to ensure a sufficient supply of cadets. The two of them had been rivals from the first day at the Academy, vying with each other for the highest scores for lessons such as astrophysics as well as in the flight simulators. It had been a while before Zaran had noticed how reticent his fellow student was about her background, and the fact that she never seemed to receive mail. He himself seldom heard from his busy parents, but other people he'd grown up with on the *Atria* sent mail, and periodically Ashwood sent long lists of books he thought Zaran should read.

Eventually, he'd challenged her about it, and she'd tried to laugh it off. When he'd just stood with folded arms looking at her, eventually she'd conceded the point. "And what are you going to *do* about it?" she'd demanded.

He'd hesitated. She was a brilliant pilot, undoubtedly his equal, and there was nobody else in the class he wanted as his wingman as much as Raffi. So he'd agreed to keep her secret, on condition that when she graduated, she quietly amend the records back to her real origins. He'd never asked whether she'd done that; by the time they'd finished their first posting together, she was cemented by his side as his number two and best friend – but never anything more. Zaran simply wasn't Raffi's type. For a start, he registered highly heterosexual, and Raffi – well, Raffi liked girls almost as much as Zaran.

He wondered now why Raffi had chosen to spend time with Medwen. Had she been taking up the responsibility he should have, acquainting the newcomer with the people and places on the *Atria* she would need to know? Or was his lieutenant just ever so slightly attracted to the dark-haired beauty?

It occurred to him at that moment that working with Raffi had made him appreciate that Elite status was nothing more than an accident of birth, and he wondered whether that was why, despite his upbringing, it bothered him less than he'd thought it should that he was attracted to a Wheeler girl.

"I'll make you a promise." He took a deep breath, holding her gaze. "I won't do anything about either Cristal or Medwen without speaking to them both. And if I need counselling, I'll talk to you. How does that sound? Raffi, someone tried to kill us," he went on, a little more heatedly. "We have to find out who, or it might happen again!"

"Zaran, half the population of the fleet hates you," Raffi sighed. "I know you didn't have any choice – I was up there with you and saw what happened to that pod. I can't begin to imagine how much damage those things could do if they got loose in the substream. But there are a lot of people who have found themselves without work, separated from their nearest and dearest, living in cramped conditions without much hope of things returning to normality any time soon. The question is, who hates you enough to do something about it?"

And that, Zaran thought tiredly when Raffi had gone and he was allowed to rest, was the big question.

Later that evening, discharged from sick bay, Zaran was summoned to the office of the *Atria's* Lord Chief Justice, Rydon. The tall, dark-haired man was seated behind his desk, wearing his formal blue robe over a lighter blue safesuit. He had a pile of printouts on the table in front of him and was fiddling with an old-fashioned gel pen. Zaran hadn't had much to do with the man since taking up his post on the *Atria*, but he'd known him quite well when he was growing up. Rydon had been a lowly prefect then, and had cautioned Zaran on a number of occasions for the kind of idiotic pranks that most youngsters committed. He'd always been just a little in awe of Rydon and found himself wondering why the justice had remained on the *Atria* when Nashira had been promoted, despite probably, like most of his peers, having been offered a promotion elsewhere in the IUP.

"At ease, Flight Commander."

"Am I a suspect for something?" Zaran asked curiously.

The justice looked up. "Why?"

"I just got out of sick bay," Zaran reminded him. "I'd kind of like to sit down."

The justice snorted. "You're the victim this time, Zaran. Yes, sit down, of course. My mind was elsewhere. I need you to tell me everything you can remember about your abduction. Where were you and what were you doing?"

"I was in the gravityball changing rooms." Zaran sank gratefully into one of the two chairs in front of the lord chief justice's desk. "I'd been summoned there by a message which I thought came from Lieutenant Raffi."

"You *thought* it came from her?"

"I did at the time," Zaran said. "It purported to come from her, but I checked with her and she says she never sent me any message."

"Hm." Rydon pulled a notepad out of the pile of paper in front of him and jotted a note on it. "Carry on."

"The message said that my gravityball team was holding an impromptu practice and suggested if I was free I might like to join in. When I got to the changing rooms, there was nobody there. I was puzzled, but thought perhaps I was simply early, and I could hear the sounds of somebody in the bubble."

"What kind of sounds?"

"Gravityball sounds," Zaran said blankly. "A ball hitting the wall, the thud of feet on the hoops ..."

"And did you investigate these sounds?"

"I did," Zaran confirmed. "I walked as far as the edge of the gravity zone. From the plate, I could see a single person in the bubble. I saw at once that it was Controller Feltspar, who you will recall I had previous dealings with."

"You mean, she's the poor soul who followed the order you gave her, the legality of which is still in question."

Zaran frowned. "I thought we'd agreed ... never mind," he continued hurriedly, off the older man's raised eyebrows. "Yes, Controller Feltspar was the person who initiated the substream shut-down – entirely on my order. I take full responsibility for that action, which I believed would protect the IUP from the blobs."

"Indeed." Rydon scratched some kind of notation on one of the printouts, and then looked up again. "So, you saw Controller Feltspar. Did you call out to her or draw her attention at all?"

"No. She was practising, and I didn't want to distract her, so I turned and walked back up to the changing room. Just as I got there, all the lights went out."

"*All* the lights?" Rydon asked. "Including the lights in the bubble?"

"Oh ... no, they were still on, but the changing room was entirely in darkness, and before my eyes could adjust, somebody threw something over my head. I think it was a fresher towel," Zaran continued thoughtfully. "It was soft and smelled damp. I tried to push it away, but there seemed to be people all around me. They pushed me to the floor, and I think I was kicked in the ribs. And I'm afraid I don't remember anything after that until I woke up in the pod."

"Did you see your attackers at all?"

Zaran shook his head regretfully. "Just an impression of several figures, I think male, but I could be mistaken."

"Did they say anything?"

"I ... can't remember. I hit my head when they knocked me down." Zaran put a hand reflexively to the place where he'd been injured. He had a sudden mental image of Medwen tenderly bathing his wounds, and winced.

"Are you still in pain, Flight Commander?"

"I ... no, I'm just a little fragile."

Rydon gave him a considered look. "And what happened next?"

Zaran described the events in the pod – how Cristal had regained consciousness first, that they'd found the comms array and most of the controls had been sabotaged, and that the navigation holo had told them nothing useful. "I'm not used to being so far away from the *Atria*," he admitted. "The star patterns were unfamiliar, since obviously we don't normally travel outward from the substream links." He described his relief at realising they were travelling at plus-light, and how he'd calculated a course that he hoped would intercept the fleet. He gave Cristal full credit for the idea, and for suggesting he fly the pod like an unnatural object. He admitted that this had caused their seronium supply to dwindle more rapidly than it might otherwise have done, but that he'd believed their likelihood of re-joining the fleet to be slim and had opted to take the chance.

"I see." Rydon made another notation on his pad and then fixed Zaran with a piercing look. "Tell me, Flight Commander, do you believe your jeopardy was genuine?"

"Since I'm told I died," Zaran said stiffly, "obviously, I do. What are you suggesting?"

"I was merely attempting to establish whether there was any possibility, in your mind, that Controller Feltspar knew you would be rescued."

"Absolutely none." Zaran thought the suggestion preposterous. "She was in as much danger as I was. I was impressed she didn't panic – I think her ability to be calm in the face of disaster has to do with her life on the Wheel. She said she had grown up very safety conscious."

"Hm." Rydon made another note, and then tapped his desk holo. "Hob, you can send Controller Feltspar in now."

Zaran swallowed as the door swished open and closed behind him. Almost immediately he could smell the waft of vanilla perfume that Cristal always wore, and he offered her a small smile as Rydon gestured her into the chair beside him, then looked away. He wondered whether the very observant Rydon would notice his discomfiture. He was a seasoned officer, he reminded himself, used to dealing with everything from minor skirmishes to very major transgressions within the IUP. It was ridiculous that one woman could have this much of an effect on him.

"Traffic Controller Feltspar," Rydon said, "please take me through the series of events relating to your abduction, starting with why you were in the gravityball dome."

"I normally practice at that time," she said. "It's just after my shift finishes, and I find it helps me unwind. I noticed the flight commander watching me from the plate and thought he probably wanted to use the dome, so I headed up to the freshers. And then the lights went out, and I heard someone shout 'get him'."

She paused as Rydon made a note on his pad and then glanced up at her. "Was it completely dark?"

"No, there was a little light coming from the dome, but it didn't tell me much." She frowned, as if thinking back to what she'd seen. "It looked like three people were attacking a fourth, but then I was jumped from behind, so I guess there must have been four attackers."

She described briefly their time in the escape pod. Zaran was relieved she didn't mention what had happened at the end, when they had both thought their luck had run out.

"Thank you, Traffic."

"Surely," Zaran said impatiently, "there must be some record of who launched the escape pod? Have the records of activity in the gravityball bubble been checked?"

"My people aren't amateurs, Flight Commander," Rydon said gravely. "Of course we've checked. The pod ... was one which originated on the *Canopus*, the vessel which evacuated the resort. The *Canopus* ended up with more people on board than it could handle, and that pod was used to transfer some of them temporarily to the *Atria* until a permanent berth could be found for them. It appears nobody had got around to returning it. As for the records from the bubble, I have viewed the holos several times. You were attacked by four persons, none of whom were in safesuits. They were wearing dark clothing and some kind of hoods which hid their faces. Identification from the holo without safesuit data is near-impossible, as you know, and there are at present a good few people on board the *Atria* who have either not been issued with safesuits, or simply might not have realised the importance of wearing them. Not everybody onboard has registered their wristcom, either. A number of shuttles arrived and departed during the time you were both missing from the *Atria*."

He sat back and considered them both thoughtfully. "From now on," he said, "I strongly recommend you not go anywhere you are likely to be alone. Try to ensure you are accompanied at all times, and do not respond to any messages of dubious origin."

"You think they'll try again." Cristal sounded concerned – understandably, Zaran thought.

"They were angry enough – and organised enough – to abduct you and set you adrift," Rydon reminded her. "Somehow, I doubt they'll have forgotten how much they dislike you both. Please ensure you wear your safesuits at all times. I will be directing members of my justice team to keep a watchful eye on you both. Dismissed."

Zaran got to his feet quickly, but Cristal hurried out before he could think of anything to say that wouldn't cause Rydon to suspect they were somehow colluding together.

He realised the Wheeler girl probably believed that any relationship between them was impossible, particularly since she must know he was matched. And he should be thinking it was impossible, too, but nonetheless he couldn't get Cristal Feltspar out of his mind. Because of the decision he'd made at Meridiana, she was very obviously in danger. If anything happened to her, he couldn't help feeling it would be his fault, and he knew he would never be able to forgive himself. But what could he do to keep her safe if she didn't want his help? They had to talk, he thought, and soon. He had to find out what she was thinking, however unflattering to himself that might be.

CHAPTER FOURTEEN

"I'm not supposed to go anywhere unaccompanied." Cristal was still annoyed that the lord chief justice thought she needed protection. She'd been looking after herself for a long time and hated the idea that she might be incapable of looking after herself.

"Are there any suspects?" Ashwood wanted to know.

Cristal shook her head. She had joined Thom and Ashwood for dinner at a small food outlet in the central core of the star cruiser, but she wasn't really hungry and found herself pushing the food around the plate. "I don't think we're exactly popular," she said. "I get a lot of, you know, glares from people. Nothing overt, but ... I understand how people would be upset with us. If I hadn't been involved, I guess I'd be just as cross. I'm worried about my sister and my father; I just hope my dad finds employment elsewhere in the Union, and Ruby ..." She broke off, a stab of sorrow interrupting her thoughts. She hadn't really had time to think about her sister earlier; now, she missed her terribly.

"You brought her up well after your mother died," Thom said softly. "I don't think she'll get into any trouble."

"Dad's so bad at keeping an eye on her," Cristal sighed. "My point is, I have just as much reason to be angry about what happened as the next person."

"I think perhaps you might mention that to Justice Rydon," Ashwood said. "If he's aware of your separation from your family, he may be thinking you could be a suspect."

"Me?" Cristal floundered for a moment. "But I nearly died!"

"That's ridiculous!" Thom stared at Ashwood as if he couldn't believe his ears.

"Obviously I don't think that's the case," Ashwood murmured. "But others might not be so ... understanding."

Thom frowned, opened his mouth, and then closed it again as his wristcom chimed. He read the message that had arrived, wiping his mouth with a tissue and discarding it into the refuse box. "I have to go," he said. "There's a problem with the nutrient balance in one of the vats. I'll ... see you later, Ashwood."

After her friend had gone, Cristal pushed her plate away. "I'm sorry, Ashwood," she said. "I just don't seem to have much of an appetite at the moment." She hesitated, looking around. It was late evening, and the cafe was practically deserted. She got the impression the staff were waiting for them to leave so that they could close. "Can I ask you something ... kind of personal?" she ventured.

"You can ask." Ashwood smiled. "Of course, I reserve the right not to answer."

"I just wondered ... whether you had any children."

"Oh." The head scientist lifted an eyebrow. "That wasn't the question I was expecting. Actually, yes, I do, largely because after I made it clear I had no intention of making a match, the trustees harassed me constantly until I agreed to give them a donation. They said they didn't want to forfeit my intelligence." He pulled a face. "I have no idea what they did with it. I told them I didn't have time to deal with children. Actually," he admitted, "I just don't have the patience to deal with anybody who can't formulate a sensible argument. Maybe when they got old enough …" He broke off, shaking his head. "I thought you'd ask about the amount of time I've been spending with Thom."

"Oh." Cristal realised somewhat guiltily she'd been thinking more of herself than her best friend. "Is there any reason I should?"

"You treat him as a member of your family," Ashwood said. "I thought you might be concerned about my intentions towards him."

"He's a grown-up," Cristal said. "It's really none of my business. But, for the record … well, he's been a good friend to me, and he needs somebody to stop him working once in a while. I just wondered … I mean, Thom's a Wheeler, and you're Elite …"

"Ah." Ashwood steepled his fingers and considered her thoughtfully. She felt her face heat. "I'm not taking advantage of him," he said finally. "I like him too much for that. He challenges my intellect." He shrugged and grinned. "As for why nobody else has commented … well, I'm given a certain amount of leeway because of who I am. And yes, that's very unfair, and I would quite understand if you were angry about it. But consider this: it will take this fleet at least ten years to get back to Union space. Some things are going to have to change significantly, and frankly Captain Asterion isn't going to bat an eyelid over romantic entanglements unless they threaten his ship."

Cristal nodded, trying to decide just how much he had guessed about her own situation. "I suppose they are," she temporised, and decided it was time to change the subject. "The message from the *Gemin* – have your people had any success in establishing what it said?"

"Let's go and see," Ashwood suggested, standing up. "I was going to offer to escort you back to your quarters anyway." At her look, he qualified, "Because you're not supposed to go anywhere unaccompanied?"

She smiled. "Thank you, Ashwood. I accept both offers."

The *Atria* didn't have a sound lab as such, but it did have an entertainment centre with associated technicians responsible for ensuring holos didn't malfunction. Ashwood showed Cristal where the relevant team had their offices, several levels down and some distance along the length of the vessel, close to the data cores. Cristal was still a little bemused by the level of luxury throughout the ship – the wood-panelled walls and beautifully tiled floors, the abundance of artworks and statuary; some of the doorways even had ornately carved architraves.

What non-Elite tended to forget, she realised, was that star cruisers were more than ships: they were towns, their population fairly static, always in flight. As well as shops, cafes, offices and living quarters, the ship had entertainment suites with a constant programme of events; it had hairdressers and laundries, a huge library, and more. Cristal wished she had more time to simply explore the gigantic ship, but her tour of duty on the bridge was a long one, and between that and the occasional gravityball practice, she had little time to herself.

And now even that was threatened, she realised. Since she was supposed to be accompanied everywhere she went, and because she shared quarters with Charra, about the only time she would be on her own would be in the fresher! On the other hand, she mused, that would mean she could avoid being on her own with Zaran, which was undoubtedly very cowardly of her but something of a relief nonetheless. She really wouldn't have acted on her attraction for him if she hadn't genuinely believed they weren't going to survive, and was embarrassed that she'd put him in such an awkward position. He was, after all, the one with a pending match, and she hoped he didn't feel too guilty about returning her kiss.

Ashwood led the way past a studio in which Cristal could see a group of young people, including several children, engaged in a re-enactment. She thought they were recreating a frame from the *Blue Daze* comic, but wasn't enough of a fan of the art to be sure.

There were four people in the sound booth. Ashwood didn't introduce them – Cristal wondered whether the chief scientist remembered their names – and they were engrossed in their study of the holo from the *Gemin*. The picture flickered so badly it was almost impossible to make anything out of it at all, but that wasn't what they were concentrating on. The broken sentences and scratchy syllables were laid out on the wall screen, and the techs were listening to the message over and over again, adjusting the knobs and switches in front of them. Despite the fact they had been working on it for hours, the message was still fragmented and unclear.

"... min control to At(ria) ... ss warming out of ... ck gigantic wails ... mm out of no ... riving ... eed them off."

Ashwood frowned at the display, and tapped one of the technicians on the shoulder. She looked up, started on seeing him, and tugged off her earphones. Distantly, Cristal could hear the fuzz of static.

"I'm not sure how much more we can do," she said flatly, leaning back and running a hand through her tousled grey hair.

"Geena, this is Cristal," Ashwood said, proving he knew at least one of their names. "Geena is one of our best sound technicians," he continued, turning toward Cristal, "and it's not even her day job!"

"I'm a metallurgist," the woman informed Cristal cheerfully.

"This makes an interesting change from looking at stress factors in firebird fuselages. I wish I could say we were getting somewhere, but as you can see, it's still pretty much gibberish. They must've realised we were too far away for the signal to reach us."

"But still they tried," Ashwood pointed out. "Whatever they had to tell us, they obviously believed we needed to hear it."

"I know it's important," Geena sighed, and indicated the screen. "But it's still gibberish. If they'd repeated the message, that would have helped, but no. Just a single burst of sound and then nothing."

Ashwood frowned, obviously having the same thought as Cristal as to why the signal might not have been repeated. It was difficult to imagine anything that could take out a star cruiser, but then nobody had conceived of the blobs that had attacked Meridiana either.

Cristal was thoughtful as she allowed Ashwood to walk her back to her quarters, but noticed that the people who passed them nodded politely to the chief scientist whilst directing uncertain looks at her. "The *Gemin* was trying to tell us something," she mused. "Something important. Something about the blobs?"

"I would imagine so." Ashwood stepped off the walkway as they reached the passageway that led to the rooms she shared with Charra. "I was never comfortable with the ease with which we left the creatures behind. After all, we never found out where they came from in the first place. We could be headed toward their colony, or swarm, or whatever it is they do."

"Swarm," Cristal said, coming to an abrupt halt. "Was that the word they used? Not 'ss warming', but 'swarming'?" She exchanged a look with Ashwood. "We should tell them," she said urgently. "It might be important!"

"It might," he concurred. "I'll call them after I've got you safely home."

"Really, Ashwood," she said, "my quarters are just around the corner and there are plenty of people around. I'm sure I'll be perfectly safe."

"Thom would never forgive me if anything happened to you."

Cristal sighed. "I'm sure it won't. And if someone did try something - well, I'm prepared, so I won't be the walkover I was last time. I'm sure you have more important things to do than hover over me."

He gave her a considered look. "If you're sure?"

"I am."

"Then I'll leave you to it," he said. "But really, do call Thom when you're safely back. He'll only worry otherwise."

"I'll do that," she promised.

She watched him hop onto the return walkway and head back the way they'd come, and then turned towards her quarters. Some people coming in the opposite direction nodded politely to her, and she felt suddenly uncomfortable, as if someone was staring at her. She told herself off for being paranoid. She tried to walk calmly, but found herself increasing speed, an itch between her shoulder blades making her think someone was watching her.

She turned the final corner and saw the pale peach door ahead of her. She resisted the temptation to run, and instead turned swiftly around and looked down the corridor behind her. It was empty, and she exhaled in relief. She keyed open the door of her quarters and went in, closing the door and leaning against it. She felt ... unsafe, uncertain and, right at that particular moment, very much alone.

CHAPTER FIFTEEN

"It sure is empty out there." Raffi tugged off her safesuit hood, leaving it dangling down her back, and flopped into one of the chairs in the ready room. Then she frowned at Zaran. "What are you doing here?"

"You're my flight," he pointed out. "You were out without me. I thought I'd wait here in case there was anything I needed to do."

"Couldn't you have done that on the bridge?" she asked. "You know, with lots of people around you, instead of – well, here on your own?"

"If I'd gone to the bridge, someone would probably have sent me to bed, like a child. I'm fully recovered, but because I was technically dead for a few seconds, people keep telling me I need to rest." He shrugged. "I did some paperwork, but I got bored, so I pulled up the flight holo and listened in. You did a good job. Made me feel redundant," he admitted, smiling.

"It's easy to lead a patrol when there's nothing out there but space dust," Raffi retorted. She hesitated, then said, "And no, we didn't pick up anything from the *Gemin*. I'm sorry, Zaran. I sent Kaitos as far back along our path as I dared, but he couldn't raise them."

"Thank you." Zaran thought, but didn't say, that his father was tough and he was sure he would survive. "I wanted to ask you something," he went on. "Later."

The bay lights were changing one by one to indicate that the firebird flight was docked and a few minutes later the five pilots that, with Raffi, formed Alpha Patrol spilled into the ready room, laughing and joking as they always did at the end of a flight. Navi and Grus were arguing about which of them had lasered the stray asteroid that had threatened to impact somewhere in the fleet, whilst Allenda just sniffed and glared at Zaran.

"Nobody's abducted you today, Flight?" she needled.

"Not that I've noticed," he replied. He wanted to add that she wouldn't be stepping into his shoes just yet, but then frowned, wondering whether … no, surely she didn't dislike him *that* much!

He was becoming paranoid, he thought. Every time someone looked at him with anger in their eyes, he wondered if they were the one and he was about to be attacked. He kept going over in his mind the reactions he'd seen at the conference when they'd been talking about the fallout from the closure of the substream gateway. There had been anger and frustration expressed, but nobody had seemed angry enough to kill … except perhaps Director Greybridge's aide, whose name he couldn't recall. He was also uncomfortably aware that Justice Rydon hadn't yet given closure to the suggestion that he might be guilty of some offence in giving the order.

He needed to speak to the lord chief justice again, he concluded; but first, he wanted to talk to Raffi. He smiled and joked with his pilots, pleased to see that none of them seemed antipathetic towards him –except for Allenda, but she had never liked him – whilst fretting about the passage of time.

Finally, he was able to get Raffi to one side. "I wanted to talk to you," he said softly, "about the *Gemin*."

She gave him a long look. "That's unexpected," she said. "I thought perhaps you wanted to talk about something more ... personal."

He shook his head a little impatiently. "This is important, Raffi. I appreciate that you thought to send someone back to see if you could communicate with them, but we're just too far away. And I got to thinking ... what would I do, if I was on the *Gemin* and I wanted to get an urgent message to us? I'd broadcast one, but I'd be pretty sure it wouldn't get through. I really wish we had better comms."

"You're thinking they'll have tried something else," she said. "But what? It wouldn't be any good sending a firebird. Our little ships don't have the range."

"No," Zaran said, "but the *Gemin* had some shuttles with pluslight drive, just as we have, and there were still some vessels on the planet dealing with evacuations and rescuing assets, for what that might be worth." He shrugged. "I guess the extra seronium would be useful."

He frowned. He had a feeling he'd just said something important, but whatever the idea was that had flitted through his mind, it hadn't registered sufficiently for him to make anything of it. He shook himself, returning to his original train of thought. "I'm thinking they might have sent someone after us."

"But they can't catch us," Raffi said slowly. "We had several days' head start, and we boosted to pluslight almost immediately. Even if they did the same, they'd still be days behind us, and they'd never catch up."

"Only if they didn't use any kind of additional booster.

What if they came up with some way of building up greater speed? After all, once one of our ships is moving, we really only use fuel to manoeuvre, and to slow down, should we need to."

"So you're thinking there might be someone out there trying to get to us? Zaran, unless they're carrying ten years' worth of supplies, that could be a suicide mission."

"I know," he said. "I think we should have a word with Ashwood, see if there's anything he can think of that might boost speed."

"Now you're thinking about going back to check." Raffi pulled a face. "And that would be equally suicidal!"

"Maybe," he conceded. "Let's ask, shall we?"

They found Ashwood, as he was so often these days, in the hydroponics unit's main office, surrounded by holos, and frowning. In the opposite corner, at the desk Ashwood had brought in for him, Thom was engrossed in what appeared to be a scrolling list of seed stocks, and didn't look up as they came in. Zaran found himself thinking that part of the apparent attraction between the two men was their ability to be totally focussed on their work to the exclusion of all else.

Ashwood waved a hand at them to take a seat, whilst he continued to tap in and out of holos. Eventually, he sat back with a sigh. "I've never been so busy," he said. "What can I do for you pilots?"

Zaran explained his theory. "Is there any way to go faster?" he concluded.

Ashwood frowned. "You know," he said, "I suppose we shouldn't be surprised, but since the substream network was developed, space travel theory has rather stagnated. I only have one astrophysicist on my team, and despite incorporating one of the GFI scientists who specialised in seronium refinement, well, I'm not sure she wouldn't be a better fit with the chemists anyway." He shook his head, obviously realising he'd side-tracked himself. "I have a researcher going through the library looking into everything relevant we have on record," he said, "and he has a team who are collating what he finds, but it's early days. I started the project in order to see if we could shorten the journey back to the Academy. I wasn't expecting to need an answer so quickly. The issue is less whether we can move faster, you know. It's how we identify and avoid things that get in our way. If we exceed the response time on our scanners, we run the risk of colliding with something." He shook his head again. "I have some hypotheses brewing, Zaran, but nothing that will come to fruition quickly enough to be of use to you in the situation you describe."

"Well, thanks anyway ..." Zaran began, but the little scientist was smiling.

"I do have a suggestion."

"Well thank goodness for that," Raffi said. "I thought you were going to let us down, Ashwood!"

"I do try not to," the head scientist said. "Look, you sent someone back in a firebird to try to communicate with the *Gemin*. Did you suggest that person check across a broader spectrum of wavebands?"

"Well ... no," Raffi admitted, looking uncomfortable. "Of course, you're right, we should have."

"Use a shuttle, not a firebird," Ashwood said. "Equip it with an extra supply of seronium so it can boost for as long as possible, but still have enough to get back. Whilst you're setting that up, I'll get Komin to run a calculation on the likelihood of getting into communication range of your hypothetical messenger ship. Even a little more information would help us to fill in the gaps in the *Gemin*'s message," he finished. "Good luck. Oh, and Zaran?"

"Yes?" the flight commander asked.

"Don't fly it yourself, boy," Ashwood said. "You have pilots to do that for you, and I believe you will be needed more here."

CHAPTER SIXTEEN

"Time for our break." Charra tapped Cristal on the shoulder, and she started. She'd been sufficiently focused on the fleet holo not to have noticed her friend come up beside her.

"Oh! Can it wait a moment?" Cristal asked. "I'm just watching Allenda's shuttle out of fleet space, in case some idiot of a captain takes into their head to get in her way."

"I still can't believe the admiral let her fly the *Gemin* mission," Charra said. "Well, I'll be in the ready room waiting for you. We need to talk about launch day."

It wasn't until several minutes later that Cristal frowned and said, "What's launch day?" Since Charra was long gone, nobody answered, and she sighed and looked around, her gaze settling on the bridge technician, who appeared to be adjusting one of the holo projectors.

"Melas? Is that urgent, or can you take over from me so I can take my break? Allenda's clear of the fleet now."

The technician, who frequently covered Cristal's breaks, waved a hand. "Just give me a minute, Cristal, I need to fix this ... ah!" She straightened from the panel she'd been working on and pushed it closed. As usual, she kept her gaze lowered. At first, Cristal had assumed the woman to be very shy, but she had discovered the reason for Melas's reticence to be quite different. Whilst she was Elite, she had a very visible genetic flaw: her eyes were different colours. Cristal thought it rather charming, but it was obvious the other girl expected to be looked down on because of it and therefore avoided making eye contact. "That should do it." Melas walked over to the traffic holo and Cristal gave her a brief update on the fleet's current situation.

"Call me if anything goes seriously adrift," she finished, and then made her way across to the ready room. Charra already had her usual cup of hot chocolate waiting for her, and Cristal relaxed with a sigh into one of the chairs.

"Allenda's away, then?" Charra asked.

"She's clear, although I'd lay odds the ear-bashing her mother gave her will still be ringing in her ears," Cristal said. "I suspect it's just as well I was the only one who could hear it, other than the two participants, of course. Sometimes I think they forget traffic control automatically listens in on anybody who's manoeuvring."

"Forget?" Charra laughed. "They probably have no idea! We never had traffic control before!"

"I hadn't thought of that," Cristal admitted. "I'd better make sure Admiral Nashira doesn't hear about it anytime soon, then."

"I said I didn't think she'd be happy." Charra tossed her empty coffee cup into the trash receptacle.

"You also said something about a launch day," Cristal remembered. "What was that all about?"

"You don't know about launch day?" Charra said blankly, and then laughed. "Of course you don't. I forget some days you're not pre-Meridiana *Atria* crew. Did you celebrate landing day on Meridiana?"

"They had a celebration on the planet," Cristal said,

sipping her chocolate. "I think it was from the first GFI vessel's arrival, which of course was later than the actual discovery of the planet, but I'm not entirely sure."

"Didn't you have any regular celebrations on the Wheel?" Charra asked.

"Oh, we had a foundation day event," Cristal said, "but since the Wheel was built over a period of time, it was a bit arbitrary when it was held, and it tended to happen around a particular date rather than on it. I'm guessing 'launch day' relates to the day the *Atria* was commissioned?"

"That's correct," Charra said. "It's our biggest celebration."

"But surely under the circumstances ..." Cristal began, but her friend her head.

"Captain Asterion told the admiral there was no way it could be cancelled," she said. "He said it was a question of morale."

"How come you know that?" Cristal had to ask. "Have you been spying on them?"

"No, they had the conversation right next to the helm." She glanced across at the door, and then said, "Between you and me, I think the way she's treating the captain is appalling. It's his ship now, not hers, and has been for some time!" She sat back. "Anyway, the event is held in the entertainment suite. I don't know if you realise it, but all the walls can be extracted, which creates a big enough space to hold a really good party. The captain usually makes a speech, and ..."

"But surely I'm not invited," Cristal said blankly.

"Why ever would you think that?" Charra asked. "Of course you're invited! You're a member of the crew, aren't you?"

"A temporary one," Cristal pointed out, "and more by luck than judgement! Besides, somebody has to man the bridge."

"Of course," Charra said. "There's usually a procedure for

that. We put the bridge into temporary stasis with just a few monitors. But I suspect under the circumstances the captain will arrange more effective cover this year."

"We can't do that with the fleet!" Cristal shook her head. "Give those ship captains ten minutes without oversight and they start to wander off course. I can't possibly …"

"I guess there'll need to be *one* traffic controller on duty," Charra said, "but why would you think it has to be you? You're not the only traffic controller on board."

"True, but …"

"Come on, Cristal! It'll be fun," Charra wheedled, not allowing Cristal to finish her sentence. "We get to wear fluorescent safesuits and drapes, and …"

"Well, there you are," Cristal interrupted. "I don't have anything …"

"We're about the same size," Charra said. "I have the set I wore last year. I was planning on getting a new one this year anyway, people tend to remember! You know …" She winked. "*Important* people!"

Cristal laughed. Charra, like a number of the other unmatched Elite women she'd met, was always trying to attract the eye of the admiral's aide, Kovis, who was breathtakingly perfect. He was tall, dark skinned, and his maroon safesuit didn't conceal the curves of some very well-developed muscles. He had short, slightly curly, black hair and dark brown eyes. According to Charra, he was rumoured to be a direct descendant of one of the first star cruiser captains. And to the chagrin of her friend and his other idolaters, Kovis appeared completely uninterested in a liaison with anyone, of *either* gender. Cristal had to agree that he was very good looking, but privately, she knew she found Zaran's lack of such perfection much more appealing.

Charra probably thought she needed to have more friends, Cristal mused, and there wasn't any way to refute her notion, although between work shifts, gravityball practice and the backlog of books she wanted to read, there really wasn't much time for a social life. And she could hardly explain to her new friend that she wasn't hoping to attract a man because she'd already realised who she wanted, and he was *matched*, and wasn't about to look at *her*.

Back at her post, nudging a couple of the worst offenders for course deviation back into line, she found herself remembering the way the flight commander's brow creased when he frowned, the jagged slash of the scar on his cheek that left the corner of his mouth permanently pulled up as if he was always just about to smile, and the slightly hoarse tenor of his voice that could curl her toes every time she heard it.

And it wasn't just his looks she liked, she thought, remembering how between them they'd released the *Iris* for its short flight away from the Wheel, and the interactions between them in the escape pod. She felt comfortable with him, despite the strange situation she'd found herself in, with so many of her friends and her family probably ten years' flight away. There was something else between them, she mused, as if they thought alike.

As if daydreaming about him had summoned him up, she suddenly became aware of Zaran leaning over her shoulder to look at the traffic control holo, and started inadvertently away from him. "Apologies, Controller, I should have advertised my presence," he said.

"No problem," she responded, sincerely hoping she hadn't given him the impression she didn't like him being so close. "Can I assist you?"

"I wondered how Allenda was getting on," he said. "Is that her shuttle there?" He indicated to the one twinkling light that was moving steadily away from the fleet, and she resisted the temptation to say no, that was the garbage scow.

"Yes, Flight Commander," she said instead. "She's well clear of the fleet now," she added, as if that wasn't obvious.

"Will you be able to follow her for a while?" he asked.

"I ... can extend the field. Although not for long, because I need to keep an eye on the, um, the fleet. But I can check up on a regular schedule, if you would like me to. For as long as she's in range," she finished, wondering if she sounded as flustered as she felt. It was the first time she'd been this close to him since the last moments in the escape pod, and she couldn't help but remember how his arms had closed around her as his mouth worked on hers.

It was, she had to admit to herself, a relief when he moved away.

CHAPTER SEVENTEEN

"Can I help you?" Zaran was in the tiny office adjacent to the pilots' ready room, trying to get on top of some of the outstanding personnel records he should have updated days ago. He had a suspicion Lord Chief Justice Rydon had been standing in the doorway for several minutes before he noticed him.

"I thought you might want an update on my investigation," Rydon said. "Oh, and on your own situation, of course."

"My ... oh." Zaran kept forgetting – possibly because he didn't want to think about – that the legality of his order to close the substream gateway was still in question.

"Relax, Zaran," Rydon said, pulling up a chair and sitting down. "You're off the hook. I've checked thoroughly and there is no legislation anywhere that insists you couldn't make an informed decision as the senior officer in the field. I had to be absolutely sure," he noted, "since I did not want to be subject to an accusation of favouritism."

"I'm sure nobody would dream of any such thing," Zaran said blankly.

"Not on this ship, no," Rydon said. "But Director Greybridge and Commander Rockspire needed to be convinced, since both are upset, for varying reasons, concerning your action. Greybridge is, of course, answerable to Galactic Fuels for losing their asset, the planet Meridiana. And Rockspire has no Wheel to be petty dictator of anymore."

"Was he?" Zaran asked, fascinated despite himself.

"By all accounts, he wasn't the most considerate of people to work for," Rydon said drily. "But neither man appears to bear you sufficient animosity to want to commit or commission a murder, although I did take a long look at Director Greybridge's aide. She's a most vituperative woman, but I'm told she's all hot air."

Zaran had to smile despite the seriousness of their discussion. Whilst as a boy he'd been afraid of the prefect, he'd also been aware that his uncle Ashwood rated Rydon highly, and as he'd grown older, he'd learned to appreciate that the slightly lackadaisical front projected by the man hid a sharp intellect. By the time Zaran had left the *Atria* to attend Academy, Rydon had already been well on the way to achieving his current position.

"So," Zaran said, "that narrows the field to everybody else in the fleet."

"I'm afraid so," Rydon admitted. "I've had my team check all the holos for the period of your abduction, and although we can pinpoint the four people responsible, we can't track them back far enough to get an identification. There are just too many people on board the ship currently who don't have safesuits." He shook his head. "I know Kora, in stores, is doing her best to ensure everybody on board has their wristcom ID properly recorded," he continued. "I appreciate that not all the regular crew on the ship wear safesuits all the time, but everyone on board must at least be registered." He leant back in his chair. "I also checked to see whether there was anybody who didn't like you for other reasons, and on that front I have a question for you."

"What's that?"

"Why did you apply for the flight lieutenant post on this ship?"

"Oh." Zaran realised he was slightly surprised this was the first time anybody had asked him. "The truth? I thought it would get me away from my mother. I grew up on this ship, and it feels like home ... and I thought it was the last place she'd want to return to."

"It had nothing to do with Allenda being here?"

Zaran opened his mouth to issue a sharp negative, and then frowned. "I never gave it a thought," he admitted. "Why *she* chose to be here, I mean. And now I may never get the chance to ask her. Maybe ... maybe she wanted to get away from our mother, too. Maybe she also thought of this ship as home." The realisation saddened him, and he shook his head. "You think she doesn't like the fact I followed her," he said. "I agree we don't really get on, and she's been resentful of the fact that I got the flight lieutenant post over her, but I hardly think that's grounds for her to want to murder me."

"Did I say I thought that?"

"You certainly inferred it."

"I doubt she dislikes you *that* much," Rydon agreed, "but she did make my suspect list. I think it's safe to dismiss your girl from the equation."

"My ...?" For a moment, because of the change of subject, Zaran couldn't think what Rydon meant, and then he felt his face heat up. "Do you mean Controller Feltspar?"

"I mean the girl your eyes follow every time you're in the same room."

Zaran sighed. "Am I that transparent?"

"Only to someone who's known you since you were a babe in arms," the justice said drily. "Aren't you the lucky one? The potential to have a beautiful match *and* a sexy mistress. Only that's not a game you can play, is it? Some Elite would. But you've never looked down on planet dwellers or Wheelers like some of your contemporaries."

"I have to do my duty," Zaran said stiffly.

"Do you?" Rydon steepled his fingers, reminding Zaran rather more than he liked of his uncle Ashwood. "Zaran, I appreciate that Nashira isn't very good at being a mother, but you have to stand up to her eventually. She'll respect you for it, you know."

Zaran shook his head. "It's not just my mother – although she can be difficult when her plans are thwarted. It's our *tradition*. We match where we're sent, and the IUP Trustees aren't about to change their stance on that. Rydon, let's focus on the problem at hand, shall we? I feel as if I've got a target between my shoulder blades. Every time somebody looks at me a bit strangely, I get nervous. It's not doing my digestion any good at all. Whoever was responsible didn't just want to kill us, they wanted us to feel helpless and alone – which is, presumably, what we've made *them* feel. They put us in a situation where we were as stranded as they are. I know it's my own fault, but there was no way I could let those alien things into the substream, and it bothers me a lot that Cristal is in the firing line because of my decision."

"They only got away with your abduction because it was so unexpected," Rydon said. "Now we're forewarned, I don't think they'll try it again – although I'm not suggesting you should relax your vigilance."

"It's fairly obvious that someone who was prepared to go as far as casting us adrift isn't going to just give up." Zaran frowned. "How do we establish who it was?"

"Justice needs to be done," Rydon agreed. "And you can't go through life waiting for someone to stab you in the back. Let me think about it, Zaran. It may be that we can find a way to force their hand. But not until after the launch day celebration. I'm sure your mother is looking forward to seeing you with the lovely Doctor Medwen on your arm."

Zaran groaned. "Rydon, I know," he said. "I'm going to do something about it, all right? Just leave that one with me."

The flight commander had to admit, a couple of days later, as he changed into his most casual safesuit and dug out the multi-coloured silk robe he wore every year for the launch day celebration, that he wasn't entirely sure what it was he was going to do. He had tried spending time with Medwen, feeling honour-bound to have at least given his potential match the opportunity to get to know him, and he her, but for all he found her pleasant enough company, there was just no spark between them. With Cristal there wasn't just a spark, there was a raging forest fire. Even if the Wheeler girl refused to have anything to do with him, he knew it wouldn't be fair to Medwen to continue to pretend nothing was wrong.

Admiral Nashira was so determined to seal the match between Medwen and her son that rumour had it she had sent the *Atria*'s surgeon general on a fact-finding mission around the fleet, cataloguing medical personnel and supplies, and placed Medwen in temporary charge of the facilities on the star cruiser, probably upsetting the other medical staff on the ship into the bargain. The dark-haired woman had been issued quarters on the officers' deck, and it was from there that Zaran collected her, as he had previously arranged.

Medwen was wearing a white safesuit with a gold over-robe. "I hope this isn't too ostentatious," she said. "I'm embarrassed to admit it's the only fancy outfit I took on board the *Gold* when I got the posting."

"It's fine." Zaran frowned a little as he tried to decide whether she was suggesting she preferred not to be on the star cruiser, and whether that was a good thing for him. He took her arm, avoiding meeting her eyes, and escorted her down to the entertainment suite. The area, normally divided into a number of smaller rooms, had been expanded to its full size, easily large enough to accommodate as many of the ship's complement as could be spared. The Wheelers and planet dwellers who had been found employment on the ship had also been invited, but the flight commander had no idea how many of them had taken up the offer.

"You know," Medwen said, as they walked, "I do like the *Atria*, but I really would prefer to spend more time on my own ship. The operating theatres here have been really busy, though. Minor injuries, mostly, suffered by people who aren't accustomed to being in space, but one or two have managed to get themselves into serious trouble. The surgeon general told me this morning about a man who managed to get himself trapped in an emergency hatch that was closing. They had to reattach both his legs and ..." She laughed. "I'm sorry, I'm talking shop, and that particular case is a bit gory."

"I don't mind." Zaran waved her into the entertainment hub ahead of him and waited whilst she exclaimed with plea-sure over the twinkling lights and familiar anthems being played over the sound system.

"Is there a live band somewhere?" Medwen looked around.

"We do have some amateur musicians on board," he explained, "but we tend to use traditional sources for our launch day celebration. Some of them might perform later."

"It looks amazing," Medwen said. "And I love that the music isn't so loud we can't hear ourselves talk! I went to a ball when I was training that was so loud I needed ear defenders." She laughed her smooth laugh. "How do I get a drink, Zaran?"

"What would you like?" He gestured towards the bar area, where for this special occasion large soda fountains dispensed multi-coloured wine into glasses. "Wine?"

"Please. With some fruit."

He added a scoop and handed her the drink. "Is that all right?"

She took a sip, and smiled. "Perfect."

Over her shoulder, way across the room, Zaran spotted Cristal. She was wearing a lilac safesuit and robe which, with her pale skin and light hair, made her look almost ethereal. He swallowed and met Medwen's eyes. She was looking at him thoughtfully and he felt his face heat.

"I'm sorry ..." he began.

"Oh, please don't be," she said softly. "Zaran, it's been obvious since I arrived that you and I aren't destined to be anything more than friends. I hope we can at least be that." She smiled ruefully. "A match between us would be ... cold and empty. If we were in Union space, I might have held to my duty, and you to yours, but we're in a whole new world now. I have no idea how long it will take us to get back to civilisation, or even if we will, and you know what? I think I'd rather find someone who wants me for myself. And as for you ... I think you've already done that, haven't you?"

"You really think I should ignore my duty?" He was startled and unsure how to react. He hadn't expected her to either notice his distraction, or be so apparently relaxed about it.

"Zaran, I'm a doctor." She smiled ruefully. "I know a thing or two about genetics. For all they talk about tradition, the reason the trustees are so strict about matching is because we Elite are becoming horribly inbred. Frankly, the introduction of some new genes into the pool would do the future a huge favour."

"I hadn't got as far as thinking about children!"

She laughed. "Men don't," she said. "But I have to tell you your mother thinks about nothing else!"

He sighed. "My mother ..."

"Has no say in this," she assured him. She wrinkled her nose. "Frankly, she terrifies me."

"Me too," he admitted, and smiled. "I do like you, Medwen. Just ... yes, I would prefer us to be friends." Over her shoulder, he again spied Cristal, who was being shown a particularly complicated folk dance by one of the other girls from the bridge crew and was laughing as she failed to copy the other girl's moves. He blinked, and turned his attention back to Medwen, only to find his uncle Ashwood smiling at him.

"Allow me to entertain Doctor Medwen," the older man said. "I wanted to ask her whether she had any idea who the very beautiful girl was who just left the party with our surgeon general ... would you mind?"

"Of course not," Zaran said. "If Medwen is happy ...?"

"I'm sure Ashwood will keep me entertained."

He smiled. "Enjoy the party, Medwen."

"Oh, I plan to." She winked at him, slipping her hand under Ashwood's arm. The chief scientist gave Zaran a knowing look as he led her away.

Zaran got a drink for himself and stood sipping it near a group of reenactors, who were moving seamlessly from one frame to another until one missed a move and they all broke into laughter. The dancers were doing the Neverine Reel, and it occurred to him that, if the music followed its usual order, the next dance would be the Exchange Reel, and a slow smile crossed his face. Looking around, he spotted Raffi further along the bar in conversation with one of the pilots from Beta Patrol. He drained his glass and returned it to the bar on his way to join her.

"Raffi," he said, "I'm sorry to interrupt, but would you mind dancing with me?"

"What, right now?" she laughed, and then saw his expression, heard the music for the Exchange Reel starting up, and laughed again. "Wait here for me, honey," she said to the pilot. "He's the boss so I can't say no!"

Zaran took her hand and led her across, counting carefully and inserting them into the line accordingly. This had always been a party trick of his, the ability to locate himself in the reel in exactly the right place to end up with a particular person. In the past, money had changed hands on whether he could do it; he had never failed.

He didn't fail this time, either. When the music finished, the girl he was holding hands with was a flustered-looking Cristal.

"I need to talk to you," he said softly, and tugged hopefully at her hand, feeling it tremble slightly in his grip. "Please?"

"All right," she said, swallowing visibly, and let him lead her off the dance floor. They had come to a halt close to a magnificent display of tree ferns, and he led her into the shadows behind it, where they were almost completely hidden from the room.

"What's this about, Flight Commander?" she asked, releasing his hand. "Have you identified the people who abducted us?"

He blinked, surprised that she would pick that as his possible reason for needing to speak with her. "Um ... no."

"I saw you come in with Doctor Medwen." She straightened, her body language withdrawn, and he thought he detected a slight tremor in her voice. "She's beautiful."

"She is," he agreed. "And she and I have just agreed we will never be more than friends."

"I'm sorry?" She looked at him blankly. "I ... don't understand." And then, before he could say anything, she went on, "I ... hope you don't think that what happened in the escape pod makes you somehow beholden ..."

"Cristal," he interrupted her, and smiled ruefully. "Believe me, what I feel when I'm near you has nothing whatsoever to do with feeling beholden." He took a deep breath, realising this was his moment of truth. "I was attracted to you from almost the moment we met," he confessed. "It just took me a long time to accept it. If I hadn't been such a coward, it wouldn't have been *you* that initiated that kiss!"

"It wouldn't?" She looked stunned, and utterly gorgeous.

"You look lovely in that outfit." He reached out his hands tentatively, palms up, open. "Do you want me, Cristal?" he asked softly. "Because I sure as all the stars in heaven want you."

"Are you serious?"

"I've never been more serious."

He watched her blush, realising that he was holding his breath waiting for her response, and forced himself to relax. After a long moment, she put her hands in his. "I think you're crazy."

"I'm fairly sure I am," he murmured, drawing her into his embrace. "Crazy about you."

Their lips met tentatively, as if, Zaran thought, they were both making quite sure it was what they wanted. His body, he was very aware, was in no doubt whatsoever about it, and as the kiss progressed, he grew so breathless that his safesuit pinged up several alarm lights. He pulled back from her, laughing a little, to toggle off the tell-tales.

"My suit thinks I'm over excited," he admitted.

"Mine too."

"Would you like to skip the rest of this party?" he asked, gesturing vaguely at the world beyond their little retreat. "I think we need to ... talk."

CHAPTER EIGHTEEN

The last thing Cristal had expected when she woke up on the day of the launch party was the way that day would end. Charra had been still fast asleep, so Cristal had tiptoed out and went to a nearby food outlet for breakfast.

As Cristal bit into her breakfast muffin, she thought over her options. She could call Jedda and suggest a gravityball practice. He'd managed to find enough players from the Wheel to make up a team, but they seldom actually got to play together because they were often working different shifts, as indeed she and Jedda were. She just wasn't as enthusiastic about the game as he was, she decided, particularly since her abduction from the practice dome.

She decided instead to go straight to the bridge to check on the progress of Allenda's shuttle. She rather thought Zaran should have insisted his half-sister take someone with her in the shuttle as co-pilot, however risky the mission, but hadn't thought it was her place to question the decision.

When she reached the bridge, she saw that the traffic holo was zoomed in on the fleet and the duty traffic controller was sitting on her stool, one elbow on the edge of the console and her chin in her hand. Anni had been a traffic controller at the port on Meridiana and had ended up on one of the last freight ships off-planet; Cristal had been delighted when she was located and transferred to the *Atria*. She straightened when she saw Cristal. "Oh, good morning. You're early!"

"I just wanted to see how Allenda is doing." Cristal frowned down at the holo. "May I take over for a few minutes, just to expand the range of the holo and check?"

"Be my guest." Anni stood up and gestured Cristal into her chair. "The last message she sent was a report that she hadn't picked up anything yet. She's almost out of communication range. How much further is she going to go?"

Cristal sat down and, after a quick check that nothing was amiss in the fleet, drew back on the holo as far as she was able, the fleet shrinking as the sensors reached out. On the far edge, almost out of range, she saw the blip of Allenda's shuttle, which as far as she could tell was still on course. She also spotted a firebird flying a holding pattern right at the edge of the fleet. She expanded her field of view and saw a second firebird further out.

"Relays?" she said thoughtfully.

"Yes, Traffic," one of the other bridge technicians said. "Probe One has firebirds out to watch her back and check for messages."

"I'm pleased to hear it," Cristal replied, nodding gratefully and wishing she could remember the young man's name. She stood up, handing traffic back to Anni. "I'll be back in time for my watch," she promised.

She paid a quick visit to Thom and Ashwood in the latter's office to remind them of the launch day party. As she had rightly suspected, they both reacted with surprise to discover what day it was. She stayed chatting to them until she was due on the bridge.

She spent most of the day on watch, with Charra counting the hours until the celebrations started. As their duty ended, Cristal watched Captain Asterion put the bridge onto minimal staffing. Admiral Nashira's aide, Colonel Kovis, was left in charge, and Anni relieved Cristal at the currently indispensable traffic control desk.

"Are you happy to take over?" Cristal asked. "Don't you want to go to the party?"

"Not really," Anni replied quietly. "I lost too many friends when the Wheel broke up. I'm going to spend the time quietly remembering them."

"I rather wish I could spend the time quietly as well," Cristal admitted, "but I promised Charra I'd go."

Back in their shared quarters, Cristal changed into Charra's lilac safesuit, feeling very strange about wearing one that wasn't her own. Although she transferred her basic medical and preference files to the new suit, she felt that it didn't know her the way her own did. She had to admit the colour suited her, though, and when she put the translucent robe over the top and spiked up her hair with her favourite iridescent gel, she thought she looked quite decent.

Charra's new safesuit was cherry red, and with her long hair loose the taller woman was, Cristal thought, very striking. They were joined by Astel, the navigator, who was wearing blue, and the three of them got quite a few appreciative looks as they made their way to the entertainment centre.

The area that had been opened up in the centre of the ship was surprisingly large. It stretched up several levels and there were balconies, flickering light shows, and music. Strategically placed plants formed cosier areas; several contained groups of children, whilst in another a group of re-enactors were moving unhurriedly through a series of simple frames. "This is amazing," Cristal had to admit, looking about herself. "It's hard to believe we're on a spaceship!"

"Didn't you have any large open areas on the Wheel?" Astel asked.

"Well, there was the star chamber," Cristal said, "but that wasn't anything like as big as this. The only really large areas were the docking bays, but you wouldn't have wanted to hold a party there – they stank of seronium and oil and sweat!"

"Nasty!" Astel laughed, and gestured to one side of the room. "Do you dance, Cristal? We usually join the reels – they're great fun."

Cristal followed her gaze and shook her head. "I know a few of the traditional reels," she said, "but I'm afraid I don't recognise the one they're doing at the moment."

"Oh, it's easy. You just follow what everybody else is doing," Astel said, looking around. "Hey, Melas! You're a great dancer – will you make up a four to walk Cristal through some of the reels?"

The solidly built bridge technician looked, Cristal thought, uncomfortable out of her uniform. She had chosen a beige outfit which really didn't suit her, as if she was trying not to be noticed. As usual, she kept her gaze firmly downcast, and Cristal thought it was a shame she was so self-conscious about her mismatched eyes. "I'll do my best," Melas said. "Have you seen the captain?" she continued, looking around. "I haven't seen him anywhere. Apparently the admiral has decided to give the speech herself tonight. How unfair is that?"

"There's a speech?" Cristal said blankly.

"Always," Charra laughed.

The foursome reel the other women tried to teach her turned out to be just as confusing as Cristal had suspected it might be, and her first few attempts ended in disastrous collisions with the others; but they were all laughing and acquired a small audience who cheerfully called out helpful – and not-so-helpful – advice. Charra finally declared her competent just as the music for the current reel ended, and the music for the exchange reel started.

"Oh, I know this one!" Cristal said with some relief, and one of the men from their audience – she had no idea who he was – led her into the line. The dance was the sort where they kept changing partners, swerving in and out of the line, and she noticed at once when Zaran joined in. He moved well, she thought, then nearly fell over her own feet and decided she'd better concentrate on what she was doing instead of watching him.

She saw him when their paths crossed, and he nodded to her, which she took as polite acknowledgement of her exis-tence. It was something of a surprise when she did the last partner exchange in the dance and found herself putting her hand into his.

His grip tightened on hers, and when he invited her to talk with him she assumed he must want to update her on the investigation into their abduction. When instead he asked her if she wanted him, for a moment she thought she must have misheard him. The way he was looking at her, however, said otherwise, and she bit her lip, hesitating, and then conceded the point. Even if this was just for one night, there was no way she was going to turn him down. When they kissed ... her heart raced, and her toes curled, just like the last time their lips had joined. She wanted this, she acknowl-edged. However briefly, she wanted him to be hers.

She was half expecting to be challenged at any moment about being in a clinch with an Elite, so when he suggested they might go somewhere more private to 'talk', it was some-thing of a relief.

"Yes," she said, and sniggered. "*Talk*, right. Do you want to leave separately and meet up somewhere?"

"No," he said, surprising her, "because I'm not ashamed to be seen with you. But it might lead to delays, and right now ..." He touched her cheek gently with his fingertips. "I don't want to be delayed," he finished huskily.

"How about," she suggested, "I sidle out from behind this tree and head for the exit over to our left? If anybody tries to stop me, I can always say I need to visit the fresher."

"I'll give you a few minutes' head start and then follow," he murmured. "But I don't want to let go of you right now." He drew her in for another long, passionate kiss.

When they parted again, a flushed and breathless Cristal said, "I'd rather be ... somewhere more private."

Scattered applause from the entertainment suite made both of them break apart in embarrassment, but Cristal realised it had nothing to do with them.

"My mother's about to make the launch day speech," Zaran diagnosed. "Normally, it would be the captain, but apparently she pulled rank on him. I doubt she has anything to say I haven't heard a hundred times, and unless you really want to listen to her, it's a good distraction. Hopefully nobody will notice us leaving."

"I definitely don't want to listen," Cristal said. "Let's sneak out." At his enthusiastic nod, she turned and walked away – a little unsteadily, she had to admit. She heard no exclamations of surprise when she emerged from behind the tree, and she saw that Admiral Nashira was standing on a raised podium on the other side of the room, holding everyone's attention with her words. She caught something about new frontiers and courage in the face of adversity, but had to admit that her mind wasn't really on anything other than whether Zaran would really follow her out.

The corridor outside was busy with people still arriving for the ball. Cristal came to a halt, half convinced she was a fool and was about to be jilted, but Zaran came out behind her and took her hand in his. He led her away briskly, and she swallowed as she noticed they were passing Jedda and one of the other members of her gravityball team. She thought he started to say something to her (or about her), but she just waved and carried on walking – a little faster, if anything.

She realised she had no idea where they were going, but chose to follow along, unwilling to destroy the moment by asking questions. She rather expected they would go to his quarters, but he hesitated and looked around, and she wondered whether he was uncertain as to where to take her. Either that, she thought, or he was having second thoughts.

After a moment, he said, "There's a garden along here. I used to play there when I was a boy ... would you like to see it?"

She wondered whether he thought her friendship with Thom made her especially appreciative of hydroponics units. "If you like," she said, trying not to sound disappointed. She'd been hoping for more, she thought a little despondently. His kisses had implied that he wanted something other than just a walk together.

Zaran led her a short distance to an arched doorway, beyond which were familiar rows of hydroponic beds, filled with – huh, looked like mostly vegetables. That wasn't very romantic.

"Their potatoes aren't doing as well as Thom's," Cristal observed, finding that she was somewhat amused. "I must remember to mention it to him."

Zaran squeezed her hand. "He's been a good friend to you."

"He's kind of like the big brother I never had," she admitted. "I think Ashwood is good for him – stops him working all the shifts without a break!"

"Have I ever mentioned," Zaran said thoughtfully, "that Ashwood is my uncle?"

She came to a halt and looked at him in surprise. "He's an actual relative? I mean, I can never figure it out because all you Elite use the surname of the ship you're on ..."

"Believe it or not," Zaran said, "he's Admiral Nashira's brother. And two more different siblings I can't begin to imagine." He leant forward and brushed his lips across her forehead, causing her to catch her breath and then swallow. "There's a secret place a little further on I'd like to show you," he murmured.

"So long as it's not a hidden control panel." She grinned reminiscently.

"Nothing so mundane."

They came out from the vegetable beds and she found herself looking at a central bed planted up with an array of shrubs. In the centre was a willow tree, whose branches stretched almost to the ceiling panels before tumbling down around it in wild profusion.

"I remember this tree when it was just a tiny sapling," he said, stepping up onto the growing medium and parting the branches. Behind was a leafy bower, the twisted trunk of the tree at its centre, fallen leaves underfoot.

"How lovely," Cristal said, allowing him to lead her into the centre. When he released the branches, the light became diffuse, and it was easy to pretend they were in the middle of a forest rather than on board a spaceship.

"I used to play here when I was a boy," he told her, his tone serious. "You may think it's weird, but this was my favourite place on the ship because here I could pretend I was just a dirt hugger."

"You wanted to be on a planet?" She resisted the temptation to point out that he had been then – as they were now – trampling all over the growth medium, and there was a good chance whoever tended the hydroponics unit had been well aware of his use of the space.

He laughed. "Being a child on a spaceship isn't a lot of fun. There are so many rules and not many places you can get actual dirt on your shoes ... but you must have experienced that yourself if you grew up on the Wheel."

"I was actually born on the planet." Cristal was surprised they were just talking to each other. It certainly wouldn't have been her first choice for making use of the secret space. "Wheeler children generally are, because it's considered a safer location to give birth – no gravity malfunctions or unexpected asteroids. But my parents took me up to the Wheel when I was just a few weeks old. My first safesuit was actually a life support cradle."

"We have those, too," he said. "I remember Allenda being put in one after she was born. We spent all our childhood on this ship. Once I got old enough to understand where we were and what was going on around us, I realised I loved being in space and grew out of the planet longing." He leant back against the trunk of the tree and drew her into his arms. She settled against him with a sigh, enjoying the feel of his arms around her. His body was comfortingly broad to rest against, and his arms nicely muscled. They were much of a height, and she thought their bodies seemed to fit together very neatly.

"I was raised by just about everyone on the ship except my mother," he said softly, his hands caressing her back.

"My mother died in an accident when I was ten, so I guess I grew up pretty much without a mother, too." She realised that his touch was making it increasingly difficult for her to focus on what they were saying. She still couldn't quite believe this was happening and gave up trying to think about anything other than the two of them, together, alone. "Zaran ... this attraction between us ... I don't know why, but I haven't been able to stop thinking about you since we met."

"It's mutual," he assured her, his arms tightening around

her. "Cristal ... for me, this isn't just about some kind of fling. I'm just not that sort of a person. I'm serious about you, and ... well, if that's not what you want, tell me now and I'll walk away."

She inhaled sharply, biting her lip, then leant back to look him in the eye. "We hardly know each other."

"I know you're intelligent, and very good at your job, and don't panic when things go wrong," he said. "And you like playing gravityball. I'm not very exciting – I work, and I read, and occasionally I go to the gym ..."

His expression was resolute and slightly anxious, and in that moment he looked very young. She lifted her hand and traced a finger down the scar on his face. "Zaran, you're Elite and I'm not," she said softly. "That does create some pretty substantial problems for anything ... lasting. Your mother will never approve."

"I honestly don't care," he said. "I don't like Elite women, on the whole," he admitted a little ruefully. "They're so superior they make me feel clumsy and awkward ..."

"So you're saying you like me because I'm not as perfect as they are?" she teased.

"No, that wasn't what I meant ..." He saw her grin and smiled back. "Or, maybe it is, but I don't mean it in a bad way. You're ... different. More real, somehow. I like looking at you, and listening to you ... and I want ..."

She put a finger to his lips, and then her lips on his. Her heart pounded as he drew her closer, one of his hands in the small of her back, the other moving up to rest on the back of her head, holding her firmly against him, his fingers running through her hair. It was incredibly erotic, and she shivered against him, seriously aroused.

"Is it me," she whispered, when their lips parted, "or is it getting rather warm in here?"

"I may be a little over excited," he murmured, and she groaned an incoherent response, snuggling against him.

"Zaran ..." she began, and then broke off, pushing him away, as, somewhere nearby, she heard the crunch of footsteps on the roughened surface of the path between the hydroponics beds.

"I tell you they definitely came in here," someone snarled. "This time, we make sure of them, all right?"

"You told us to make them suffer," another male voice replied, sounding angry, "and we will." They were coming closer, Cristal realised, clutching at Zaran in shock – not so much because of what the men were saying, but because the first person who'd spoken had quite unquestionably been Jedda Granit.

CHAPTER NINETEEN

Zaran hadn't intended to end up in hydroponics in a clinch with Cristal – which is to say, he'd intended the clinch, but not the location. He would have preferred to take her to his quarters, but they were right across the ship and he wasn't entirely sure she wouldn't think he was taking her for granted. Had she just been a casual date, he might have gone there without another thought, but he wanted Cristal to under-stand that she meant more to him than a quick bedding. Since he'd conceded the point to Medwen, he'd finally accepted that he was head over heels in love with the Wheeler girl. He'd found himself at a loss to decide what to do about it, and only the sudden realisation that they were close to his favourite garden had resulted in them ending up under his – he always thought of it as *his* – willow tree.

That said, it seemed like the perfect location: private without being too pushy, somewhere romantic they could talk and kiss and cuddle without any need to rush anything. He nuzzled her neck, inhaling the vanilla scent she wore. He remembered with affection the first time he'd laid eyes on her, never realising then what she would come to mean to him. The desire to possess her was a dull ache at his very core, an absolute certainty that she was the right girl for him.

Holding her close, caressing her through her clothing, feeling her breath on his cheek and her warm length pressed to his was like a promise, an anticipation of something more amazing yet to happen. He was enthralled by her, enraptured by her, and when she pushed him away for a moment his breath caught - and then he heard the voices dispassionately discussing disposing of the two of them.

Zaran cursed himself for putting Cristal in this jeopardy. He'd thought she'd be safe with him – no, that wasn't true, he realised. He hadn't been *thinking*; he'd just wanted to get her on her own. With the bridge crew at a minimum and everyone at the celebration, there wasn't even anyone to notice they were missing – something he had thought of as a benefit but which was more likely to prove the opposite.

He hesitated to com for help. The people searching for them were too close. Indeed, they seemed to have come to a halt adjacent to their location, apparently puzzled as to where they had gone. He didn't think he recognised either of the voices, but thought there might be more than two of them – there had been four, the last time. Rydon's suggestion that they might be able to set up a situation where their attackers would give themselves away had been accurate. Unfortunately, Zaran realised he'd jumped the gun and given them their opening by allowing his hormones to overcome his common sense. He looked into Cristal's eyes and shook his head slightly, trying to decide what was the best action for them to take. His safesuit had an emergency button, but it was hardly a silent alarm and triggering it would immediately tell the men where the two of them were. He could key one of his saved contacts, but needed to speak to explain why he was doing so, and nobody was likely to call him in the middle of the celebration. The party was so big they probably hadn't even noticed that he and Cristal were no longer there.

"Maybe they went out another way," a third voice suggested from the other side of the tree. Both Zaran and Cristal flinched, realising they were surrounded.

"Nobody's used any of the other doors recently," one of them – he wasn't sure which – said. "I've just pinged the core to check."

"Aren't we lucky we have a hacker on our team?" the first voice said. Zaran frowned, thinking there was something vaguely familiar about that voice but unable to place it.

"They must be hiding. Let's spread out and look for them. Penn, go stand by the archway so they can't get out. Keep your circuit open and yell if you see anything of them. I'll stay here in case they break cover."

"Sure."

Penn, Zaran thought. He didn't recognise the name but found himself vaguely relieved that it *wasn't* someone he knew. He wondered whether, if he and Cristal remained perfectly still, the men – and from their voices they appeared to all be male – would fail to find them and give up looking, but he thought that unlikely. If the men believed he and Cristal were still in the room, they would also be aware that their conversation was likely to have been overheard. Having given themselves away, they weren't going to just give up.

He felt Cristal heave a silent sigh. She waved a hand to attract his attention, then pointed to herself and then out. He shook his head frantically, pointing instead to himself and out. She shook her head equally firmly and repeated her action, then pointed to him and tapped her wristcom. He realised she was suggesting that if she created a diversion by giving herself up, it would give him sufficient time to call for help. And he was more likely to get hold of someone who *could* help, he accepted with a sinking sensation in his stomach. She only knew a few people on the ship and probably didn't have their call codes keyed into her wristcom. He closed his eyes and swallowed. She was right; it was probably their only chance. She gave him a wan smile, reaching up to kiss him softly on the lips before turning and taking a deep breath. He let go of her reluctantly and watched her race out through the willow fronds, shouting as she went, "No, please, don't hurt me! It wasn't my fault, he made me!"

Which was true, as far as it went, he thought, frantically keying Rydon's call sign and adjusting the settings so that the holo would pop up above his wristcom with its volume reduced.

"Made you? *You* pushed the buttons!"

Cristal was still shouting, repeating herself over and over again, and there was the sound of a struggle. Zaran swallowed, resisting the temptation to run out after her. She was obviously trying to make enough noise to drown out his call for help.

It took a long moment for Rydon to reply, and when he did his holo was greyed out and his voice angry. "What do you want, Zaran? It had better be urgent!"

Zaran lifted his arm so the Justice could see him, put a finger to his lips and hushed the man.

"What? *You* called *me*, at the most *inopportune* moment ..."

Zaran waved a frantic hand, turning up the gain so that Rydon would be able to hear the commotion Cristal was creating, somewhat muffled now as if the man holding her had his hand over her mouth. He was cursing her and calling for his friends.

"You're in trouble," Rydon realised. "Wait." His holo vanished for a couple of heart-stopping seconds and then came up in focus. Zaran didn't want to guess what the lord chief justice had been doing, but his hair was sticking out in all directions and he appeared to have his robe on inside out. "Where are you?" Rydon asked.

Zaran said softly, "Hydroponics, Area 6."

"Where's ...? Never mind. Leave it with me. We'll be there shortly."

Zaran wondered how long 'shortly' would be, and since he could hear Cristal still struggling and shrieking and he couldn't stand it anymore, he burst out of his hiding place to confront her attacker.

The man trying to restrain Cristal was slender and of average height, but from the success he was having in containing her he had to be quite strong. He was swearing at the girl as she kicked out at him and twisted in his grip. Two more men were converging on them – and on him, Zaran thought. Cristal's captor wore a safesuit, but the other two men were in identical dark outfits to the ones their earlier abductors had worn, only with the hoods open so that their faces were visible. They were complete strangers to Zaran, but he thought he recognised the man holding Cristal – he believed him to be one of the Wheelers who had been working on the bridge as a traffic controller on the beta watch. Zaran realised he had even spoken to him once or twice and had never noticed the man display any particular animosity towards him.

"Leave her alone!" he snapped, moving forward, only to be brought up short as the two new arrivals grabbed hold of him. "This is all my fault," he said, resisting the temptation to struggle in their grip. "I gave the order. She had no choice but to do what I told her."

"Of course she had a choice," spat the man holding her.

"Yes," she said, quietening now Zaran was out of hiding. "Yes, I had a choice, Jedda. I could have let the aliens get into the substream; I could have let them loose on the whole

Union. I chose not to do that. Nothing else would have made any sense."

"But you knew the scout was on his way," Jedda responded, his face screwed up with anger. "I was going to be a star on the Circuit. He would have known as soon as he saw me play. Now, by the time I get back to the Union, I'll be too old for the Prime Circuit!"

"That's what this is about?" Zaran said disbelievingly. "Gravityball?!" He yanked a hand free and hit the emergency alarm on his suit, which helpfully lit up and started to rev up to the ear-splitting whine it emitted at full power. One of the men holding him cursed and hit him, and the next moments were a chaos of flailing limbs and painful blows. Even though he was outnumbered, Zaran thought he had a chance of getting away from the men, but then a fourth man – presumably the one who'd been sent to watch the archway – jumped in, and he saw that Jedda had Cristal's throat in his grip.

"Struggle any further and you get to watch her die," Jedda bellowed over the noise Zaran's suit was making.

"You're going to kill us both anyway," Zaran responded bleakly, wondering how long it was going to take Rydon to get there.

"Either she goes first, and you watch, or you wait and both go together," Jedda shouted. "And shut off that hellish noise!"

Zaran considered his options briefly, then hit the cut-out switch. The alarm siren wound down, and the silence, when it came, was almost a relief. "We know what your complaint is," he said. "But what about your friends? I assume they weren't expecting gravityball contracts."

"You stranded them," Jedda said, relaxing his grip on Cristal slightly. Zaran held himself perfectly still, afraid that if he moved at all the other man would tighten his grip on

Cristal's slender throat. "What more reason do they need to hate you?"

"Elite need to be knocked off their pedestal," one of the others growled.

"And I *told* you to leave our girls alone," the fourth man snarled. Zaran stared at him for a moment in bewilderment, and then recalled his face. He was the man who'd said much the same thing to him when he'd been having lunch with Cristal on the Meridiana Wheel.

"So what happens now?" Zaran thought he detected movement at the periphery of his vision, and found himself crossing his fingers, hoping that meant help was close at hand. He didn't like the way Jedda was holding Cristal. He had big hands – useful in gravityball – and Cristal wasn't actually choking, but she was gasping for breath, and it wouldn't take much for the man to do her serious harm. Jedda held her so that she was almost on tiptoe, limiting her ability to struggle against him. "Are you planning on stranding us again?" he demanded, thinking it might be a good idea to get the man to condemn himself.

"Depends." Jedda glanced at one of the men who was holding Zaran.

"Nah, no emergency craft near enough," was the reply. "We're near the centre of the ship here. It wasn't the best place to capture them."

"They gave us the perfect chance," Jedda returned. "Sneaking off for a quickie behind a tree? So much for the great Elite warrior tradition!"

Zaran resisted the temptation to deny the other man's assumptions; in all honesty, there was a measure of truth in them.

"So what, then? Should we just finish them here?" The man who spoke had the unmistakable rough accent of Moksha, one of the inner planets of the Union on a different substream chain to their present location, and Zaran wondered what had brought him to Meridiana. He might have been on one of the trader vessels, or perhaps a seronium carrier.

"I want them to suffer," Jedda said stubbornly. He held Cristal away from himself and looked her up and down. "Maybe we can strip them and tie them up and stuff them under that willow they were hiding in. Nobody'd find them there, I bet. They'd starve to death ... eventually."

Cristal was staring at her fellow Wheeler as if she'd never seen him before. "I don't understand," she croaked, clawing at the hand he still had around her throat. "We've always been ... well, not friends, but at least team-mates ..."

"I was going to be a star," he growled. "You knew how important that was to me. You're not a bad player, but you let me down, Cristal. You let this arrogant Elite nobody seduce you." He glared at Zaran. "You're not denying it, are you, Flight Commander?"

"There hardly seems any point since you've obviously made up your mind."

"Strip him," Jedda said offhandedly to the men holding Zaran, groping for the fastening of Cristal's safesuit. Zaran gave a bellow of absolute rage, struggling to free himself, and for his troubles got a whack around the head that left him seeing stars.

"Now!"

Prefects seemed to appear from nowhere to grab at the four men, catching Jedda sufficiently off-guard to get Cristal away from him without her taking any further harm. Zaran managed to struggle free of one of his captors and kick the other firmly in the crotch, giving rise to a satisfying howl of pain. He got within range of the two prefects restraining Jedda and let fly with a roundhouse punch that connected in a very acceptable manner with the traffic controller's chin.

Jedda fell back with a cry of pain, and Rydon caught Zaran firmly by the collar and pulled him away.

"That's enough, Flight," he said sternly. "The situation is under control."

"What kept you?" Zaran growled. "Cristal ...?" He turned, held out his arms to her, and she fell into them with alacrity and hugged him tightly.

"I'm fine, I'm fine," she reassured him, the hoarseness in her voice and redness of her throat rather contradicting her words.

"Is she really?" came Thom's anxious voice, seemingly out of nowhere.

Zaran looked around to find Cristal's friend standing with a large prefect holding his arm, preventing him from getting too close to the action. Ashwood stood a little further back, his arms crossed and his expression thoughtful. Where they had come from and how they had managed to arrive at such a pivotal moment would have to be a story for another time.

Rydon was busy co-ordinating the activities of a number of prefects. They were securing the now rather battered-looking prisoners in restraint holds prior to, presumably, taking them away to the brig.

"Someone called for a medic?"

Medwen came striding past the potato beds, a medikit in her hand. Raffi, who was following her, looked around with interest and, Zaran thought, some amusement. "You held a party and didn't invite me?"

"Three would've been a crowd."

"And six wasn't?"

"Four of them weren't invited," Zaran responded drily.

"Let me have a look at those grazes." Medwen extracted Cristal from Zaran's arms and examined the marks on her neck. "Hm, nothing too serious. Your safesuit should deal with any pain, and I'll prescribe you a tincture for that sore throat. I needn't have brought my medikit after all." She smiled, and then turned to Zaran as Thom came to give Cristal a hug. "How many fingers am I holding up?"

"Four," Zaran said, correctly. "I have a headache, Medwen, but nothing worse."

"You were both very lucky," Thom said.

"Yes, I know I said we needed a sting operation to bring the villains into the open," Rydon said drily, "but I had rather intended for it to be at a mutually agreed upon time rather than right in the middle of the launch day celebrations!"

"I just can't believe," Cristal said shakily, "that Jedda did all this to us because of nothing more than gravityball!"

CHAPTER TWENTY

Now the dust had begun to settle, something was nagging at Cristal. The villains were lined up preparatory to being marched away under the stern eye of the lord chief justice. Medwen was packing away her unused medical equipment, and Thom and Ashwood were investigating the damage done to the hydroponics beds during the struggle, but Cristal was sure there was still some detail of their situation that nobody had spotted yet, something unresolved ...

If she hadn't been looking around, trying to establish exactly what her subconscious was warning her she was missing, she wouldn't have spotted the pinpoint of light of the laser targeting mechanism, and she wouldn't have flung herself without a care for her own safety straight at Zaran, causing him to fall backwards with her almost on top of him. Despite her quick action, as she fell she suffered a searing pain along her arm and felt Zaran convulse beneath her. She landed on her knees and grabbed frantically at his arm, which was spouting blood in an alarming manner, uncaring of the fact her own arm had been grazed by the laser beam. She heard Thom swear – something she had never heard him do before – and then a crackle of laser fire, and then ... silence. She gasped in a desperate breath, and a moment later Medwen was kneeling by her side, putting her hands over the gushing wound in Zaran's arm. "I spoke too soon about not needing my medical bag," she said calmly. "Leave this to me, Cristal."

"Oh ... I ..." Cristal rocked back on her heels, a wave of darkness and dizziness sweeping through her.

"I'll be fine. It's not serious," Zaran said, but the quaver in his voice gainsaid his words.

"Cristal, stay where you are." Ashwood bent down to put an arm around her. "Rydon's people got the shooter. Nobody's going to die."

"There had to be another man," she said, a little wildly. "Four men tried to abduct us, but Jedda was on duty on the bridge then. There had to be a fifth man!"

"Well reasoned." Ashwood patted her rather awkwardly on the shoulder. "Good job, well done."

One of the prefects emerged from between potato beds. "That one won't be bothering us anymore," she said. "I've summoned Adam to remove the body to the mortuary."

"Thank you, Sierra." Rydon turned toward Medwen. "Doctor, do you need assistance getting the flight commander and his friend to sickbay?"

Medwen had efficiently stemmed the flow of blood from Zaran's arm. "I don't need to go," he said. He managed to sit up, the unsealed, blood-soaked arm of his safesuit dangling, but it was obvious from the way he swayed from side to side that the world wasn't yet quite steady for him.

"Yes, you do." Medwen frowned at him as he staggered to his feet. "Your arm has a deep slice through it, and although it's partly cauterised, every time you move even slightly the blood vessels are opening up. I'd rather not seal the wound here. I need a full body readout and a better level of sterilisation."

"We can help." Ashwood nodded Thom in the direction of Zaran whilst himself started to assist Cristal to stand up. Her initial dizziness was passing as her safesuit administered medication, and with his help she was able to stand, although she still felt confused and distressed.

"We'll be taking these miscreants away then, Flight," Rydon said briskly. "Please try and stay out of trouble for the foreseeable future, yes? And if you don't, I'd regard it as a personal favour if you managed to arrange it for a more convenient time!" He turned and followed his prefects out.

"She was a blonde," Raffi observed, watching the lord chief justice leave.

"Blonde?" Medwen said blankly, standing up and watching critically whilst Thom and Raffi between them got Zaran more or less upright.

"The woman Rydon left the ball with." Raffi winked at Cristal. "I think you may have interrupted the beginning of a wonderful friendship, Zaran."

"How very wicked of me," he replied, his tone rueful.

Cristal was grateful for Ashwood's assistance in getting to sickbay. Although her wound was relatively minor and her safesuit had dispensed enough painkillers that she could barely feel it, she was shaken up from the revelation that it was Jedda Granit who had been responsible for her and Zaran's earlier abduction and for tonight's attack. Her knees hurt from where she'd fallen to the floor, and her throat was still very sore. She kept coughing, and mercifully Ashwood didn't try to talk to her. The two of them followed Thom and Raffi, who had Zaran propped between them. He was stumbling a little and looked very pale. Cristal wanted to ask if he was all right – knew he wasn't, but wanted to ask anyway. He kept turning his head as if checking she was still there, and she hoped he wasn't in too much pain.

They finally reached sickbay and, after a quick glance at the status board, Medwen led the way to a vacant triage area. "Cristal, take a seat," she said, pointing to a diagnostic chair. Tapping her wristcom, she summoned a quiet nurse, murmuring instructions to him.

Ashwood assisted Cristal to sit down, and she managed a smile as she thanked him.

"My pleasure," he assured her. "My nephew would never forgive me if I let anything happen to you."

Medwen looked up at the readouts above Cristal's chair, which had automatically linked to her safesuit, and then gave the nurse further instructions. Cristal watched as Thom and Raffi helped Zaran onto the diagnostic bed opposite. The readouts above it lit up, and Cristal squinted at them, wishing she had some idea what they indicated about his condition.

"Let me see your arm," the nurse said, bending over Cristal. She unsealed the arm of her safesuit whilst he tapped instructions into the small replicator to one side of the room. As he turned back to Cristal to swab and medicate the charred graze the laser had left on her arm, the unit extruded a container and a small measuring cup. The nurse turned to collect it, unfastening the container and carefully dispensing a dose of its contents into the cup. "Drink this." Cristal obediently swallowed the cup's contents, something honey-flavoured, cooling and soothing, which even seemed to clear her head a little.

"That's good stuff," she said approvingly, finding a weak smile for the nurse.

"I'm glad you like it." He closed and handed her the container. "One measure morning and evening until the bottle's empty. Doctor Medwen says that should deal with any lingering damage."

"Thank you."

Meanwhile, Medwen was bent over Zaran. From where she was sitting, Cristal couldn't clearly see what the doctor was doing. She found her eyelids drooping as tiredness swept over her. She sat listening to the murmur of Medwen's voice as she administered to the flight lieutenant's wound.

"He'll live," Raffi observed, and Cristal opened her eyes to find the lieutenant grinning at her. "I think he's made the right choice," she added, and winked.

"You'll be fine," Medwen told Zaran. "The laser nicked several veins in your arm, but everything's sealed now, and the wound shouldn't cause you any further trouble. Go and get cleaned up and then get some rest, and try not to do anything *too* strenuous until the wound has had a chance to bond." She looked across at Cristal. "He's all yours, Controller."

Cristal got up cautiously, relieved to find she already felt quite a lot better, although she suspected she'd find some spectacular bruises when she took off the borrowed safesuit. Zaran sat up, swinging his legs over the side of the bed and resealing his blood-soaked sleeve. He held out his hand to Cristal, who took hold of it, squeezing his fingers gently in her own.

"Are you alright?" he asked.

"I'm fine," she assured him. "I really did just get grazed, although Charra may never forgive me for the state of the safesuit I borrowed from her. You were far more badly wounded than me."

"It would have been *much* worse if you hadn't intervened," he assured her. "How did you know?"

She sighed. "It suddenly occurred to me that Jedda couldn't have been one of the men who abducted us, although he was obviously the ringleader, because he was on duty at the time. There had to be a fourth man somewhere, and it was just dumb luck that I spotted his laser about to fire."

"You were amazing," he said quietly, gazing into her eyes. She felt her toes curl just from the expression on his face. "Twice you were amazing. When you ran out to distract the men whilst I called for help – and then, at the end, you probably saved my life. I adore you. Will you have my children?"

Her eyes widened as he spoke the traditional Elite phrase that proposed a match. He couldn't be serious, she thought, and she laughed a little incredulously. "What, off the record?" she asked.

"No," he said quietly. "*On* the record. I have a very high-risk job and, frankly, quite probably a short life expectancy. This – tonight – this isn't how my life normally is, but every time I take out a flight there's a good chance I might not come back. Maybe I'm being unfair, expecting anyone to want me, knowing that, but ... I want to be with you, Cristal, all the time we can have. I don't want to waste a single minute." He smiled wryly. "Besides," he finished, a little louder, "it will really annoy my mother!"

"What will annoy her?" Ashwood asked, coming into his line of sight. "And what are you two whispering about? You really should do what the doctor said, my boy –go and get some rest."

"I would love to have your children," Cristal said thoughtfully to Zaran. Because, she realised, she felt the same way. After nearly losing him, she just wanted to be with him for as long as possible. And if this turned out just to be a medication-induced dream, she might as well be honest about how she felt.

Both Ashwood's eyebrows shot up, and he cleared his throat. "Ahem ... I appreciate that someone is bound to ask sooner or later just what the two of you were doing alone in hydroponics during the launch day celebrations. However, you really don't need to ..."

"Oh yes, we do," Zaran said, squeezing Cristal's hand. "Can we do it now? We're in the right place to do the blood tests, after all."

"Are you delirious?" Ashwood asked, exchanging a look with Thom. "You just got shot. Can't this wait?"

"I'm not confused," Zaran insisted, getting cautiously to his feet and putting his unwounded arm around Cristal. "I don't think I've ever felt quite so sure about anything. Ashwood, you told me to stand up to my mother – oh, sorry, that may have been Rydon, but I'm sure you'd agree with his suggestion. And Medwen, you're all for new genes in the pool ..."

"What about you, Cristal?" Thom asked, his expression concerned. "Are you sure about this? He's Elite and you're not. It's not just his mother who's going to be angry about the flight lieutenant matching with a Wheeler!"

She smiled up at her old friend, knowing the calm she felt was genuine and had nothing to do with Medwen's medicine. "I'm quite sure." She looked at Zaran, wondering if her expression was as besotted as his. "Things have changed so much, Thom. Maybe it's time we stopped being slaves to the old ways."

"Good choice," Medwen said approvingly. "I'll be happy to witness, if you'd like me to."

Zaran hesitated, turning to look Cristal in the eye. "Am I rushing you?" he asked.

"Yes, but please don't stop," she said. "I always wanted to be swept off my feet!"

He leant toward her, ignoring Raffi, who was sniggering. "Is that all you want?" he asked softly.

"You know it isn't!" she murmured back.

Zaran straightened. "Ashwood? Raffi? Thom? Would you also be our witnesses?"

"I think the module's online in the adjacent bay," Medwen said, glancing at her wristcom. "Yes, it is. Apologies; this isn't my own sickbay!"

"Where *is* the surgeon general?" Zaran wondered, having only just registered his absence.

"Last seen leaving the ball with a mysterious woman," Ashwood said. "Most of his team are out reviewing the medical provision on other ships and assisting with the people who were injured in the blob attacks on Meridiana or were injured subsequently. However happy we are," and he gave both Zaran and Cristal a long look, "we should remember that there are others for whom the situation we're in is less than a picnic."

"I haven't forgotten," Zaran said quietly. "Cristal, I'm sorry your father and your sister can't be here for this. I hope they'd approve of me."

"Ruby would," Cristal said. "I'm not so sure about my father! He and your mother ... well, never mind."

Zaran smiled at Medwen. "I'm glad you're here," he told her. "However irresponsible I think my mother was, leaving the order for your ship to follow us, we need an extra doctor used to dealing with emergency situations. I guess keeping you here on the *Atria* was my mother's idea."

"I'm grateful for the opportunity to get to know the equipment available on the star cruiser," Medwen said. "And at the moment I know I can do more good here than on my own ship. *Gold* is designed to be a response vessel in the event of an incident. We carry good supplies of drugs and equipment but don't have a lot of bed space."

"All this is very interesting," Raffi said, tapping her wristcom pointedly, "but if you need me to witness something, Zaran, you'd better get on with it. Beta Patrol's on its way in, and I need to be ready to take Alpha out."

"What's going on?" Zaran asked, frowning.

"Nothing that need interrupt your plans, Flight," she said. "Doctor's orders are to rest." She grinned broadly. "And I suggest you do as you're told for once."

"You know I won't be able to rest until I know what's happening," he said sharply. "Has something been heard from Allenda's shuttle?"

"No, it's nothing like that," Raffi assured him. "Just a build-up in the number of asteroids we're seeing. The captain thinks the fleet may need to make a course change shortly to avoid something up ahead."

It was Cristal's turn to be alarmed. "Course change?" she said. "When? Oh!" The sudden realisation was like a stone in her stomach. "He's down a traffic controller," she said worriedly. "Am I needed?"

"No!" Raffi exchanged a look with Ashwood. "It's all in hand, Cristal. Anni's on duty, and she's good – although not as good as you. Honestly, I think you two deserve each other. You're both far too fixated on doing your duty!"

"Thanks," Zaran said. "I think!"

"Everything's ready," Medwen announced. "But I'm going to give you both one last chance to change your minds. Zaran, you're Elite and entitled to an Elite match. Cristal, you're a Wheeler, and there will be people who disapprove strongly of you marrying an Elite. Please tell me you've given this your full consideration and you're not rushing into something you'll come to regret."

"People already disapprove of me for closing down the substream," Cristal sighed. "I'm getting used to being glared at."

"It'll only get worse," Medwen predicted. "So, one last time, do either of you want to delay this?"

Zaran looked down at Cristal, his expression anxious, and she smiled a little helplessly. "I don't want to delay."

"Good," Zaran said. "Because I don't, either. Let's do this thing!"

It all seemed rather clinical, Cristal thought. She and Zaran gave small amounts of blood, and the machine declared the match within acceptable parameters.

"Note!" it intoned. "One participant is recorded as having a potential match on record. Delete prior match?"

"Oh my goodness, yes!" Medwen said, laughing and stepping forward to enter her authorisation code.

"Delete prior match," Zaran confirmed.

"Match approved. Do the participants wish to continue with the match? Please answer clearly."

"I, Zaran, confirm I wish to proceed," Zaran said firmly, taking hold of Cristal's hand.

"Um, I, Cristal, confirm I wish to proceed," she said, her hand trembling a little in his, still not entirely sure she wasn't dreaming.

"Match is agreed. Record match?"

"Yes," said Zaran.

"Yes," echoed Cristal.

The four witnesses added their names, and Zaran leant across to murmur in Cristal's ear, "So clinical!"

"Zaran, Cristal," Ashwood said, a twinkle in his eye, "I offer you my blessing, for what it's worth. I will inform your mother, Zaran, if you wish."

"You just want to see her face!" Zaran laughed.

"There is that," his uncle grinned.

"But thank you," Zaran continued, sobering. "I doubt she's going to be very pleased, but I've lived my life without her approval, so I'm quite sure I can cope without it now."

Ashwood shrugged. "I think she does care," he said. "But she's not very good at showing it. Well, boy, if I was you now,

I'd take my new match and go and lock myself in my quarters for as long as I could possibly get away with."

"You," Zaran told him, "get away with a great deal more than I do! Cristal?"

"Sounds lovely," she admitted.

"All right, then. Let's do it!"

CHAPTER TWENTY-ONE

Zaran was well aware that he was rushing Cristal, but being shot at had brought his life into sharp focus. He wanted this lovely girl more than he'd ever wanted anything, with the possible exception, he had to admit to himself, of desiring to be a pilot – but there was a difference. Being a pilot was what he *was*; being with Cristal was what he *needed*. Someone who seemed to perfectly complement him.

He was very aware, as he led her into his meagre quarters, of how inadequate they were for a couple. There was only one desk, and he'd never bothered to do much in the way of decoration. The fresher was functional, and the bed was large enough for two, but only if they were very friendly. There were others elsewhere in the fleet who must be much worse off, he told himself. And freeing up the spare bed in Charra's suite would mean some other girl would get a decent space.

"Last chance to change your mind, Cristal – are you absolutely one hundred percent sure about this?" he asked, making sure the door was locked and his comms unit was set to emergency only before turning to put his arms around her.

Medwen had done an impressive job on his wound, he noticed absently. It barely hurt at all now.

His new match leant into him, her arms encircling him. "Sure?" she said. "I think I died and went to heaven! What are you *doing* to me?"

"Nothing yet," he teased. "Soon … everything! But first," he noted, wrinkling his nose, "we both need to get clean. I don't know about you, but being covered in my own blood doesn't seem particularly sexy." They had got some very strange looks on the walk from sickbay, he thought ruefully. "Why don't you go first? I'd love to suggest joining you," he added, pressing a kiss to her forehead, "but frankly the fresher cubicle isn't big enough for two."

"It's a funny thing," she said, a little tremulously, "but I never feel entirely comfortable not wearing my safesuit. It's because I lived on the Wheel," she went on, blushing. "You just don't, there. There's always the threat of a stray asteroid, or a more than usually idiotic freighter pilot damaging the structure."

"Are you telling me you don't want to take off your safe-suit?" he asked a little blankly.

She chuckled. "Not at all," she said. "I just wanted to warn you that I might wake up in the night and be a bit … disoriented, without one."

"I promise, if I have to wake you up in the night, to make sure I remind you where you are." He grinned.

She reached up to kiss him, and he half-groaned into her mouth. "I'm not trying to rush you," he said, "but … hurry back?"

"I don't plan to dawdle," she said, and then looked down at herself. "But you're not to laugh if I'm all over bruises."

"I may have a few myself," he said. "I promise not to laugh. In fact, I promise to kiss them all better." He gave her an exaggerated wink, which sent her into the fresher laughing.

He took the opportunity, whilst she was out of the room, to pick up a few items that were lying around and put them away, then turned back the sheet on his bed. It really was going to be cosy for two, he thought. Even if there were no bigger quarters available, he'd have to have a chat with the storekeeper about upgrading the bed. He sat down at his desk and tapped his fingers impatiently on its surface, listening to the hiss of the fresher.

When Cristal reappeared, clean and wearing no more than a towel, he was torn between the desire to sweep her into his arms and the knowledge that he needed to take his own turn in the fresher first. For once, common sense won over urgency.

"I need to get out of this safesuit." He glanced down at the arm, the fabric of which was looking a little less blood-stained. Given enough time, the safesuit would absorb the cells, but of course it wouldn't do so until they were completely lifeless. "Have a seat," he offered, gesturing to his bed. "Oh, if you don't mind, that is."

She grinned at him. "One of the things I like about you," she said, "is that you're not all domineering. You're not what I always thought an Elite man would be like. Are you really atypical, or were my preconceptions completely wrong?"

"I don't know," he said, frowning. "I guess I never thought about it. I'm just me."

"Well, I like you just the way you are."

He bent to give her a quick kiss. "I'm so very glad you do!"

Zaran had to admit he felt better once he'd removed the bloodstained safesuit and allowed the fresher to do its work. It was invigorating as well as cleansing, but he had no desire to linger when Cristal was waiting for him. He retrieved a second towel to wrap himself in, and returned to the main room.

He drew her into his arms and inhaled the scent of her - warm flesh, the lingering aroma of vanilla, her hair damp and, clean of its iridescent gel, pale and soft as he drew her head towards his. He could feel her tremble as his mouth claimed hers, feel her breath against his cheek. He watched her eyelids flutter as their kiss prolonged, and heard his own breathing quicken. He told himself not to rush, to savour each and every moment of this night.

When their mouths parted, she reached up to touch the scar on his face. "I keep meaning to ask," she said, "where you got this ..."

"Pellan." He shuddered slightly at the memory. "I was trying to pull a pilot out of a crashed ship."

"Oh." She frowned. "I remember the holos ... I hadn't realised that was you. What you did was heroic!"

"That's what they called it," he gritted out. "I lost almost my entire squadron. I can't call that a *success*."

"But didn't you stop the cult that was murdering traders?"

"Yes, but I'm not sure it was worth the price," he sighed. "There must have been a better way ... and I never deserved the praise for it, or the promotion. I tried to tell them ..."

She frowned, obviously puzzled, but then her eyes widened. "You weren't given a choice about the promotion, were you?" she said. "You're ... Elite. Worse than Elite, you're the son of two star cruiser captains. You're expected to be ... sort of super Elite. And not just ..." She hesitated, then continued, "I guess you felt like you couldn't let either of them down. Hell's furnace, Zaran! I don't envy you your demons!"

He exhaled hard, and a little of the tension he hadn't realised he was feeling went out of his shoulders. The corner of his mouth twitched upward ruefully. "Not such a hero?" he said.

"My hero," she told him, her thumb brushing across his lips. "I've got a few demons in my past, too. I've never been sure what happened to my mother, whether when the Wheel was breached she was trying to get back to me and my sister … your mother was distant, my father was too absorbed in his work … I think we have a lot in common."

"We do," he agreed, caressing her gently, avoiding her bruises.

"I suspect," she said, "your mother is going to be furious about this."

"Let me," he said firmly, "worry about my mother." At least Ashwood had gone to break the news, he thought, and he wouldn't have *that* hanging over him!

He lost himself in her, kissing her and caressing her, enjoying the feel of her warm skin against his. He couldn't remember ever feeling this way before: his whole being rapt by her, every sense that he had focussed on her, touch, sight, hearing, taste …

"I adore you," he murmured, laying back with her on the bed, their towels discarded, their bodies pressed together. He explored her with his fingertips and mouth, every little gasp of pleasure she gave enhancing his own arousal.

"You're *mine!*" he told her.

And shortly afterwards, she was.

Much, much later, he lay beside her, temporarily sated, his arm around her, feeling her soft breath against his shoulder. She was tucked against him, asleep, and he knew he should be sleeping too, but he couldn't stop looking at her. They belonged with each other, he thought, and marvelled at the circumstances that had brought them together.

His eyes were finally drifting shut when he became aware that his com alarm was flashing. He shifted Cristal gently away, smiling as she curled into the warmth he left, and got to his desk before the audible alarm cut in. "What is it?" he asked.

"Flight Commander." Captain Asterion's holo popped up. He didn't blink at Zaran's state of undress – the pilot figured he'd probably seen worse.

"Sir?"

"I need you on the bridge." The captain scratched his cheek. "A rumour tells me you may have Controller Feltspar with you. Is that the case?"

"Um, yes, sir," Zaran said, a sinking sensation in his stomach.

"She's needed here as well, Flight Commander. I'm sorry," the captain continued, sounding weary, "but this is an emergency."

CHAPTER TWENTY-TWO

Cristal didn't want to be on the bridge being glowered at by Admiral Nashira. She wanted to be back in Zaran's bed, with him, touching his skin, sliding her hands down his back, pressing him against her. She wanted to feel his lips brushing her neck, sliding lower, his tongue flicking her nipple, his hair brushing against her. She wanted to put her head on his chest and listen to his heart race just as hers was racing. Neither of them had been innocent, but somehow what had happened between them had seemed, to her at least, so much more intense, more *real*, than anything that had ever happened to her before. And somewhere in the midst of it all, she remembered telling him she loved him, and his passionate response.

Later, when she'd awakened in his bed, she had been disappointed to find him not beside her but instead leaning over her, fully dressed, his expression anxious. "I'm sorry, my heart," he said, "but we've both been summoned to the bridge. Some kind of emergency, Captain Asterion didn't elucidate further."

"That's awkward," she replied ruefully.

"Why?"

"Because I have nothing to wear!" she pointed out. "I can hardly turn up in Charra's safesuit. You'd better go ahead. I'll run by my quarters and get my uniform safesuit. I'll only be a few minutes behind you if I run."

"I wish we didn't have to go," he said, bending to kiss her gently. "We'll get back to this later." He gave her his best grin.

When Cristal had reached her quarters, she had found Charra sitting in her chair watching a holo. She'd paused it when Cristal came in. "And where have *you* been?" she asked. "I'm guessing you had a *really* good launch day celebration, so tell all …"

"Charra, I'm sorry," she blurted out, "I just came in for a clean safesuit. There's a meeting on the bridge I have to go to. I'm really sorry about your outfit - I *think* the laser burn is mendable …"

"What?" Charra exclaimed blankly.

As she stripped off the ruined safesuit and clambered into a clean maroon uniform, Cristal filled Charra in as best she could in the few minutes available.

"I can't believe so much has happened in so short a time," Charra said. "When the emergency is over, I'm going to expect a full account!"

And so she'd arrived finally on the bridge, her hair on end and her clothing clean but hardly neat, to be greeted by Admiral Nashira looking daggers at her. The admiral stood talking to Captain Asterion, who was in his favourite position near the navigation holo alongside Jheron, the Beta Watch commander. The captain, she realised, looked worried, and she reminded herself that, no matter how unfortunate the timing of whatever this emergency was, her duty had to take precedence over her personal life. But that didn't mean she had to stop wishing things were otherwise.

Zaran, she saw, was standing talking to Raffi by the door to the ready room, and she thought he looked alarmed and anxious. Anni was on duty at the traffic control holo, and assuming that she'd been called to take over, she went to join her.

"I said ten degrees, Captain," she was telling the holo of an elderly woman Cristal recognised as one of the more difficult merchants. "You've got the *Banefire* on your starboard bow. If you don't hold course, you're going to collide, and don't tell me I didn't warn you!" She glanced up at Cristal and shrugged elaborately, silencing the feed. "That one's never going to listen!" she complained.

"Most of them aren't used to space being so crowded," Cristal murmured placatingly.

"Controller Feltspar." Asterion strode across to her. "I need you to listen in on the briefing in the ready room. Give some thought to the best deployment pattern for the fleet."

"Sir." The duty bridge crew were Beta Watch, most of whom she knew only by sight, and she thought they were giving her odd looks as she followed the captain, the admiral and Colonel Kovis into the ready room.

Inside, the tables had been amalgamated into the conference configuration, and Cristal found herself taking a seat between Kovis and Zaran. She kept a polite smile fixed on her face, despite wanting to wilt under the glares directed at her by Zaran's mother. She reminded herself that whatever his mother might think, Zaran loved her and their match was solid. Ashwood arrived, his hair ruffled as if he'd dressed hurriedly, followed by Director Greybridge, minus, Cristal was relieved to see, the latter's annoying aide, Dolor Stile. The two of them took the remaining seats and Captain Asterion leant forward and placed the palms of his hands on the table.

"Thank you all for responding so quickly. It seems that trouble comes in pairs." He paused, and Cristal swallowed, afraid that the emergency was one that might threaten her happiness. "Firstly," the captain said, "I know some of you will be aware of the increasing reports of asteroids in our path. Lieutenant Raffi?"

"There's always a little space debris around," the lieutenant said, "but over the last day, the frequency has increased to alarming proportions. I sent an advance scout to check our path, and there's a big debris field out there. Something big broke up, but the pieces haven't fully dispersed. Trying to get the fleet through intact could be … interesting."

"Do we have the firepower to create a safe passage, Ashwood?" the captain asked. Nashira was saying nothing, Cristal noted; she presumed that the admiral and Asterion had already agreed on who would do the talking at this briefing.

"I've looked at the density reports and done the math. Theoretically, we could do that," Ashwood replied. "It would, however, use up an excessive amount of seronium. Not so much that we couldn't get to our destination," he added, "but that presupposes not having another emergency down the line. I am concerned that we are having this problem so early in our exodus. I have my people looking at alternative fuels, and early reports are encouraging, but I have no idea how long it will take to develop anything useful. Or find a seronium deposit we can mine," he finished scrupulously.

"Why do we need to go through the field?" Zaran asked. "Couldn't we avoid it by making a course change?"

"We could," Asterion said, "but that brings me to the second of our problems. It would seem that the blobs aren't the only alien life form in this part of space. One of our relay firebirds received a faint message from Allenda half an hour ago. She reported that she had been unable to make contact with the *Gemin*. However, she witnessed something – she described them as gigantic bulbous creatures – following a stream of blobs and scooping them up as if they were in some way harvesting them."

"Considering the fact that up until now the blobs corroded everything they came into contact with," Ashwood said, steepling his fingers, "it does sound as if this second type of life form is somehow impervious to, or even feeds on, the first type."

"Are they headed this way?" Zaran sounded alarmed. "Is Allenda on her way back?"

"Since her contact with us was too tenuous to allow us to give her further orders, Allenda reported that she has opted to continue in search of the *Gemin*," Asterion said flatly. "I'm afraid she's out of range now, and the relay ships have been recalled." He paused for a moment to let the implications of that sink in, and Cristal noticed Colonel Kovis had put a hand on Nashira's arm, as if comforting her. Perhaps that was why she was so quiet, Cristal thought. Her only daughter's fate might never be known. "At least one of the second type of creature is indeed headed this way," the captain continued. "The earlier message from the *Gemin* referenced 'things like gigantic whales', and we infer from what we were able to decipher that Captain Decrus intended to lead them away from the fleet. However, Allenda's message indicates he was unsuccessful. It would seem the new life forms can move considerably faster than the fleet. Beta Patrol has been sent out to see if they can get a visual on the creature or creatures."

"So it's going to catch us up," Director Greybridge said. "I think I understand why I was included in this meeting. You want my authority to use my company's seronium to take the direct route through the asteroid belt."

"Oh!" Zaran's exclamation was one of sudden, horrified realisation, and Cristal saw that his face had paled.

"What is it, boy?" Ashwood asked.

"Seronium," Zaran said. "We're idiots. They're after the seronium. Director, on the planet – they were first seen at the refineries, weren't they?"

"That's correct," Greybridge said. He, too, had paled. "There and the spaceport."

"Where there were ships loaded with seronium," Zaran said. "During the fight over Meridiana, one of my pilots took a hit to the fuel tank and jettisoned it. Once he'd done so, the creatures ignored his ship. I wish I'd realised earlier. We might have avoided further contact …"

"How?" Admiral Nashira asked, speaking for the first time, leaning forward. "We need seronium to manoeuvre the fleet, Flight Commander. And many of our unwilling passengers are expecting to be paid with the proceeds of the extra seronium on the carriers when we reach Bendos."

"The seronium is an asset of the GFI," Greybridge put in. "We can't just jettison it!"

"No," Ashwood said thoughtfully. "But we could, hypothetically, use some of it to lure the space whales into a trap. If they're like the blobs, they won't take damage from our lasers, and it would be difficult to persuade them to dip into the radiation field of a star. But luring them into the range of an active asteroid cloud would, I am sure, at least slow them down. We could reconfigure the fleet so that the vessels with laser capability were on the outside of the cylinder and plot our safest course using our full computing functionality." That was her task, Cristal realised, and the reason she was a part of this briefing. She frowned, considering. "Once the thing is in the asteroid field," Ashwood continued, "we can alter the trajectory of one or two of the larger rocks and collapse the field onto it."

"How long have we got?" Zaran asked, looking across at Cristal. There was anguish in his eyes, and with a sinking sensation she suspected she knew who he would suggest pilot any vessel used to set the kind of trap Ashwood was talking about.

"Impossible to be precise," Ashwood said, frowning.

Greybridge put one hand to his forehead. "Flight Commander Zaran," he said, "I was tough on you for initiating closure of the substream gateway. I wish to apologize. If those things eat seronium, had they got loose in the Union, it would have been catastrophic. Seronium is the lifeblood of our society. Untold billions could have ended up without a reliable source of energy. It would be barbaric – the end of our world, our way of life. You were right to close the gate. I regret ... that I didn't see that earlier."

"Director Greybridge." Admiral Nashira leant forward and fixed the man with her steeliest look. "I must ask you – will you allow us to use your company's primary asset in this way?"

He heaved a visible sigh. "If it's a question of our survival, I don't see how I can say no - but it's going to cause considerable discontent amongst our passengers. The company employees are already concerned that they've lost their livelihoods. If they find they've lost their share of the profits as well ... I think we could see ..." He broke off as one of the bridge crew put their head around the ready room door.

"Captain? Beta Patrol has sighted something."

They all spilled out onto the bridge. The traffic control holo was still focussed on the fleet, but the navigation holo was zoomed right out and there was *something* right out on the fringe of it. Several firebirds could be seen in a holding pattern. Zaran went across to stand beside the captain.

"... like the blobs, just an amorphous *thing*," the flight leader was reporting. "Sort of pale blue colour. No response to hails – not that we were expecting one, really. The thing is on the same course as the fleet, and it's definitely gaining."

"Sir," Zaran murmured

"Yes, Flight?"

"Can I recommend Beta Flight attempt a strafing run across the path of the thing?" Zaran suggested. "I'd like to see if we can get it to veer off."

Asterion nodded. "Good call," he said. "Your flight, Commander."

Zaran moved to one of the bridge stations and popped up the pilot holos. "Flight Commander to Beta Flight – let's see if a strafing run across the front of this thing will get its attention. Don't aim to hit it at this stage; just see if it can be deflected."

"Yes, sir!"

Cristal hesitated for a moment, not sure what she should do. The meeting had broken up before she'd given any input, but she knew what would be expected of traffic control and how long it would take to reconfigure the fleet. She had better, she decided, make a start. She moved quietly across and tapped Anni on the shoulder. "I know it's not my watch," she said, "but if you want me to, I'd be happy to take the fleet. There's likely to be some panic when they hear about this new threat."

Anni relinquished her seat with obvious relief. "All yours, Controller!"

CHAPTER TWENTY-THREE

Zaran's attention was focussed on the holo in front of him. He itched to be out there with the pilots, knowing he would understand the situation much better if he saw it in person rather than second hand. "Beta Leader, can you confirm your flight is carrying probe missiles?" he asked.

"Yes, Flight," the beta leader replied. "You want us to drop one into that thing?"

"If it doesn't respond to the strafing run, yes."

"And ... no, sir, no response to our strafe. It didn't even change course. No hails detected."

"Launch the probe. Let's see if we can find out anything about the inside of that thing." Zaran looked at Captain Asterion, who nodded approval. His gaze swept around the bridge, noting approvingly the calm atmosphere projected by Beta Watch as they worked.

Director Rockspire, who had been fidgeting about by the podium, said, "I'll identify an appropriate vessel for you to use for your entrapment. I'll com you once I've got agreement. I'll be as quick as I can."

"Thank you, Director," Asterion said. "Traffic ..." He paused. "Ah, Cristal, good. How long will it take to get the fleet into a tighter formation? As discussed, we need the more vulnerable vessels at the centre and laser-equipped ships on the outside to take out anything large enough to get through the pluslight field."

"I can get you that formation in ... if there are no problems, around an hour." Zaran looked across at his match, wishing with all his heart that they could have had longer together before this new disaster loomed. He took a moment to admire her professionalism, since she apparently knew enough about the capabilities of the fleet's ships to undertake the task, before turning his attention firmly back to the active flight.

"Thank you," he heard Asterion say. "Helm, if we continue at pluslight, how long now before we reach the edge of the debris field?"

"We're already in the edges of it," the helmsman replied, his hands steady on the big ship's steering dome. "I'd say it'll be approximately two to three hours before the density of the asteroids affects our flight path."

"I'll get Corporal Komin up here," Ashwood decided. "He can work with navigation on course projections. He's our fastest programmer, and those asteroid paths are likely to be very erratic."

"Captain, where do you want the *Atria* in relation to the fleet?" Cristal asked.

"We need to lead the fleet," Admiral Nashira replied. Glancing across, Zaran saw Asterion raise an eyebrow, and winced in sympathy. Then he realised this was the first time his mother had ever spoken directly to Cristal, and he felt his shoulders tense, half expecting some kind of confrontation.

"The ships are going to realise there's something going

on," he heard Colonel Kovis observe. "How much should we tell them?"

"At this stage, just a general broadcast in relation to manoeuvring in order to negotiate the debris field," Asterion suggested. "Telling them we've got space whales coming up behind us might cause some panic."

On the holo projection, Zaran saw one of the firebirds blink out of existence. "Beta Leader, report!"

"We lost Sergeant Bellus." The flight was some distance from the fleet and the flight leader's holo was breaking up, but Zaran could still see the distress on his face. "That thing just *elongated* and swallowed his ship whole! We've lost contact with him … and the probe we sent, sir. It stopped broadcasting when it came into contact with the thing."

"What's your fuel situation?" Zaran demanded.

"We need to turn back."

"Acknowledged and approved." Zaran knew it was his duty to notify Bellus's next of kin, and he tapped a quick enquiry into his wristcom before straightening to look at the captain. "I'll detail firebirds to fly a scouting pattern. There could be more than one of those things out there."

"Yes, there could." Asterion was standing straight, his hands clasped behind his back, whilst Commander Jheron directed Beta Watch. The two men seemed to work well together, he thought.

"I'm not going to scramble all of Alpha Patrol." Zaran stretched to relieve the tension in his shoulders. "We're going to need as many pilots fresh as we can get." He alerted his patrol, then turned to Ashwood, who was peering at the holo and counting on his fingers. "Any idea how long that thing will take to reach us?"

"I hate to be imprecise," his uncle said, "but at current speed, I estimate six hours, give or take. It really depends on whether it maintains its current speed and course."

"I'll prepare a reassuring broadcast," Admiral Nashira said. "Captain Asterion, the fleet is your prime responsibility. Please oversee the passage through the asteroid belt. Ashwood, I'll expect your Corporal ... what was his name? ... to ensure we're in no danger. Once Director Rockspire tells us the identity of the vessel he's prepared to sacrifice to protect us, ensure that it drops back into position at the rear of the fleet. Flight Commander, you'll be directing the outside operation. I'd prefer it if you remained on the bridge."

"I can't do that," Zaran said firmly, glad she hadn't phrased it as an order. "This could get very complicated; I need to be where I can see the field of ..." He hesitated, unwilling to commit to the word 'combat'. "Engagement," he decided. He glanced across at Asterion. "I have an unpleasant but necessary duty to discharge, Captain. It shouldn't take me more than half an hour. I'd be grateful if you could keep me advised of any changes to the situation."

"Of course, Flight."

"I'll advise when I've finished briefing my pilots." He tapped his wristcom. "All pilots assemble in the ready room in thirty minutes. This is not a drill." He hesitated for a second, looking across at Cristal, but she seemed focussed on her complicated task, and he gave Raffi a quick nod before turning to leave. His match needed to work, he thought. He shouldn't distract her.

He had only got a few steps down the corridor when his mother caught up with him.

"Zaran," she said, "I really would prefer you to remain on the bridge. I don't want to lose *both* my children!"

"I'm sorry about Allenda," he offered, "but ..."

"Yes, so am I. But I'm sure the *Gemin* is fine, and she'll rendezvous with it, and we'll see them again."

"I'd like that to be the case," Zaran said cautiously. "Admiral – Mother – I have to be out there. This is much too serious for us to take chances. I have always operated better when I can see what's going on first hand, rather than relying on holos. Please don't order me to stay on board."

"Your father would say it was your place," she pointed out, and he realised she was furiously angry.

"You still ... think of Decrus," he offered, a little lamely.

"He told you, didn't he?" She paused, and took a long breath. "I did my duty, Zaran. I accepted my mistake, and I did my duty." She hesitated. "I need to go, but when this is over, you and I are going to have a long talk about this *girl.*"

"I realise she's not what you wanted for me," he said, "but I've made my match. I wish you'd try to like her ..."

"I don't particularly *dislike* her, Zaran," she said, but he rather thought her tone indicated otherwise. "But she's not Elite and your children – will there be children?"

"I certainly hope so."

"They won't be Elite."

"Does that really matter?" Zaran straightened. "It's done, Mother. Please don't treat her badly. And I don't have time to discuss this any further now. I have to go and tell a nice lady that her husband won't be coming home."

Nashira actually looked taken aback, and Zaran wondered if she'd taken in the fact a pilot had died. She shook her head slightly, and said, "We *will* talk about your ridiculous decision when this mission is over. I know I can't stop you leading from the front, but please endeavour to come back in one piece."

"I certainly plan to." He watched her walk away, and shook his head. He couldn't remember his mother ever being so honest and open with him, but he no longer felt some indefinable responsibility to be the perfect son she seemed to want. He realised that, whilst he might never fully forgive her for the lack of interest she'd shown in him when he was small, at least now he had an inkling as to why that had happened. He believed she had loved his father; perhaps she had simply been afraid of loving his son too much at the expense of the daughter she'd produced as a duty. He wondered how much of her bitterness stemmed from listening to her head rather than her heart.

Half an hour later, his condolences given to a now-grieving wife and mother, he arrived in the ready room. Alpha Patrol were all there, including Raffi, and also present were several unassigned pilots and three cadets. "Something's up," one of them accosted Zaran. "If there are firebirds, can we at least protect the fleet?"

"We don't have the firebirds," Zaran said flatly. "But we do have some shuttles with laser capability. Slow and steady, but we're taking the fleet through an area of space that's littered with debris, and dealing with any encroaching asteroids is very important. Does that satisfy your need to be involved, cadet?"

"Yes, sir!" the girl said, straightening, a smile on her face. "Thank you, sir!"

"I'll get the ground crew to allocate shuttles," Raffi said.

"Thank you." Zaran straightened, projecting as much confidence as he could, knowing there was a chance, as there always was, that he could be sending these men and women out to die. He knew it was his job, but he didn't have to like it.

"People of the fleet." Before he could start his briefing, Admiral Nashira's holo popped up over the fleet-wide broadcast circuit. Everybody looked up, several with expressions of surprise and dismay. They might not know how bad things were, but they were intelligent enough to realise that if the admiral was making a broadcast about it, something serious was up. "We are about to pass through an area of space where there is considerable debris," the admiral continued. "You will all be aware that the impact from any asteroid large enough to get through the pluslight field could cause damage to your ship. The convoy is being reorganised so that ships with the firepower to destroy anything that threatens our integrity are on the outside of the fleet, with unarmed vessels to the centre. Please listen to and obey any course changes given to you by Traffic Controller Feltspar, who is acting with the full support of Captain Asterion and myself. I appreciate that the manoeuvres you will be undertaking will eat into your seronium supplies, and I assure you that all ships will be refuelled as required. There is no danger so long as you all follow instructions. I repeat, there is no danger imminent from the space debris. Thank you."

"Space debris?" Sergeant Navi Redwind said, pulling a face. "Is that all this is about, Flight? That's not very exciting."

"It would be if one of the asteroids hit this or any other ship in the fleet," Zaran replied darkly. "But no, that isn't the full story." They quieted, looking at him, and he went on to explain that there was something – nobody quite knew what – coming up behind them.

"Beta Patrol lost a ship to it," he said. "We lost Corporal Bellus." He paused to allow the pilots a moment to express their dismay, and to grieve, before continuing, "It's dangerous, and I don't want any heroics. We need to slow it down long enough to set up a trap for it. Grus, I want you to take out the two-seater firebird. I'll give you more orders later on." As the sergeant nodded, he finished, "Pilots, to your ships, and … may order prevail."

He watched them all move to the airlocks of their firebird cradles, and then walked across to his own, tapping his wristcom.

"Cristal?"

"Yes?"

"I ... will do my best to come back, my heart."

He heard her sigh. "Don't make promises you can't guarantee you'll be able to keep. Fly well, Zaran. I love you."

CHAPTER TWENTY-FOUR

Entering the asteroid field was like going into a kaleidoscope. The space debris was tightly packed, and there was no straight path the *Atria* and its attendant fleet could take. There were going to be dozens of course changes, which would have to be communicated to the right ships at the right times. Add to this the flitting firebirds, and the occasional darting vessel on the outer edge of the fleet diverting to take out a piece of threatening space debris, and the result was a task that could give anyone nightmares. Cristal signalled yet another captain who was drifting off course, and glanced up as Captain Asterion came into her line of sight. He gave her an approving nod.

"You're doing an excellent job, Traffic. Will you stay on duty for the duration of this emergency?"

"Of course, Captain," she said. She glanced at her wristcom and was surprised to see that her duty period had started.

"I've asked Tamrel, the Beta Watch tech who was shadowing Granit, to come on duty early so that you have someone to spell you. She's inexperienced, but capable of taking over so that you can take breaks."

"Thank you, sir."

"And do take those breaks, Traffic." He turned away to speak to Charra, who had taken over the helm. Cristal noticed the bridge technician, Melas, dodging deftly sideways out of his path, her gaze as always firmly on the floor.

Corporal Tamrel, when she turned up, turned out to be an attractive blonde girl around Cristal's own age. She pulled out a seat and sat down beside the traffic holo. "I hope you don't mind me watching," she said. "This is a new configuration for me. Wow, you've got them pretty neatly lined up. How do you do that? Jedda was …" She pulled a face. "I should say I'm sorry about what Jedda did, shouldn't I? Sorry, I'm babbling."

Cristal laughed, finding herself liking the woman. "No problem. His actions were crazy, frankly. We're getting our overall course from Astel and Komin …" She nodded across at the portly data analyst, who looked uncomfortable, either because he didn't like being on the bridge and the focus of attention, or because Ashwood was hovering over him like an anxious mother bird with a fledgling in the nest. The corporal was typing at speed on his virtual keyboard, with Astel beside him on navigation checking his calculations. "And it's just a question of keeping a watchful eye on the out-riders. Do you want a turn?"

"What, now?" Tamrel looked alarmed.

"Sure. Before things get too hectic. Use the focus to correct for the field fuzzies."

Tamrel nodded. Cristal handed over the station, and then sat back and stretched. The bridge was quiet, but everybody appeared on edge. Captain Asterion was standing with the science officer, Ferris, the two of them conversing quietly. Ziff, at the comms station, had a whole line of department heads up in holos and appeared to be giving them some kind of briefing. Alpha Watch were all on duty now, and she wondered whether Beta Watch would actually get any rest knowing the situation the fleet was in.

"Traffic?" The captain came across to her.

"Sir?"

"The captain of the seronium carrier *Swiftwing*, call sign G7291, has volunteered for the entrapment mission. Her crew are being transferred to another ship; she'll fly the mission alone. I've ordered her to start dropping back through the fleet."

Cristal frowned at the holo. "Ah, I see her," she said. "Where does she need to be, Captain?"

"She's to hold steady at the rear of the fleet and await further instructions."

As the captain moved away, Tamrel said, "Entrapment mission?"

"You haven't been briefed?" Cristal shook her head. "Sorry, probably my job." She explained about the thing approaching the fleet from the rear, and Ashwood's plan to use the asteroid field to at the very least slow it down. "Flight will ensure the captain is taken off before the thing gets too close," she concluded, trying not to let her concern for Zaran show. He was doing his job, as she had to do hers.

"We could have gone round this field," Tamrel murmured, frowning at the holo. "This is why we haven't, isn't it? What's the thing coming up on us? One of those blobs?"

Cristal shook her head. "No," she said, "it's something that *eats* blobs. It's big, blue and we have no idea what it is. We're going to deal with it. We hope."

Tamrel nodded. "Order will prevail," she said calmly.

It occurred to Cristal, as she watched Tamrel's performance, that nobody she'd met on the star cruiser had asked her if she had any religious belief, or indicated where she might go to worship if she had. She rather had the impression that the Elite didn't do religion to any great extent. She seemed to recall hearing Zaran use 'may order prevail', a Balancers' phrase, when sending out his pilots, but he'd shown no other indication that he held any strong belief. She made a mental note to ask him. Wheelers tended to be self-reliant and keep any beliefs they had to themselves; perhaps the Elite did the same.

Whilst the tension built, time seemed to drag. Tamrel seemed very competent, and Cristal thought that, whatever else she might think of Jedda Granit, he did seem to have done a decent job of training her. She made a mental note to commend the woman to the captain when the emergency was over. Cristal made sure they both took regular breaks, and replaced her preferred chocolate drink with a more stimulating spiced chai to ensure she stayed alert.

As the fleet penetrated further into the belt of spinning space debris, the ships with laser capability were stretched to keep up with the quantity of fragments. One or two small pieces got through, and a team of emergency workers had to be ferried to one of the trading vessels to patch up a hole in the hull that had already resulted in several deaths. The captain of the vessel in question called Captain Asterion several kinds of idiot for taking the ships into the field. Then the thing that was the real problem – the space whale – became visible on navigation holos, and chaos erupted. Ships at the rear of the fleet demanded to be relocated further away from the thing, ships at the front refused to give up their primacy, and Cristal was stretched to the limit trying to keep them from colliding with one another.

Admiral Nashira, who had returned to the bridge, made a second broadcast to all the ships of the fleet from the relative quiet of the ready room, excoriating the captains for their selfish behaviour and resorting to tongue-lashing when sweet-talking failed to quieten their protests. "The *Atria* will be moving to the rear of the fleet to ensure you are fully protected," she finished.

Captain Asterion and Colonel Kovis exchanged a look, and then the captain said, "Navigator Astel and Corporal Komin, please chart us a course that will take us to the rear of the configuration." He tapped Zaran's holo. "Flight, *Atria* is headed for the tail end of the fleet to offer protection. Can you detail off some ships to take point in our place?"

"I'm reluctant to reduce my flight at this time," Zaran returned. "I suggest you launch Beta Watch. They haven't had their full rest break, but apart from taking out the occasional piece of space debris they only need to hold formation."

"Good thinking, Flight. I'll give the order. *Atria* out."

The captain liaised with the deck chief to ensure the second watch's firebirds had been fully checked and refuelled, and then roused, with remarkably little difficulty, the Beta Watch pilots. Cristal wondered if any of them had actually gone to bed.

In the time it took to get them airborne, she and Tamrel had their hands full keeping the ships of the fleet in line. Constant threats that they would be struck by space debris if they wandered off course seemed to be the only way to prevent them, and Cristal was very aware that the captain and admiral were watching her. She wondered if she'd be castigated for bullying tactics when it was all over.

She would have liked to spend some time watching Zaran's firebird. Alpha Watch were formed up around the rear of the fleet, where the *Swiftwing* was now dropping back out of the formation. Soon it would come to a halt, the seronium would be released to entice the whale and … actually, Cristal wasn't too clear on what would happen next. Ashwood had several of his people running calculations with Admiral Nashira's aide, Kovis, standing beside them, hands clasped behind his back, frowning at what they were doing.

Ashwood, prompted by Komin, informed Asterion that a suitable course for the *Atria* had been identified, and the big ship began to slow down so that it dropped back through the fleet, with Charra holding it on a steady trajectory. This made Cristal's job even more interesting, as her perspective on the fleet was no longer linear. She adjusted the focal point on her holo.

"You're sure about this course?" Asterion enquired thoughtfully.

"What? Why?" Komin looked up from his calculations, and paled as he saw the asteroid the command holo had just picked up heading straight for them. "Where did that come from?"

"Calm down, boy," Ashwood said, patting him on the shoulder. "It's just a rogue. Mm, a useful one. Could we ...? No, perhaps not. I suggest you shoot at it, Captain."

"Really?" Asterion said, his voice heavy with sarcasm. "I'd never have thought of that." He tapped a holo. "Bridge to gunnery, target asteroid." He gave the co-ordinates. "Helm, stand by to manoeuvre," he added.

The *Atria*'s marker in the holo yawed to one side as Charra rolled the big ship to line up their lasers, and Cristal inadvertently gripped the edge of the podium, half expecting to feel the ship's movement. A moment later she released it, feeling embarrassed - of course, with artificial gravity nobody could actually *feel* the movement.

"Fire at will," Asterion said pleasantly. A moment later, the asteroid split into a snowflake on the holo.

"*Swiftwing* is stationary at the planned co-ordinates," Cristal reported. "Fleet is moving away steadily."

"Beta Patrol reports the density of asteroids is thinning

noticeably; the edge of the debris field is in sight," noted Ziff, the tall, laconic communications chief.

"No further course changes required," Ashwood informed them all. "Nice work, Komin," he added, causing the portly computer tech to blush visibly.

"Estimated time for the fleet to clear the asteroid belt completely is twenty eight minutes," Charra reported.

"Everything seems to be going to plan," Admiral Nashira observed from the doorway of the ready room.

Which was, of course, the signal for things to start going very wrong indeed.

CHAPTER TWENTY-FIVE

Despite the potentially disastrous situation they were in, Zaran found his heart soaring as his firebird dropped away from the *Atria*. There was nothing – almost nothing, he amended, thinking of his new match – that he loved more than the feeling of flying, nothing between him and the universe but the cockpit cover of his vessel. It was the first time he'd seen the fleet from this perspective, and he marvelled at how neatly Cristal and the other traffic controllers had got the ships aligned. The core of the fleet was the *Atria*, several large freighters, and a group of seronium carriers. Around and behind those were the medium-sized vessels: traders, *Gold One*, heavy hauliers and people carriers from the Meridiana Wheel, together with a few smaller, unarmed vessels. Finally, encircling and guarding those, were the smaller, laser-enabled ships, including the *Atria's* three shuttles, all travelling at pluslight against a backdrop of space debris. Hanging silently, this picked up enough light from distant stars to be visible as a morass of rocks, some the size of small moons, others barely more than grains of sand, and all being disturbed by the passage of the fleet, by the debris being pinged back into the jumble to collide with and change the trajectory of other debris, so that it was all on the move, a dangerous disarray.

"Alpha Patrol, spread out around the tail of the fleet," he instructed his team. "Fire at will at any debris that appears to be on a collision course with any of our ships. Raffi, with me." Her firebird fell in alongside his as he moved out toward the whale creature.

His first sight of the thing shocked him. It was vast, far larger than he had been prepared for. It was vaguely teardrop shaped, like a whale, but lacked any visible extrusions. The surface of it was veined in pale blue, so that it stood out against the stars behind it. Like the blobs, the thing had no visible means of propulsion, but where the blobs had been merely frightening, this was terrifying. It was immense, unknowable and utterly alien.

"What's causing it to be lit up like that?" Raffi wondered.

"I'm guessing bioluminescence," Zaran replied, pulled out of his introspection by her calm voice. "But I'm not a scientist."

"How close do you want to get to it?" Raffi asked.

"I don't think we should get any nearer than we are," Zaran said. "I just wanted to get a clear look. Holos don't do it justice. But I don't want to attract its attention." He tapped the *Atria's* holo. "*Atria*, has the whale changed course or speed at all?"

"Not since we started tracking it, Flight." He was surprised when the reply came from not the duty comms officer, Ziff, but from Colonel Kovis. He guessed that meant his mother was planted firmly and immovably on the bridge, and hoped she wasn't spending her time glowering at his match.

The patrol held its station as the minutes ticked by. Zaran found himself watching the dance of the fleet, irrationally proud of how well Cristal was managing the jumble of shipping. Traffic Control, he had come to appreciate, was a specialised skill. It was one a star cruiser didn't normally need, so it was just as well his match appeared to have it by the bucket load, or there might have been a lot more ships taking damage.

"So, are you happy?" Raffi asked him on their closed link.

"If you mean with Cristal, I've never been happier," he said. "If you mean out here in the void looking at something I can't even begin to comprehend – not in the slightest!" He broke off to deal with a communication from Captain Asterion about the *Atria's* change of position within the fleet, and frowned as a ship began to drop back through the other ships in order to reach the rear of the fleet. The whale was closing slowly and had yet to reach the debris belt. The *Swiftwing* – sister ship, as he understood it, to the ill-fated *Brightwing* – was moving more slowly than the rest of the fleet and was now close to being the last vessel in the line.

Zaran executed a sideways roll so that he could target a stray piece of debris. He noted absently the twenty eight minutes it would take the fleet to clear the asteroid belt, and the fact that the seronium carrier was now in a holding position at the centre of the debris belt. So far so good, he thought to himself, and then his eyes widened as he looked at the whale.

"Raffi, am I imagining it, or ...?"

"If you are, we both are," Raffi returned. "It's changing shape ... elongating ... only it's not getting any smaller ..."

"It's dividing," Zaran realised with horror.

"Dividing? How? Be more precise, boy!" came Ashwood's voice from the *Atria* holo.

"Like an amoeba," Zaran said. "I'll turn on my nose cam, but you'll have to wait until I get back to the ship to see the recording."

"I've *got* to figure out a better way to transmit data," came Ashwood's parting shot.

"The weird thing is," Raffi said, ignoring the chief scientist's comment, "that the second whale looks like it's going to be as big as the first one. So it's as if it's duplicated itself rather than split in half. Oh, and I think it might be about to do it again ..."

"You're right," Zaran said. "At present, the second whale is just following the first one," he continued. "And the third one ... is going to be just as big as the first two."

"I don't know what's happening with Captain Hera," Sergeant Grus reported. "She's saying that the whales are stealing all her oxygen and she has to get off her ship now before they kill her. She's threatening to open the valves on the seronium prematurely."

"It's too soon," Zaran said. "*Atria*, can you speak to Captain Hera?"

"I'll try and calm her down," his mother said. Zaran winced. His mother's idea of calming was usually more akin to bullying.

"She's a volunteer," he pointed out.

"I think she's hyperventilating," Grus said. "*Atria,* her flight suit's alarm is going off!"

Zaran swore and hit Grus's holo. "Sergeant, you'd better get her out of there. Dock and extract."

"But what about the seronium? Wasn't she supposed to ...?"

"We'll fire on the ship if need be. Get her back to the *Atria*." Zaran flicked icons. "Emergency medical team to the ready room, please."

"We seem to have stopped at three whales," Raffi said. "For the moment, at least."

"Flight, our holos indicate the whales are changing course and ..."

"Wow!" Raffi breathed incredulously. The three objects had begun an intricate, swooping pattern around each other, as if they were revolving around a central point. The whirling grew faster, and Zaran swallowed as he realised that somehow the manoeuvre, which in any reasonable universe would have slowed them down, was in fact having the opposite effect.

"They're moving faster!" he said. "Grus, what's your status?"

"Just docking, Flight," the sergeant replied. He sounded surprisingly calm.

"Don't hang around," Zaran instructed him flatly.

"Wasn't planning on it."

"Raffi, let's give these things a bit more room," Zaran said. "Drop back toward the barge."

"No reply to request to cycle the lock, Flight," Grus reported. "I'm going to have to blow it. Deploying safesuit."

Zaran swallowed, wishing there was something he could do. Their increase in speed meant the alien creatures were gaining rapidly on the fuel barge, and he needed Grus to not only have removed the captain from the ship but also to have got himself clear before he could assess their best next move.

"Ah, boy?" asked Ashwood.

Zaran tapped the chief scientist's holo, which had popped back up on his screen. "Yes, uncle?"

"I'm sending out three probes into the asteroid field. They're going to impact with particular asteroids and knock them off course to nudge others off course to close up the gap we came through. The whales should be caught in the middle, and hopefully that will slow them down long enough for us to get clear."

"You're going to throw rocks at them," Zaran translated slowly.

"That's correct."

"Was that always the plan?"

"Pretty much, yes."

Zaran sighed. "It would've been nice to know earlier," he said. How far we've come, he thought. Left our home planet, travelled to the stars, become comfortable out here, and the first time we're faced with an alien threat, we resort to throwing rocks at it. He shook his head. Well, he supposed if Ashwood thought it might work, it was worth a try, and nobody had had any better ideas.

"We're calculating on the hoof," Ashwood said. "We need the debris field to be relatively stable before we can finalise the calculations and release the probes. I would consider it a favour if you could avoid firing on anything unless you absolutely have to."

"Right." Zaran hesitated. "You will give Sergeant Grus's firebird time to clear the seronium carrier, won't you?"

"If we can, boy."

Zaran swerved to avoid a piece of space debris, calculating that it wasn't about to collide with the seronium carrier, then fired on another piece that would have done if he hadn't deflected it. Raffi's firebird was still alongside his, and together they circled the *Swiftwing*, mimicking in some respects the way the three whales were rotating around each other.

"Grus, progress?" Zaran snapped impatiently.

"Five ... minutes ... Flight!"

"Make it less!"

"She's ... heavy!"

Zaran tapped his fingers impatiently on his firebird's helm, dispatched another small piece of space debris, and pulled up the specs of the seronium carrier, working out how best to place his laser fire to release its precious load.

He wondered if it would even be necessary; the whales were still closing on it, now within the edge of the debris belt. Zaran divided his attention between incoming debris and the whales, trying to see whether any small asteroids struck them, and if so what the outcome was. The probe they'd fired into it had just disappeared; it was possible they could absorb the debris just as easily. He guessed Ashwood's concept was that they might deal with one or two, but not if the entire asteroid belt was collapsing on them.

And, if Grus didn't hurry, on the three hovering firebirds! Zaran wished he'd flown the two-seater himself, that it was him hauling the captain's inert body back to it, or that he had some magical weapon that would at least delay the space whales ... order's bane, he might as well imagine himself safely back in bed with Cristal, he thought gloomily. He shook off the thought that that was somewhere he might never be again.

"Got her, Flight," Grus reported, sounding more like himself. "Just taking off now. It appears her suit's the only thing keeping her alive. Looks like a problem with her heart."

"I'm not surprised," Raffi observed. "Mine's been pretty shaken by all this, too!"

"*Atria*, estimated time to probe impacts?" Zaran asked.

"Six minutes." It was Captain Asterion who responded this time. "We need those whales focussed on the barge, Flight. Can you release the seronium?"

"I'm on it," Zaran said. "Raffi, start back. I'll be right behind you."

"You'd better be!"

Zaran watched her flip her firebird and set off after Grus's two-seater, then rolled his own ship and accelerated toward the *Swiftwing*. He blinked away a sharp memory of the *Brightwing* breaking up over Meridiana and focussed on targeting his laser.

One moment he was perfectly lined up to take the shot, the next he was rolling sideways as a piece of space debris he'd simply not seen spun out of the field to his left, collided violently with his cockpit, bounced off it, and neatly removed his port thrusters.

Which made manoeuvring his firebird kind of tricky.

"Flight, are you damaged?" Zaran winced, using his remaining thrusters to roll his vessel back toward the barge. With less manoeuvrability, he realised he was going to have to get closer before he fired.

"I'm on target, *Atria*," he responded.

"You have three minutes before you need to get clear, Flight. We'll count you down."

No rush, Zaran thought, babying his vessel into firing range. The *Swiftwing*, now presumably on autopilot, ploughed majestically onward through the swarm of rock, jerking and juddering, making targeting its seronium pods ... interesting.

"Two minutes."

Zaran jinked his firebird to avoid a rock ricocheting from the *Swiftwing* and took a moment to wipe a hand across his forehead. He didn't need to have sweat dripping into his eyes.

"Preparing to fire," he reported.

"Thirty seconds ... "

Zaran engaged his lasers and banked his firebird, racking his fire across the *Swiftwing's* seronium pods. One wobbled visibly and then split open, spilling its contents in drifts of droplets, and he made a second pass. He didn't have time to check whether the whales were responding. The countdown from the *Atria* was at zero, and the asteroid field was blossoming, rocks flying in all directions as the stability of their orbits was disrupted. He kept firing, just targeting the barge generally now, unable to steer enough to line up with it. A second pod actually exploded, the detonation wave throwing his firebird about as if it was made of paper.

"The whales are closing on the barge," Colonel Kovis reported. "Flight, what's your status? You need to get out of there!"

"Tell me about it," Zaran muttered. He concluded he could do nothing further with the *Swiftwing* and turned toward home.

It was seat-of-the-pants piloting with space debris all around and one thruster out. Zaran rolled and zigzagged and dove, his full attention on trying to stay out of the way of anything big enough to do serious damage to his ship. He didn't even dare take his hands off the controls long enough to hood-up his safesuit. He avoided using his lasers – the debris belt was already responding to far too many stimuli without adding any more. Cause and effect, he thought. Knock one rock into another and that one hits something else until the initial energy input is spent. Only the explosion waves from the three probes, the barge, and the activity of the whales injected more forces ...

He was, he knew, at least headed in the same direction as the fleet, but every second that passed, the gyration of the debris around him increased and his chances of successfully dodging it grew less. It would only take one slip, one misjudgement, and it would all be over. He knew he was a good pilot, but he also knew he was only human. It was probably only a matter of time ...

His firebird juddered as something hit it amidships, and another thruster went out, reducing the manoeuvrability of his small craft even further.

"*Atria*, I've taken damage," he reported. "Still on course to rendezvous."

As if things couldn't get any worse, he noticed there was an especially large piece of debris – one of the largest he'd seen in the field – on the same trajectory as him, and catching him up fast. No, he amended, trying to spot an escape from its path but not finding one, not just travelling in the same direction but rolling along, spinning. As it turned, he noticed a black, uneven patch on the surface, which was probably ...

Oh.

Oh!

He let his ship slow, freed a hand to pop up his safesuit hood, and tapped the *Atria* holo.

"*Atria,* Flight. My situation is poor, but I have a thin chance of escaping the debris field. Don't wait for me, but if you can leave a rescue shuttle, appreciate it. Look for my safesuit emergency beacon. And if I don't make it ..." He broke off, and when he continued, it was a real effort to get the words out. "Cristal, I'm sorry. I love you."

CHAPTER TWENTY-SIX

Cristal froze at her station, her hand going to her mouth. She had been focussed on believing – believing absolutely, no matter how increasingly unlikely it seemed - that somehow, miraculously, it would all be all right, Zaran would take his shot and then escape the debris field in one piece. After all, he was an ace pilot.

The fleet had practically cleared the belt of rock when Ashwood's probes detonated, the explosions altering the trajectories of the particularly large fragments so that they tumbled spectacularly into others, setting off a chain reaction in the debris field. The head scientist hovered anxiously over the holo, Corporal Komin beside him, initially excited that their calculations – with *so* many variables, Ashwood said, you could never be *entirely* sure – had proved accurate. That excitement increased when the whales reacted to the release of the seronium from the *Swiftwing* by altering course and converging – or whatever you called it when three things were moving together in a complex pattern – on it. But then Raffi and Grus docked, and the very ill captain of the barge was transferred to sickbay, and Zaran stopped answering hails …

That his ship was still visibly manoeuvring had given her hope – perhaps he had simply lost his comms array – but now he had finally communicated with them, and it didn't sound good at all.

Cristal jumped as someone put their hand on her shoulder. "Hold on, controller," came Kovis's calm voice as he withdrew his hand. "Flight's not lost yet, and I have every confidence in him. You need to make sure he's got a fleet to come back to."

Reminded of her duty, even though fear sat in her stomach like a stone, Cristal forced herself to take hold of the edge of the traffic control podium and refocus on keeping the many ships on course. Now that they were clear of the debris belt, the more difficult captains had quieted down somewhat, but several ships had sustained damage during the passage and repair tugs and shuttles were busy ferrying equipment and personnel around. There was a particularly obnoxious young trader pilot who had spent the entire transition getting progressively more drunk, and Admiral Nashira wanted him removed and replaced as soon as possible – which would be a lot easier if he wasn't also the ship in question's owner.

"Captain?" It was Raffi Forrester calling from the ready room. "Emergency shuttle is fuelled and launching now. Sergeant Kaitos is with me."

"Thank you, Lieutenant," Asterion replied. "Don't take any unnecessary chances. Keep us advised if there's any sign of those whale things coming through the debris field. Charra, hold us steady on our current course."

"Sir."

Admiral Nashira was pacing back and forth, her robes swishing in an irritating fashion, her hands clasped behind her back. "He'll be fine," she said abruptly. "I refuse to believe anything else."

"Of course, Admiral," Kovis replied. His face was so

expressionless that Cristal couldn't decide whether he genuinely believed his own words or was just putting a brave face on things.

The fleet was still in the formation adopted to pass through the debris belt and, not having been given any instruction to revert to the earlier configuration, Cristal found herself going through the motions, her eyes straying constantly to the one blip moving away from the fleet, back in the direction from which they'd come.

"There's no sign of anything coming out of the debris field except debris," Raffi reported. "We're seeing Flight's emergency beacon, but there's no sign of his ship."

"Surely he can't have abandoned it?" Ashwood looked pale and anxious, and Corporal Komin was fidgeting by his side. Cristal suspected the latter would like to leave now his calculations were no longer required, but without an order to do so, he was stuck where he was.

"What can you see, Lieutenant?" Asterion leant over the comms holo, a frown on his face.

Cristal realised that her tour of duty was long over, but knew there was no way she could leave until she knew, one way or another, whether this day which had started out as the best of her life would turn out, after all, to be the worst. She tried to achieve the zen-like state Charra seemed to reach to fly the big star cruiser, but couldn't stop her hands from shaking a little.

"Captain." Everyone on the bridge part-turned toward the comms desk as Raffi reported in. "We've located Zaran's firebird ... it may not be good news."

"Proceed, Lieutenant," Asterion said. "Tamrel, please take over Traffic."

"Thank you," Cristal heard herself whisper. She staggered to her feet to allow her relief access to the holo controls, but couldn't bring herself to move any further away, all her attention focused on the tiny dot that was Raffi's shuttle. She started to count silently, pretending it wasn't the seconds she was counting, seconds that seemed to drag past slower and slower as she waited, with everyone else, for Raffi's next words.

"There's a huge asteroid just leaving the belt," came the pilot's voice. Her holo showed her peering forward anxiously. "It looks like Flight's firebird has collided with it. The wings are spread across the face of it, but the body appears to be wedged in a crevice."

"Is that Asteroid B?" Komin remarked to Ashwood, and half the complement of the bridge turned to stare at him.

"One of my catalysts?" Ashwood said. "Yes, I believe it is."

"One of the pieces you set moving with a controlled explosion?" Captain Asterion was obviously seeking clarification.

"Yes, yes."

"We're trying to come alongside it," Raffi said, "but it's rolling."

"Interesting," Ashwood murmured. "There must be an anomalous mineral spread to have caused it to rotate ..."

"Ashwood," Asterion snapped, and the head scientist fell silent.

"Corporal Kaitos is suited up and prepared to investigate the wreck," Raffi said.

"Take care, Lieutenant." Cristal wondered whether the captain was thinking they couldn't afford to lose more pilots with combat experience on account of the weird life forms they were encountering, and then cringed at her thought that he wouldn't be that concerned about any of his crew going into a dangerous situation.

"Of course, Captain." Raffi sounded affronted by the suggestion they might be doing anything else.

On the traffic holo, Cristal could see the emergency

shuttle manoeuvring in the vicinity of the rogue boulder. She stood with her hands clasped, wanting to believe that Zaran would be fine, that he'd come back to her, but more certain as the moments passed without word that she'd never see him again. She was frozen in place, heart thundering in her chest, braced for the worst possible news.

"*Atria*, we've got him!" Raffi sang out. "He's alive!"

Cristal slumped, almost in shock, becoming aware that tears of tension and relief were dripping down her face.

"Come with me, Traffic," Colonel Kovis said, his tone kind. He put a hand under her elbow and drew her away from the traffic holo.

"But ..." She made a vague gesture towards the control console.

"You've done enough," Kovis said. "Anni is on her way to take over, and Tamrel can hold things together until she gets here."

"I ... thank you." She stumbled along beside him, off the bridge, along the corridor and up the steps into a travel pod, barely aware of where they were, until somehow they were in sickbay. The blond counsellor she'd spoken to what seemed a lifetime ago guided her to a chair and, once she was seated, handed her a mug of hot chocolate.

"Drink," he said, looking up. "Thank you, Colonel."

"My pleasure," Kovis said. "Take good care of her – she's the best traffic controller we've got."

And how did that happen? Cristal wondered. She'd thought her job on the Wheel was ... well, a little tedious on slow days, to be honest, and not especially important. If she hadn't drawn the short straw, she wouldn't have been one of the skeleton crew left to man the Wheel after the majority of the crew had been evacuated. Guiltily, she wondered where her father and sister were, whether they'd stayed at Bendos or been evacuated further into the IUP, and whether they missed her and were worried about her. It had been days since she'd last given them more than a passing thought.

Knowing that Zaran's lieutenant would take good care of him and that he would be brought to sickbay as soon as she got him back to the *Atria*, Cristal leant back and closed her eyes. It seemed forever since Zaran had woken her that morning with the news they were needed on the bridge. Since then, she had run back to her quarters to change into her uniform safesuit and been cross-examined by Charra as to where she'd been all night. When she'd admitted that she and Zaran were matched, her friend's mouth had literally fallen open – and stayed open as Cristal had told her about Jedda's betrayal.

Charra's only complaint about the news had been that she'd have to find another roomie.

Cristal was distantly aware that the counsellor was hovering nearby, presumably keeping an eye on her, and she was almost nodding off when the door swished open and Medwen came in alongside a gurney carrying a battered but conscious Zaran. Cristal gasped, getting so quickly to her feet that she almost ended up wearing the remains of her hot chocolate, but the counsellor rescued the mug from her.

"Zaran!" she blurted, stumbling toward the gurney as Medwen directed the man pushing it to transfer her match to a diagnostic bed.

"I'm fine," he said, coughed a little, and laughed weakly. "Well, maybe not fine, but alive, and that's more than I was expecting at one point. I'm sorry …"

"It's all right," she told him, starting to take his hand and then looking to Medwen for permission.

"You can hold his hand," the doctor said, frowning at the diagnostic readout. "Cracked ribs, possibly some metatarsals in your right foot, nasty crack on the head … and you were getting low on oxygen." She busied herself giving him an injection.

"I had a dumb idea," he said. "Probably saved my life."

"What idea?" Cristal asked, barely noticing when the door opened again, and Captain Asterion came in with Admiral Nashira.

"I nearly got totalled by a big asteroid," Zaran said. "Then I saw it had a hole blown in it ... I guessed it was where Ashwood detonated one of his probes. I'd lost thrusters and I knew I'd never make it out in one piece. Then I thought I'd let the asteroid take the hits. I tried to put my firebird in the hole." He snorted. "Took both wings off and the anti-collision foam deployed, but I was in one piece long enough to get clear of the debris. Raffi says she's getting bored with rescuing me seconds before my oxygen runs out. I owe her my life. Again."

"I'm very glad you do," Cristal said.

"So am I," he agreed. "I wanted to get back to you. I wanted to share so many things with you ..."

"There will be time," she promised him, before straightening to meet Admiral Nashira's cold stare. The admiral shook her head once before turning her attention to her son.

"I am beginning to have considerable sympathy with your father's desire that you should direct your pilots from the safety of the bridge," she told him. "I am, however, relieved to see that you survived this particular piece of heroism."

"So am I," Zaran said. "Thank you."

"Zaran needs to be unconscious so I can work on the bones he's broken," Medwen said briskly. "Admiral, Captain ... he's going to be fine. I'll let you know if the breaks are worse than they appear. And *you*, young lady," she finished, frowning at Cristal, "need to get some rest. You can take the empty cot in that room." She indicated one of the empty chambers around the diagnostic hub of the sickbay. "So you won't be too far away when your match wakes up."

"Thank you," Cristal said, giving Zaran's hand one last squeeze before stepping back and allowing the doctor to do her job.

CHAPTER TWENTY-SEVEN

Zaran wasn't entirely sure why his mother had felt it necessary to throw a dinner party but hadn't been able to think of a good reason not to attend. It had been eight days since the fleet left the asteroid belt, and there was no sign of anything pursuing them – so far, at least. As Captain Asterion had remarked, it had taken the 'space whale' a while to catch up with them before, and it was possible there was something even more inexplicable pursuing *that*.

Despite her threats, Admiral Nashira had yet to confront Zaran about his choice of match, and had even included Cristal in the invite to this meal without any comment. He suspected she might still have hopes he'd change his mind, but he was sure that was never going to happen. He couldn't imagine being with anybody but Cristal; just looking at her made his heart sing. Now they were living together, every day seemed to have an extra sparkle to it. Between tours of duty, they talked, and laughed, and made love, in perfect harmony with each other.

They walked side by side now, her hand in his, as they approached the guest suite. It was the first time in years that

Zaran had had reason to go there, and he'd forgotten how extensive it was. There were several doors off the exquisitely decorated atrium; one, which was open, led to a large conference room. The single, huge oval table inside was usually, to his knowledge, only used for business purposes. Today it had been set with the ship's best china and cutlery, and the normally bright lights had been dimmed. It hadn't occurred to him, he realised, that his mother would be housed in the guest suite. Somehow he'd imagined her in the captain's quarters, where she had lived throughout the latter part of his childhood and until she was promoted off the *Atria*, but obviously those were Captain Asterion's rooms now.

Zaran had opted to wear his dress robe, and was pleased to see that the captain and Colonel Kovis, who had arrived before him, were similarly dressed. Cristal looked stunning, he thought, in the maroon uniform that made her part of the *Atria's* crew, and he squeezed her hand reassuringly as Admiral Nashira glanced across at them. Her only acknowledgement of them was a nod, but as far as Zaran was concerned, that was fine. If she chose to challenge his choices, he'd deal with it when it happened.

More guests arrived: the Galactic Fuel director, Artur Greybridge, and Commander Rockspire from the Meridiana wheel; the senior administrator who had been in charge of the resort on the planet – Zaran could never remember her name; Lord Chief Justice Rydon, escorting a smiling Medwen; Ashwood, arm in arm with Thom, who, Zaran had heard, he'd invited to share his quarters; a portly man he didn't recognise who was wearing a dark crimson coat liberally embroidered with gold and silver patterns, a style which indicated that he was a well-established merchant; and finally an elderly woman wearing neutral colours, the only person present not also wearing a safesuit. Looking around, Zaran found himself missing his sister. However cold their relationship had been,

she had always been there, part of the family, and he hoped
she had found the *Gemin* and was safe.

A soft chime announced the arrival of the meal, which
was plain fare, served by two cadets. Zaran carefully chose
seats for himself and Cristal halfway down one side of the
table opposite Ashwood and Thom, where he was likely to be
able to avoid making eye contact with his mother, who took
the seat at the head of the table. The others settled into the
remaining seats.

Ashwood beamed cheerfully at Zaran and Cristal. "How
are you settling into your new quarters?"

Zaran smiled back. His uncle had, he was fairly sure, been
responsible for ensuring that he and his match were moved
from his rather cramped room to a larger suite closer to the
Atria's control room and a short distance from the other
pilots. He had a suspicion his mother had been originally
responsible for ensuring there was a larger room vacant and
available for him, although he had no doubt it had been
Medwen she'd expected him to be sharing it with, not a
Wheeler girl who'd never even – he'd been astonished to
discover – travelled anywhere by substream.

"I've never had reason to," she'd told him. "My life was on
the Wheel. I grew up there and went to school there, and
when I was small vacations were always taken on Meridiana.
After my mother died, we didn't really take any more
holidays."

She was probably the only person around the table who'd
never seen the Union in all its debatable glory, Zaran thought.
He'd seen far more of it than he liked, the good and the bad,
and found he was almost enjoying cruising through unknown
space.

"Why are we here?" the resort director asked as the first
course was placed in front of her. She was a middle-aged

woman with a smile Zaran thought looked professional rather than genuine.

"I'm sure there will be time to discuss that when we've eaten," Kovis, who was seated opposite her, responded.

The resort director – what *was* her name? – looked less than impressed with this answer. Cristal leant towards her match. "That's Saria Parker," she murmured.

He gave her an astonished look. "How did you know ...?"

"You were looking at her and frowning."

He shook his head. "I can't tell you how happy it makes me that you already know me this well!"

The conversation whilst they were eating was mostly polite small talk. Nashira congratulated Medwen on her efforts to survey medical staff and recruit first aid providers to ensure that all the ships in the fleet had some coverage, a project which the doctor assured the admiral was actually being led by the surgeon general, Nazif Atria. Although she had arrived with Rydon, Zaran was aware his near-match was spending a lot of time with Raffi Forrester – and good luck to the two of them, he thought, smiling at Cristal, whose contribution to the conversation was mostly about gravityball. She had tried out for and been accepted by the *Atria's* team, since after Jedda Granit's arrest the Wheel team had agreed to disband. The five men involved in the plot against Zaran and Cristal had been tried and found guilty. Both Jedda and the man who'd fired at Zaran had been sentenced to confinement in the brig until such time as they reached Bendos, when they would be transferred to local custody facilities. Their three accomplices had been dispersed to ships around the fleet, sentenced to performing menial tasks under close supervision for the foreseeable future.

Once the meal was complete and after-dinner drinks were served, the admiral rose to her feet and raised her glass. "A toast," she said, "to a successful journey and a safe return to the Union."

Everyone drank, and then Nashira continued, "I'm please you were all able to accept my invitation to join us for this meal." She sat down again but still commanded every eye in the room – something she usually did, Zaran thought, schooling his face to neutrality and reaching out to clasp Cristal's hand.

"Now we have the time," the admiral said, "I thought we should discuss fleet management. Whilst we were in an enhanced threat situation, obviously the IUP took the lead; but I am conscious that much of the fleet's personnel are drawn from civilian locations. Your employees, Director Greybridge, and yours, Commander Rockspire. As well as a number of supernumerary planet dwellers ..."

"Layabouts and eccentrics," Greybridge snorted, glaring at the plainly dressed woman, who looked back at him placidly. "Ex-GFI employees who decided they preferred life off the grid to putting in an honest day's work."

"Nevertheless, they should be represented," Nashira said.

"Represented?" Greybridge seemed to finally catch the drift of the admiral's conversation. "You mean ... you're suggesting we form an oversight committee, as if we were a planet?"

"We're going to be in transit for some time," Nashira said. "Obviously, the IUP must retain the option to act unilaterally, should another threat situation arise. However, Director, you and Commander Rockspire, and Administrator Parker ..."

"My correct title, as I have repeatedly told your *aide,*" the woman half-snarled, glaring at Kovis as if she had some difference of opinion with him, "is Resort Leader."

"I do apologize," Nashira said in her sweetest – and therefore most irritated – tone of voice. "*Resort Leader* Parker. You and the two gentlemen are all invited to take seats on the oversight committee. Captain Block." She nodded to the portly man in maroon who had said little during the meal. "I'm told you are the most senior captain from the merchant ships in the fleet."

"Oh no," the man said, his mouth twisting. "That would be Captain Mertens."

"Order's bane, no!" Rydon muttered, rather too loudly; but when half the guests looked at him, his face was expressionless.

"Well, we can sort that out later," Nashira said, with what her son judged to be a rather forced smile. "And Celebrant Sharra, I'd like to invite you to represent the non-GFI inhabitants from Meridiana."

"Well, that explains why you invited a nobody like me," the woman said with a rueful smile. "I'll ask them, but I think they'll agree to your choice."

Nashira blinked, presumably unaccustomed to having her diktats challenged.

"Of course I've been taking care of my staff," Greybridge said. "But it's not easy. Everybody is so spread out, sometimes only one or two to a ship, and not all of them owned by Galactic Fuel." He turned to look at Rockspire. "I assume you are in a similar position, Neno."

"The evacuation was somewhat chaotic," the Wheel director agreed. The two men seemed comfortable with each other, and Zaran remembered that when the blobs had chosen to attack the original evacuation from the planet, they had been absent from the bridge having a business meeting of their own. He thought the Wheel director — according to Cristal, promoted to that position from a much lower one simply because everybody senior to him had already chosen to evacuate the Wheel – was being overly obsequious towards the planetary director, although how Greybridge felt about it was unclear. He had the perfect businessman's face, Zaran thought - capable of a limited range of emotions, just enough to underline whatever his stance was on a particular subject. At present, he was smiling in polite agreement.

"Of course I'll be happy to represent my staff," Parker said. "We are less dispersed since, of course, we had our own ship standing by to evacuate us – the *Canopus* under Captain Windwist. I will also be happy to represent the last guests at the resort, who remained in the hope that things would return to normal. Sadly, that moment never came." She glared at Zaran in a way that made the flight commander feel she held him solely responsible, and he sighed inwardly. Another person who would never forget that he was the one who gave the order to initiate the shutdown of the substream gateway. "Some of them have, however, been moved to other berths," she noted. "The *Canopus* is a large ship, but an old one, and some areas are unsafe for passenger use."

"Chief Engineer Harp and I have a team visiting ships around the fleet, undertaking repair work," Ashwood put in. "I can ask them to include the *Canopus* in their schedule."

"I'm sure Captain Windwist will ask if he thinks that's necessary," Parker said, frowning a little. Zaran wondered why she didn't like his uncle's suggestion.

"The *Atria* has its own command structure," Nashira said, "but I'd ask Captain Asterion, Chief Scientist Ashwood, and Lord Chief Justice Rydon to represent the flagship. I will chair the committee with Colonel Kovis as my assistant."

"Justice is going to be stretched thin, with many ships in the fleet suffering from overcrowding and potential culture clashes," Rydon noted. "I'd like to recruit some extra prefects. There are prefects from Meridiana spread around the fleet, and there may be other suitable candidates to whom a probationary period could be applied."

"Of course," Nashira said, interrupting when it looked like Rydon would have said more. "Order must be maintained."

"There are other decisions that need to be made." Ashwood steepled his fingers and looked around the table. "We need to convert as much space as possible to hydroponics, or the food supplies will run out long before we reach Bendos. We have the seed and the components to expand, and beds can be replicated, but we need space and recruits to operate the new facilities."

"Space is limited," Greybridge said. "People are already crammed in to much smaller spaces than is comfortable, and if you try and take more away from them it could lead to considerable disquiet."

"There must be space we can use," Ashwood argued. "Storage areas not currently in use, and some of the social areas. Some traders may have cargoes that can be discarded or recycled ..."

"You can't ask us to just jettison our livelihoods," Captain Block objected, rising to his feet in obvious indignation.

"It could be a matter of that or starvation," Ashwood said bluntly. "Nashira, can you not, as senior representative of the Union, guarantee compensation to any captain who is willing to assist us in this way? I'm sure the Trustees will be willing to underwrite the cost when we regain the substream."

"I would be committing the Union to what could be considerable expense," Nashira said, frowning; but then her expression smoothed out. "But of course I'd be returning their citizens and their ships, including the *Atria*. Let's table that for discussion at our first committee meeting."

Zaran was well aware that he hadn't been invited to join the oversight committee, and was rather glad of the fact. As flight commander, he sat on the *Atria*'s command group, but his skills weren't in the kind of administration the fleet was going to need. Should they encounter further problems, however, it would be his responsibility to formulate any necessary battle plan. He thought about mentioning it, but Nashira saved him the trouble.

"Flight Commander Zaran," she said, "will, of course, be invited to present to the committee on any deployment of his pilots. Hopefully the existence of a strong and specific chain of command will prevent any further *rushed decisions* on his part."

Oh, and there's the veiled dig, he thought. Obviously her brief expression of concern about his welfare after the asteroid flight had faded. He would have liked to express indignation, but Cristal squeezed his hand. He realised her warning against insubordination was right, and just nodded.

"And what can the science department offer us?" Nashira asked her brother. "Aside from hydroponics," she finished pointedly, with a sideways flick of her eyes to Ashwood's chosen mate, who shifted uncomfortably in his seat. Zaran saw his uncle put a hand on the other man's knee, and he relaxed visibly. Yes, he thought, those two are good for one another.

"Science offers many things," Ashwood said. "I have people working on the potential of other elements as fuels, and a whole team now dedicated to endeavouring to improve long distance communications. It's ridiculous that we can't speak to one another over distance. Even within the fleet, some digital transmissions are substandard." He sighed. "We have drifted into stagnation," he said. "We – humanity – built a network that covers light years, but having built it, we reached a point of balance. We have sufficient resources, land, adventure, of a sort, and experience, and so we looked no further than what we had. And yet the universe is infinite, and beyond our safe little network of planets who knows what wonders may exist?

"These things we have seen," he went on. "The blobs, the whales – we still have no idea what they are. We may never know. But where they exist there might be an infinite variety of life forms we have yet to meet. There were always rumours of generation ships that went out before the substream was discovered, from which nobody has ever heard again, and ships have gone missing since. The star maps we have are sadly deficient. They show us the areas the probes passed through when the substream gateways were created, but beyond that are distinctly lacking in precision."

"You sound ... excited by our journey," Greybridge observed.

"Of course it excites me," Ashwood said. "I'm a scientist and I love it when the universe challenges me. It's going to take us ten years at best to get back to Bendos, and away from the safety of the substreams who knows what else we'll find, what scientific breakthroughs we'll achieve!"

Ten years, the flight commander thought. A lot could happen in ten years. He squeezed Cristal's hand, turning his head to smile at her. As far as he was concerned, the best thing that could happen already had, and he couldn't remember ever feeling so content. Despite the situation the fleet was in, despite a future that threatened shortages and hardships, he couldn't imagine being anywhere else. With Cristal by his side, he thought, he could face anything the universe could throw at them.

Zaran looked around at his fellow travellers and grinned. "Bring it on!"

AUTHOR'S NOTE: ABOUT THE UNCHARTED SERIES

Most of the action in this series takes place on or around the *Atria* (pronounced At-tria, not Ay-tria). It's a gigantic ship, and it's ugly on the outside. Inside, it's a small city with IUP crew and civilians.

The series takes place at an undefined time in the future – civilisations have risen and fallen, so there will be no more than passing references to our history. One of those civilisations developed the substream network – it's a bit like the London Underground, with nodes at systems with useful resources along unconnected lines all starting from (or terminating at) Sol system. The people who live permanently in space, either on ships or on inhabited platforms (such as the one at Bendos), are 'Elite'. The people who crew the Wheels that oversee the substream gateways at 'Wheelers'. The people who live on planets are planet dwellers (politely) or dirt huggers (impolitely).

Technology wise, aside from the substream, which shortens the travel time to far-flung systems, most ships have pluslight and sublight drives. Gravity plates are standard in ships and at locations without appropriate natural gravity.

Replicators are also widely used, although naturally produced products are also traded.

The IUP (Interstellar Union of Planets) is run by a Board of Trustees based on Sol Platform (which is in one of Earth's LaGrange points, probably the one the Webb telescope currently inhabits), where Sol University is also located. The star cruisers cruise the substream carrying updates for system databases with the latest news, media, laws, medicine and science.

If you want to read a short novella set before this book, please visit my website at https://jamortimore.com/ and sign up for my newsletter, which will advise you when the next books in the series become available.

ACKNOWLEDGMENTS

Many thanks to all the friends I've made in the SF and media worlds over the years, and new friends in the book world. Special thanks to Penny and Lynn, who have to live with my writing, and to my cats, who are good at getting in the way of it, and to Vicky Brewster, my editor.

Extra special thanks to the members of the Rebel Authors slack channel - you are the best author friends a girl could hope for! I'm not going to name anybody specifically, you're all wonderful. I am eternally grateful for all the help and support you have given and continue to give me.

ABOUT THE AUTHOR

J A Mortimore (Judith) stated writing stories at a young age and has never stopped. She wrote fan fiction for many years in a number of fandoms, all pre-internet. She has been active in science fiction and fantasy circles for longer than she cares to think about. Now retired, she lives in Gloucestershire, UK with two friends, some prima donna cats, and far too many books, sewing projects and half-written manuscripts.

She has a story 'When the Circus Came to Town' in the Rebel Diaries Anthology (2022).

With Penelope Hill, she has co-written a fantasy novel 'The Vanished Mage' available from Elsewhen Press.

Printed in Great Britain
by Amazon